This is for the children who never felt the arms of a protective parent; who were left alone in their cribs, wet, hungry, and unloved; and for those children and adults who suffer the effects of RAD (reactive attachment disorder).

We are all born with a sacred place in a small, dark corner of our brain that grows and develops into something much larger and brighter when our mothers or fathers answer our cries, hold us when we're frightened, feed us when we're hungry, and love us unconditionally. But if our cries go unanswered, that corner in our brain remains dark and undeveloped. We never learn how to ask for what we need because when we do, no one listens. Eventually, our cries grow silent; we grow into a child and then an adult and forever stop seeking that which we desperately need. Only when, by the grace of God, someone truly amazing steps into our lives and shines light in that darkness, do we have a chance to feel the safe hands of love.

Chapter One

Kazak, Russia
1999

Stealing is common here. It's survival.

The vendors know this and are suspicious of everyone, including me, even though I'm only thirteen. Rows of displayed goods on tables line the dusty streets between tall run-down buildings, their walls swirled with fat graffiti. Mama's sister, Aunt Ludmila, and I are careful not to go to the same vendor twice and have learned to playact.

Today, a black crow caws overhead like he's mocking me. He perches on a shattered streetlamp and watches with his beady eyes. It's like he knows what I'm about to do. Like he's tattling to the vendor, daring me to get caught. I don't want to steal, but I must.

The cool shadows give me a reason to wear my coat with the inside pocket. A harsh breeze causes dirt tornadoes at the side of the road, filling my nostrils and making me thirsty. The wind carries the smell of the subway up through the traffic.

Aunt Ludmila nods toward the fruit stand and distracts the lady vendor who has plump peaches on her table. I can almost taste their sweetness and feel the juice dribble down my chin. I reach for two, fit them in the palm of my hand, and curl them toward my pocket.

"Hey, girl!" a man shouts.

The peaches tumble from my grasp and roll into the dirt. The gray-haired man steps toward me from the back of the stand. "You can't take those without paying for them." The crow cries again, laughing at me. I want to throw a stone at him.

Aunt Ludmila slaps me across the face, knocking my head back. My flaxen hair spills out of my hood. "What are you doing, child? Apologize to these nice people."

The man and woman stare with their mouths agape. I put my hand up to my face and feel the heat. The sting shouldn't shock me because I've felt it before, but it does. Tears fill my eyes. They're a part of the act, but they're also there because each slap reminds me that Ludmila is in control and not Mama.

"You don't have to hit the child." The man offers me a handkerchief. His Russian sounds different from ours. He speaks slower, as if our language is difficult for him to speak.

Ludmila snatches the handkerchief and hands it back to the man. "Yes, it's the only thing she understands. I'm sorry for what she does. Her mother is with child, and she steals for her benefit." She grabs my arm and turns me to face the man. "Apologize."

I curtsy in the old-fashioned way Aunt Ludmila taught me. "I'm sorry, sir. I'm worried about Mama and how long it's been since she's eaten. She's weak with child." Although this is an act, Mama really is pregnant, and she hasn't eaten in a long while.

Kindness reflects in the wrinkled corners of his eyes. He comes around to the front of his stand and picks the peaches up off the ground. He brushes them with his sleeve, puts them in a sack, and hands it to me. "Here is one for you and one for your mama." He scowls at my aunt. "Go now." He waves us off.

I thank him, and we turn to go.

"Wait." The man approaches again. "I'm the pastor at the Orthodox church on Bauman Street. Do you know where that is?"

I nod.

"Come there around five o'clock tomorrow. We have a soup kitchen. You bring your mama too."

Free food? I don't believe him, but I want to. I nod and smile. I will go to this soup kitchen.

We turn away and walk down the long row of booths where other merchants sell their wares. Once we're out of the man's view, Ludmila grabs the sack from my hand, takes a peach, and bites into the fruit. I loathe her. My mouth waters. I turn away and tuck the other one inside my pocket for Mama. If only I could convince Mama to make Ludmila leave us.

A young man who's leaning against a tall brick building next to a vendor whistles at me. Other men who are huddled around him gawk too. A few make obscene noises.

Ludmila gives them a hard stare and turns to me. "Tuck your hair back into your hood. Keep it there."

My hair is as white as the snow, almost unnatural.

We spend another hour going up and down the aisles of this street market. I don't look at the young orphanage children who sit on filthy threadbare blankets along the edge of the road. They look younger than me, but they are street-smarter. They're trying to sell copper wiring that they've probably ransacked from the guts of a building, abandoned due to arson.

On our way back to Mama, a greasy-haired man smoking a cigarette stops to talk to my aunt. He whispers in her ear and she giggles. I stand off to the side, pretending not to notice him or listen to what they are saying. He pats her bottom and she squeals. Then he nods toward me and asks her a question I can't hear. His stare makes me feel dirty. I turn away to walk back to our apartment.

I haven't gone far when Ludmila approaches from behind me, placing her heavy arm on my shoulder. She's out of breath because she's large and her legs are thick.

"Do you think you're too good to walk with me?" She takes my face in her hands and pinches my cheeks until they hurt. "You stay away from that man, you hear?"

"I'm not interested in him." He repulses me. No man is to be trusted. Ever.

#

The next day before five p.m., Ludmila goes out to work—probably to visit with men. Thick makeup cakes her cheeks under the rouge. Blood-red lipstick lines her lips. She wears heels and a low-cut blouse. Besides stealing, this is our only way to survive.

Mama rests on the bed in the corner of our room on an old tattered mattress that we found several days after the occupants left the place where we are now staying. This is our third home in two months. We must hide from the authorities that threaten to lock us away unless we pay them off. Ludmila, Mama, and I live together. We have no other family.

Two years ago, Sergey, a teacher at the university, fell in love with Mama. He seemed different from the others, lavishing her with jewelry, paying for our apartment, and filling it with silly trinkets. He was kind to me and bought me the first gift any man ever had—a silver bracelet. I wore it every day.

But when Mama got pregnant and her stomach grew and her face swelled, Sergey came around less and less, until one day he didn't return. Mama made excuses for him, saying, "He'll be back. He's busy with his students."

But I knew he wouldn't. I saw him on the street with his arm around another woman—a younger woman—laughing, whispering in her ear, and kissing her on the mouth. I froze in the street, blocking his path, my jaw slack. His eyes met mine, but he didn't pause. He sidestepped me as if I were a tree standing in his way, an inanimate object without feelings, without a heart, someone he'd never met before.

I tore the bracelet off my arm, threw it on the ground, and stomped on it, crushing the cheap silver links into tiny pieces and scattering them on the grimy street. I wished I could squash out the memories of his fake love as easily.

The landlord threw us out of the apartment. Mama stumbled in her grief, letting Ludmila tell her what to do and where to go.

Now we live in a dark condemned building full of other poor people like us. Some are my age, but I don't look for friends because we won't stay long. We never do. Sometimes if I turn a corner fast, I see rats scurrying down the hallways. They don't scare me though. Some aren't afraid of me either.

Our apartment smells like wet socks. It's one large room with a small stove, a sink, and a separate tiny bathroom. We each sleep in separate corners of the room. My bed is the torn sofa.

I tell Mama I'm going out but will be back soon. She barely stirs, but nods. I walk ten blocks to the church on Bauman Street, passing homeless men sleeping in the alleys, heroin needles lying beside them, their hunched backs slacked against spray-painted buildings. Taxis bounce and weave in and out of traffic, their tires hissing as they pull away from the curb.

When I arrive, there's a line five meters long of poor, decrepit people waiting to go inside the church hall. No one looks familiar. A sign on a stand says Soup Kitchen 5:00 p.m.

The air smells of cabbage and potatoes, making my stomach growl and burn. The gray-haired man I met at the market welcomes the people and dishes out food from the bins. He introduces himself as Pastor Kostia.

Will he remember me? I reach for two plates at the end of the line and wait.

When it's my turn I say, "One is for Mama."

His eyes meet mine. "Why didn't she come with you?"

"She's tired and as big as a cow."

He nods. "Oh, yes. You're the girl who came to our fruit stand. No?"

"Da."

"What's your name?" He fills my plate and Mama's.

"Oksana."

"Where is your aunt?"

"She's looking for work." I continue through the line, avoiding his eyes.

"How soon will your mama deliver this child?" he asks, as he serves the next person in line.

"Soon, very soon."

Chapter Two

For several weeks, I see Pastor when I go to his church for food. He's kind and gives me extra food for Mama. He introduces me to his wife, Hannah, and I remember seeing her at the market. She is big-boned with broad shoulders and short legs. She smiles, and I see that she's missing a tooth, but she smiles big anyway.

One day, when I'm in line and Pastor sees me, he says, "Oksana, fill up your plate and follow me." He tells Hannah he'll be back shortly.

I put the potatoes and sausage on my plate and follow him into the large cathedral. Lit candles throw shadows on the wooden statues. The ceiling is so high I can't see where it ends. Way up at the front, a spotlight shines on a piece of art—a limp man nailed to a wooden cross. Why?

I was in a church only once when I was twelve. We were hiding from a woman who wanted to fight Ludmila for stealing her boyfriend. It was dark that night, and I didn't see much of the building. I don't understand what people do in a place like this, why they come here.

This cathedral smells like old shoe leather and candle wax. A humming noise startles me. It's followed by the sound of a loud instrument playing music. The chords echo off the steep walls. Someone sings. Her high notes are shrill and make me want to cover my ears. Pastor doesn't seem to notice so this must be normal. He takes me through the church, through a door behind the altar, and leads me into a small room.

"This is where Hannah and I live, our dining room. Please sit down." He motions to a small table and chair, and I sit there with my food. He takes the chair across from me. "You must be hungry, so eat. I'll give you more to take back to your mama." He stares at me.

I shift in my seat.

He gets up. "I'll be right back. I have something to show you."

I take small bites so my stomach feels fuller, but I want to inhale my food. I haven't eaten rich food like this since the last time I came.

A drawer opens and closes in the other room. Pastor returns with a photograph in his hand, places it on the table in front of me, and points to the lady in the photo. "This is my niece and her husband. They live in America—where I am from."

I nod.

"They want to adopt a baby from your country. They can't have children of their own."

I nod again.

"Do you know what your mama will do with the baby?"

My fork clinks on the plate. I pause. "I don't understand."

"You are poor and your mama doesn't work. How will she take care of the baby?"

I shrug and look away. I don't want to look poor.

His eyes roll over me. "I can tell you are not fed enough. How will your mama take care of an infant too?"

Blood pools on my cheeks. My fingers quiver. It's like he's looking at me through a glass jar, like I am a trapped insect. I know we are poor, but it makes me ashamed.

"My niece and her husband have money, food, and a good home. They have love and are kind." He stares at the photograph and tells me the lady's name, and her husband's and the dog's, but I don't hear him.

"Do you think your mama would let this family adopt her baby?"

"Adopt?"

"They could take the baby and raise it like it was their own. They would give it their name."

"Why?" I ask.

"They can't have any of their own."

Shaking my head, I stand. The room is warm. My stomach

aches. "No." I can't think about giving Mama's baby to strangers. I've heard from kids on the street what Americans do with Russian children.

Pastor shows me the photo again. The man and woman smile in front of a large home with green shutters. The people lean into each other like lovers. A big gold dog sits on the grass next to them. "See how happy they are? Your mama's baby would go to nice schools and wear nice clothes and never worry. Don't you want your brother or sister to be happy?"

I can't finish my food. "No! Mama would not do that. The people will chop the baby into parts and sell its insides."

Pastor's eyes get large and he laughs.

What is so funny?

He says, "No, that is not true. They would only love the child." He rests his hand on my shoulder.

I cringe from his touch and turn to go.

He removes his hand and backs away. "I'm sorry I upset you. Stay. Eat. You talk to your mama later. I won't mention it again. But maybe my niece could help you, give your mama money."

When he takes a seat across from me, I slowly sit and finish eating. Would he really give Mama money for the baby?

He talks about his family in America. He says he's a missionary who helps the Russian people learn about God. When I'm finished eating, he says, "Come, let me get food for your mama."

I am happy to leave. We go through a little yellow kitchen and head toward a side door, which Pastor opens. "Anytime you need something, you knock on this door."

A cold breeze whips in my face and the outside swallows me, just one girl in a world of so many. Murmured voices of those gathered in the alley float toward us, wafted by the wind.

We return to the deserted food line. Pastor makes a plate for Mama, scraping the bottom of the bin and scooping the remnants onto a plate. He hands it to me. "God bless you and your mama." He smiles. "Come back soon. Bring your mama."

I give him the smile I think he wants to see.

Chapter Three

On the way back to Mama, darkness presses me to hurry, and thoughts of what Pastor said hover in my mind. How will Mama feed the baby? I stow the food inside my coat and walk toward our apartment, hoping no one will smell the food and jump me. I rush faster, keeping my eyes low to the ground, wishing I could be invisible. I sigh in relief when I finally reach our building and climb the three flights of stairs to our apartment. I'm out of breath when I reach our door.

Ludmila's voice booms from the inside. "You have no other choice."

I hesitate outside the door, listening, but I can't hear what Mama says, so I enter. "About what?"

Mama lies on the mattress on the floor, pillows propped behind her. "Never mind. Where have you been?"

"To the church." I show her the food beneath my coat and set it on the table next to her bed. Potatoes, sausage, and a slice of bread are heaped on the plate.

"Did you get this from that man again?" Ludmila asks.

"Pastor."

"Is the line still open?" she asks.

"No, it closes at seven."

"Why didn't you bring any for me?" Ludmila asks.

I look at Mama and then down at the floor. "I didn't know you'd be here. Besides, you could have gotten your own."

"I was working. I'm the *only* one working," Ludmila says. Her face turns crimson like she's angry, and she squints at Mama. I think if Mama wasn't here, Ludmila would slap me again. She turns back to me. "You could have brought it and kept it in the cooler."

Mama frowns. "Here, Ludmila, you can have some of mine." Mama hands her the plate. "Take half."

"No!" I snatch the plate from my aunt. "This is for Mama."

Mama says, "I can share. I'm not very hungry."

She's lying.

Ludmila turns to me and smiles.

Oh, how I want to scratch her eyes out! She thinks she owns us since she works, but she works to please only herself.

#

The next morning, Mama sleeps and Ludmila is out, probably looking for men. It's Saturday, and I have nothing to occupy my time. There are no kids hanging around the building, but even if there were, I wouldn't care. Cigarette smells trickle into our room, choking me. It's disgusting. A baby cries somewhere in the building, and a man shouts. Little kids laugh and play in the hallway.

I've never been to Pastor's home in the morning, but I decide to go. After throwing on my coat, I run down the stairs, hungry. As I head toward downtown, the sun is only a smudge in the sky, hidden in the shadows of the bleak and shapeless clouds. I avoid the eyes of strangers and choke at the thick exhaust from cars and buses passing on the street.

When I get to Pastor's, I hesitate outside the door. Did he really mean it when he said I could come anytime?

I knock, squeeze my eyes shut, and hold my breath.

Hannah answers. She flashes me her missing-tooth smile. "Oksana. Come in, come in." She wears a flowered apron over her plump body. Flour powder dusts her hair and the tip of her nose.

I curtsy. *"Privyet. Spasiba."*

The warmth of her kitchen envelopes me, and the sweet smell of apples fills the room. I can almost taste the flavor. My mouth waters.

"Have you ever peeled apples before?"

"*Nyet.*"

"I'll show you how. You can help me until Pastor gets home.

First, wash your hands over there in the sink."

I unzip my coat, set it on the chair, and go to the sink. Following her instructions, I run warm water over my cold hands, savoring the warmth against my skin. The smell of pie dough and the sweet apples lying on the counter makes me drool.

"Go ahead. Eat one." She nods toward an apple.

I pluck the biggest and take a bite. The tartness makes me pucker, and the insides of my mouth pinch. Closing my eyes, I try to memorize the flavor. It's been so long since I've tasted an apple.

When I'm finished, Hannah hands me a knife and shows me how to peel one. She makes it look easy and she's fast. I move my knife the same way she does, but I'm slow and jerky. I peel one to her five, but soon we're done, and she shows me how to slice the apples and add the sugar, flour, and cinnamon. She tells me to reach in for a few slices when we're mixing them. The sugar and cinnamon flavors run together and sweeten the tartness. It's so good that I want it to last a long time.

I like Hannah because she is cheerful and kind. She hums as she works, and when she laughs her whole body shakes.

Pastor returns and raises his eyebrows when he sees me in his kitchen. "Hello, Oksana."

I curtsy. "May I work with Hannah in exchange for more food?"

He meets Hannah's eyes and nods. "Sure, she could use the help. Why don't you come at noon each day to help her cook for the homeless?"

For another few weeks, I help with the church meals. Each time, I put aside the food for Mama and Ludmila before the line forms so we guarantee there's enough left over. So many people are hungry and have no jobs. I'm not sure why Pastor and his wife are so kind to me, but I think it's because they want Mama's baby. But they don't talk about it again.

I bury that thought because I don't want their kindness to be for that reason. I want it to go on forever, but I know that it won't last because something this good never does. I must find work, but what can I do? I don't want to visit with men.

Mama slowly gains strength, but her legs swell at the ankles. and some nights I hear her moaning. I curse Sergey. Why did he have to leave? He told Mama he could get her a job at the university too. Liar. Just like all the others. Mama said he must have gone back to his wife. I never told her the truth. Why? It would only hurt her more. Her beauty cursed us all, but her stupidity angered me. Why did she believe the lies?

But I knew the answer: it was the hope of a better life, that someone really cared, that this time would be different. I believed the lies too. But never again. No one could give me that. Ever.

I tend to Mama now, bringing her water to keep her cool. I shoo away the rats and roaches that crawl in and out of the holes in the walls.

One day when I'm coming home and standing outside the door, I hear Mama and Ludmila quarreling.

"I won't do it," Mama says.

"You have no other choice," Ludmila says.

When they hear me enter, they turn silent.

"What are you talking about?" Even though I ask this question, I know the answer, but I won't admit it to myself for fear it will come true. Ludmila wants me to live in the orphanage.

"Nothing, come here and let me see what you brought me tonight." Mama extends her arm and motions for me to sit beside her bed. She's wearing an old T-shirt that hangs to her knees and covers her round abdomen.

#

A few days before Mama's baby is due, I return home and hear her screams coming from the hallway. I run into the room. The baby is coming. When her pain stops, Ludmila hands her a bottle of vodka and tells her to sip between the pains.

Ludmila grabs the food I've brought and tells me not to give Mama any because it'll make her sick. She shovels the food into her mouth. "When her pains get closer together, go up to the fourth floor and bring Sasha."

"She's gone. I saw her moving last week."

Ludmila primps in front of a cracked wall mirror, applying her makeup and reaching for a brush like she's going out.

My stomach tumbles. "Where are you going?" I panic. My heart gives loud thumps in my chest.

"I have other plans right now. You'll have to manage. When her pains get worse, give her more vodka. It's on the table." She changes into a low-cut blouse and a tight skirt. I can see the dimples in her butt cheeks through the thin fabric. When she slips on her coat, my heartbeat quickens. I glance at Mama. She has deep wrinkles in her forehead and a line of perspiration above her lip.

I follow Ludmila. The room spins. "I don't know what to do."

"Didn't you help Sasha deliver babies?"

"Yes, but that was different. I only watched. I never did it alone." The air in my chest thins. I can't breathe. What if the baby comes? I don't have any supplies.

"I'll only be gone a short while. Labor takes hours. She probably won't be totally ready until later tonight, and I'll be back by then." Her hand is on the doorknob.

A warm wave of heat surges through my body. I'm sweating and my mouth is dry. I pull her arm toward the room, reeling her around. "Mama would never leave *you* like this!"

She yanks her arm out of my hold. "You don't understand. We need the money. She'll be fine until I return. I have to go." The door slams.

She lies. It's not the money she wants. It's the men. She wishes she were as beautiful as Mama, always trying to win the men's approval. *Oh, how I wish I could find a way to get her out of our lives, for Mama to get a good job.*

Mama groans. I rush to her side. She sits up in bed, swings her legs around, and tries to stand.

"Stay still." I push her chest so her back leans against the pillows. "Lie down."

She lies back and pants—short shallow breaths. I go to the sink, rinse a rag in cold water, return to her bed, and place it on her brow. "I'm here. I'll help you."

Visions of the delivery with Sasha howl in my mind. I must keep my wits about me, or the smell of pain and blood will gag me. What will I use for supplies? What if something goes wrong? What if Mama dies?

Chapter Four

Mama screams and sucks in a ragged breath.

Tears flood my eyes. She's never moaned like this before. Her face reddens, and the veins on her neck bulge. I choke back the ball of phlegm in the back of my mouth. I hate Ludmila for leaving. My fingers tremble as I place the cool rag on Mama's forehead.

"Sasha made Katya breathe when she was in labor. Breathe, Mama. Like this." I pant in short bursts.

Mama pants with me, her eyes bulging and as round as coins. She wails and then slowly relaxes. When her breathing returns close to normal, she points to the vodka bottle, breathless. "Bring that here." She pats the space next to her, and the bed creaks as she shifts her weight to a sitting position, her back leaning against the wall.

I don't want to give her the bottle. She'll fall asleep. But she's waiting and smacking her lips like I'm going to give her a candy bar. The look reminds me of when dogs wait for the butcher to throw them a bone, drool frothing from their mouths.

"Oksana!" She reaches further toward me. There's a sharp edge in her voice. "Hand it over."

I give it to her.

She twists off the cap and throws back a swig. A long swig. She pinches her eyes and shivers, but then smiles and recaps the lid. "I'll be okay. Go get some towels, scissors, and thread from the box over there. She points across the room to her little sewing box and places the bottle next to her, her palm resting on it. For a second, I think maybe she'll stay in control.

But then she groans low like a growl. It's sudden, as if she's surprised she's having another pain. Sasha counted the minutes between Katya's pains, but I don't need to. I know it's been less than two. Her pains are close. Already. I breathe with her.

When her spike in pain ends, she reaches for the bottle and chugs it again, then collapses onto the pillows.

I kneel down beside her and push back her long stringy hair that's matted to her face. She's wearing one of Sergey's old cotton shirts. It's missing buttons, and she's naked from the waist down. I prop her up onto the pillows. and she bends her legs, exposing her bottom. A small bloodstain appears on the sheets.

I gag and swallow. I must stay strong.

I hurry across the room and gather towels, the scissors, and thread, then go to the sink to wash my hands, all the time thinking of the blood. Katya had so much blood. *I can't do this. I can't.*

Mama moans and cries again, then takes another swig. "Oh, it hurts. It hurts so bad."

Whimpering, I bite my lip and return to her, flicking the rag off her forehead and rinsing it again before I replace it.

She pushes it aside like she's angry, and shakes her head. "Owwhh . . . the pain . . . it's coming again. Give me another swig." She reaches for the bottle.

"It's almost gone." I snatch it out of her hand. "Breathe." I blow again. She locks her crazed eyes on mine and pants with me.

When the contraction dies, she falls limp on the pillows again. "I can't do this. It hurts too badly. Go find Sergey," she slurs.

"He's not coming back. It's just us now. Remember?"

She cries, and her eyes cross before they roll up, only showing the whites. "I'm too tired." Her eyes close and her body goes limp.

I want to say, "No, you're too drunk," but I shake her arm and raise my voice instead. "Mama, you have to do this."

She whines with her eyes pressed shut.

Sasha had me boil water. I go to the stove, fill a pan with water, and set it on the stove. I must look to see how open her bottom is and how close she is to delivering the baby, but I shudder and twist my hands. No, Katya took hours to have pains this close. Ludmila was right. The baby won't come this soon.

But Mama growls again, and I run to her side. Her knees are bent, and she's curling around her thighs like she's going to push. No! I force myself to look at her bottom and gasp. "I see the top of the baby's head! Oh my!"

The room spins.

Mama clutches my wrist and squeezes until I think she will snap my bone in two. Her face turns almost as red as the blood trickling on the sheets. "Grrr!"

My arm burns where she's holding me. "Let go, Mama. I need to get the towels, the scissors."

Finally, she releases my arm and falls back onto the pillows. "I can't do this." Her voice is shrill, and tears stream down her face.

The boiling water gurgles on the stove. I throw the scissors in and turn it off. Sasha had other tools in the water, but all we have are scissors. I gather the towels and the thread and set them on the bed.

Mama's eyes are closed again, and her legs have fallen open like she's unconscious.

"Mama?"

Her eyes flit open.

I exhale, relieved, but not for long. Katya's eyes had stayed open the whole time. The vodka has cursed Mama.

She reaches for her bottle, but there's nothing left. She tosses it on the floor. It clanks but doesn't break. She closes her eyes again and falls limp.

Tears stream down my cheeks as I go to the stove and scoop out the scissors with a spatula and return to the bed.

I shake her. "Mama, the baby's head is almost out." I brush the wetness off my face. "You have to push. Don't stop."

Her eyes open.

"Keep pushing!" I shout.

Her head bobs. She curls around her legs and screams.

Somewhere in the crowded building a man curses and shouts, "Can't you shut that woman up?"

"Grrreeeoooowww . . ." Mama screams again, and the baby's head pops through the opening, dangling. It's bluish, full of white slime and red goop. I cradle the head in my palms, feeling the warm liquid.

Mama pushes again and the shoulders rip through, the entire body slipping into my trembling hands and onto the towels. The warm slime has saturated my fingers and forearms. "It's a girl."

Mama smiles faintly, closes her eyes, and falls back onto the pillows, limp.

My tears have turned to sobs because I am both excited and scared. My sister needs to cry. Why isn't she crying? I'm the only one who can save this child. "Mama! What do I do?"

She doesn't flinch. "Mama!"

I grab the baby by her feet and hold her upside down like Sasha did and give her one smack on her bottom. She cries, but it's weak and garbled like there is fluid in her mouth. Sasha used a suction tool to get the fluid out. I don't have one. What am I going to do? She's going to suffocate!

Whimpering and talking to myself, I rub her face, nose, and mouth with a towel. "Come on, baby. Breathe." I use my finger to scoop inside her mouth and around her nose, then she squeals louder and faster, her fists pummeling the air. The fight for her life has begun.

"Aahhh," I cry out, relieved, and lay her on another towel. Her arms and legs move in jerky movements.

I feel the cord. It's pulsing like a heartbeat. I can't crimp it yet. I must wait until it's no longer beating.

Mama stirs, her eyes still closed. "I'm so tired. I can't—"

"Look at her, Mama. She's beautiful—like you."

Her eyes open like slits, and she glances at my sister long enough to take a glimpse, but the pains return and she screams. Sweat lines her brow, and the veins in her forehead bulge. She pushes long and hard and growls like an animal again. I barely recognize her, her face is so swollen. She pants and pushes more, but then falls back onto the pillows. The color drains from her face, and her eyes are closed. Her head falls to the side like she's passed out.

Rapid-fire breaths scrape against my throat. She can't sleep now. The birthing sack hasn't come. Is she too drunk? Sasha said if a woman doesn't deliver the sack, she can fester inside from an infection that could kill her.

"Mama, wake up!"

My sister cries. I wrap her tight in a towel until she calms, then shake Mama. "You need to push the sack out. You're going to be done soon. Don't fall asleep yet."

What happens next will haunt me for a long time, but I can't tell anyone. Ever.

Chapter Five

By the time Ludmila returns, it's almost dawn. The sun's glow is rising in the horizon, but not my spirits. I haven't slept. I'm lying on my bed, facing the wall, thinking of what I've done. The room is hot and smells of blood even though I've removed the bloodied towels and thrown them in the garbage dump.

Ludmila gasps when she enters. "You've had the child?"

Her footsteps sound across the floor. I'm so mad at her I pretend to sleep so I don't have to see her, afraid I might attack her. It helps that my back is to her.

Mama stirs. "Ludmila? She looks like Sergey. No?" Her words are slurred.

Now Mama wakes?

There is a pause, and I assume Ludmila is looking at the baby, who lies at Mama's side.

"She's a tiny thing," Ludmila says. "I expected you to still be in labor. It is good that this is over. We must move on now."

"No. I can't think about that right now."

"Maybe not, but soon enough you will have to think about it. That good-for-nothing Sergey won't be back. We can't count on him. This child will only add to our burden."

I hear this, and I know that what I did was the right thing, but I'm worried what will happen next.

When I know they're both sleeping, I quietly arise, dress, and run to the church. A loud ringing in my ears follows me. My heart beats faster than it should. I pound on the door to Hannah's kitchen.

Tears streak my cheek, and my ears burn from the cold. It takes several minutes before Hannah answers.

"What is it, child—what's wrong?"

"They are making me go away. I know it. Ludmila—I hate her—is going to take me to the orphanage. I heard her telling Mama."

"No, maybe you're wrong?"

"No, it's true."

Pastor comes through the kitchen door. He stops when he sees me crying and Hannah's arms around me. "What's this about?"

I tell him the news, and I see the sadness in his eyes. "I know that you can't help me, but will you show me—one more time—the photograph?"

He leads me to a desk in a sitting room off the kitchen and pulls out a book full of names, numbers, and addresses. Then he pulls out a photo book from a shelf above it. He shows me the same photograph again of the young smiling couple standing in front of a large brick home with flowering trees.

Have I done the right thing?

"Here, take this photograph with you. I will write the address on the back. If this is true—that you will go to live in an orphanage—maybe someday someone will come from America to adopt you too." Pastor shrugs and glances at Hannah, who is crying. "You never know what can happen when God is in your heart."

"No, no! I'll never go to America. I want to stay with Mama. She needs me."

Pastor sits at the little desk chair and scribbles something on the back of the photograph. He reaches in his pocket and pulls out a small key chain. After finding the key he needs, he slips it into a locked drawer. Inside is a metal case with paper currency. He tucks the money and the photograph in an envelope and says, "Keep this safe. Maybe it will comfort you."

Then he says, "Let us pray." He and Hannah take hold of my hand, and Pastor bows his head. "Dear Heavenly Father, bless Oksana and her family and keep them safe from harm. Guide them with your love and give them strength to endure your will. Help Oksana to see and feel your spirit, in Jesus's name, amen."

I don't know anything about this God or Jesus. But Pastor believes, and it gives me hope.

Chapter Six

Several nights later, Mama lies in bed with the baby next to her in the corner. I'm lying on the sofa, ready to fall asleep. Aunt Ludmila is out. The only light in the room comes in through the window from the streetlamp outside, dim and forlorn, like me. Mr. Bushcka shouts in the apartment above us. His heavy footsteps clump across the floor, and then glass shatters and more shouting rings out.

I want to tell Mama what I did, but I don't know how. Since the birth, she seems lost, like she's in a faraway place—like she's sad all over again, like when Sergey left. I don't want to add to her pain. Maybe it will be better if she never knows. Ludmila ignores the baby, like she wishes my sister had died during birth. She doesn't care about me either. She doesn't care about Mama, but Mama is beautiful. Ludmila needs her.

Mama says, "We'll name her Natalia, which means actress, or a movie star. It'll be her destiny."

"What does Oksana mean?"

Mama sighs. "You were named after your father. Your name means traveler."

"Was my father a traveler?"

"Yes, he didn't stay long. You look like him."

"Was he tall?"

"Yes, very tall, but he had wide shoulders too."

"Was he nice?"

She sighs again. "Yes, he was good, kind, and funny. He made me laugh."

I want to ask, why didn't he stay, what happened to make him go, but I fear the answer. It was probably me.

Mama's breathing turns soft and shallow. She's fallen asleep. I think of my father and what he was like, what he would think if he saw me, if he thinks of me now, but then my stomach knots in anger. Why did he have to leave? I never knew him. Mama said he left when I was a baby.

The doorknob rattles and Ludmila returns. Mama stirs. I pretend to sleep, facing the wall again, my back to my aunt. Ludmila breathes heavy, probably from carrying her fat body up the stairs. She huffs like she does when she's reclining into the sofa.

She speaks low to Mama. "Elaina, it's time. I will take them tomorrow and that's that."

Bile rises from the pit of my stomach.

Mama cries softly.

I fall in and out of fitful sleep. The shadows in the room chase me, following my thoughts. I toss and dream of strange faces, dark tunnels, and a faceless man who walks beside me. I can't find my way home. I'm lost.

The night passes slowly like the fog beneath the bridges where I've slept before, and I wake to my sister's cries. My shirt is damp with perspiration. Shafts of light stab through the window, momentarily blinding me. Dust flakes swirl in the air.

Our door is ajar, and Ludmila's voice trickles in from the hallway. She's talking to Irina, our neighbor. Mama's bed is empty. She must be in the bathroom.

I rise to see. No, the door to the toilet is open. Mama is gone.

My sister's arms and legs flail. Her face is red. Why didn't Mama nurse her? Maybe she did, but her milk isn't satisfying. My stomach is empty too. I take off Natalia's soaked rag and see her chafed red bottom. She's tiny and barely has a crack between her buttocks cheeks. Her arms and legs jerk in angry movements.

After rinsing the cloth, I drape it on the back of the chair. I wrap Natalia in a towel and she grows silent for a few minutes, just until she knows I have nothing to give her except my finger, which she spits out. She wails again until she's exhausted enough to fall asleep.

A man's voice sounds outside the door. It's Pastor. I gasp. He's talking to Ludmila. I hold my breath. He came. He's really here. He will tell Mama the secret. I hide Natalia in a basket in our tiny bathroom and run out to the living room, behind the door.

Ludmila says, "She's gone to look for work. What do you want with her?"

I peer through the crack. Ludmila stands with her hand on her hip, glaring at the man.

"I don't want to talk to you. I came to talk to Oksana's mama."

"She's not here. Talk to me. I handle all her affairs."

Pastor hesitates. His eyes meet mine as I'm peeking through the slit. I shake my head.

He turns to Ludmila. "No, I will come back. When will she return?"

"I don't know. That depends." Ludmila crosses her arms.

"I will try back later." Pastor turns to go. Natalia fusses. I move away from the door and hurry to the bathroom. After I pick up my sister, I sway her in my arms and she quiets again.

Ludmila returns to the apartment and closes the door. "What did he want?"

I shrug.

Natalia fusses, like she knows what I've done.

Ludmila says, "Come. We will go." She doesn't look at me.

"Where?" My stomach clenches.

She takes Natalia from my arms, still not meeting my eyes.

I grab my coat off the floor in the corner, slip my arms into the sleeves, and feel for the envelope in my pocket. It's there. My heart beats so loud I can hear it in my ears. I follow Ludmila out of the building.

The wind whips my hair into my face, a sign that winter's chilly bite is close. I button my coat and lift my hood. "Where's Mama?"

"She's looking for work."

"Where are we going?" My voice cracks.

"We must take Natalia to the orphanage."

"No!" A knot forms in my throat.

"We cannot feed her. The authorities will come and take her if we don't. Her best hope is for me to put her in the baby home. She will get fed there."

"Mama will be angry."

She steps ahead of me, her thick legs moving with purpose. The dark deep wrinkles around her pinched mouth warn me of her quick temper and her impatience. She holds her head high, and her dark hair falls in jagged wisps across her face. She smells of sweat and onions.

We walk in silence for at least two miles toward the center of the city and pass the orphans huddled along the edge of the road. School doesn't start for another hour. One little girl watches me, locks her eyes on to mine. I pause for a brief second, hitching in a breath as I recognize the despair in the shadows above her cheeks.

The sun's rays peek between the clouds and heat up the day. My coat makes me hot and weary, but it was a gift from Mama, so I keep it on to feel close to her. We pass cluttered yards in front of shops with broken, boarded-up windows and moldy shingles, and garbage-choked alleys until we get to the other side of town, where trees line the street. Their crooked branches droop over the road like bent fingers waiting to pluck us off the ground. We take a narrow path off the main street that winds into what looks like a forest. I dodge weeds growing between the cracks in the sidewalk.

Natalia sleeps in Ludmila's arms. Soon, the sidewalk ends, and on the other side of the trees there are larger buildings. Like dark secrets, they're hidden away.

We continue to the largest building sitting on a hill. An old black iron gate guards the entrance. One of its hinges has lost a bolt, and the door stands crooked in the dirt. Ten small windows on the front of the building face us. A deserted playground sits to the side. This must be the baby home. Tall weeds and seeded dandelions have grown up around the slide and the swings. There are no footpaths leading there.

Ludmila points to the curb in front of the building. "You wait here. I will be back."

"No. Please, you can't leave her here!" My arms reach for Natalia, pulling her toward me. She wakes, and her weak cries make my heart beat faster, but there's nothing I can do.

Ludmila yanks her out of my grip. "Stop this." She waddles toward the gate to the orphanage. Tears spill down my face. I drop my head.

The crooked gate creaks when she pulls it open to let herself in, and then it shakes until it finds a resting place in the dirt. After she's in the building, I walk the same way she did, through the gate, but I go up the sidewalk and around the side of the building. I tiptoe in the grass to a window and cup my hands around the glass, peering inside. My tears make the room blurry. I wipe them away, wishing I could wipe away my fear for Natalia.

There's a large room full of cribs—rows and rows of cribs. The windows are ajar and there are no screens, so I can hear, but even though there must be fifty babies in the room, none are crying. It's eerily quiet.

One dark-haired baby looks at me. He doesn't smile. He only stares and flaps his hands. I can see that his diaper is soiled, and he wears no shirt or pants. He has no blanket. Around his ankle is a piece of gauze—maybe from a scrape—which I can tell has started to cut off the circulation because his foot is a shade darker in color than the rest of his body. A fly buzzes around him.

A lady in a white uniform sees me. She has reddish hair and fat dimpled arms. Her eyebrows run together, and it looks like she has one long, thick one. She scowls at me as she approaches the window holding an infant. "Go on, get out of here."

This is where my sister will live?

My legs tremble back toward the sidewalk, through the gate. I shuffle back to the curb. My stomach aches. I memorize the surroundings. "I'll be back, Natalia. I promise." Without me, my sister has no one.

Shortly after, my aunt returns. She doesn't speak. I follow her, but we don't leave the way we came. A heavy feeling spreads through me, seeping like dissonant chords on a violin, screechy and alarming, tasting like bile in my throat.

She's going to leave me too, isn't she?

Chapter Seven

My heart is thumping louder and faster. Aunt Ludmila and I continue on the dirt path through the trees in silence. She doesn't look at me.

"Where are we going now?"

"You'll see."

More silence. My tongue feels dry and tastes like the dirt in the road. I lick my lips repeatedly until their chafing burns.

Then she says, "We cannot feed you either. You must go to the orphanage, where you will study and get fed. It's your only hope right now."

My stomach aches like someone kicked me. The wind gushes out of me. I can't breathe. I stop, my feet weak from hunger and the thought of what will happen next. I want to run, but there's nowhere to go, and my feet are frozen. "You'll only leave me for a little while, right? When Mama gets better, she'll come and get me. She needs me to take care of her."

Ludmila's chin juts forward. She stares ahead. "I don't know how long it will be. I'll take care of your mama. Don't worry about her."

I reach for her arm. "Promise you'll return soon and bring Mama. Please!"

She yanks her arm out of my grip. "We'll see."

"There's something I have to tell her." How can Ludmila pretend to flick me off, shoo me away like a fly? "If you don't come soon"—I choke back a sob—"I will leave and come find you."

She stops and turns to me, her cheeks flushed. “No, you won’t find us. I don’t know where we will be living. You have to stay there and wait.”

I hate Ludmila. This is all her fault. “Does Mama know where you’re taking me?”

”She knows. She agreed that this is the only way.”

“I don’t believe you!” My fists are clenched. She lies. Mama wouldn’t let me go to a cruel place. She, like me, has heard from the street kids that the children in the orphanages are beaten. I could run and hide, but where would I go? “I will find Mama and ask her.” I turn to run, but Ludmila clutches my wrist.

“You will not!” She twists my arm tightly and pins it behind my back, speaking between her teeth into my ear. “Enough. You must go.”

Pinching my eyes shut, I squeeze my tears and swallow the lump in my throat. I will not let Ludmila see me cry. Somehow I have to find a way to tell Mama what I did.

Ludmila yanks me forward, dragging me.

As we continue on the sidewalk, I try to rip my arm from her hold, but it’s impossible because Ludmila tightens her fat grip. I close my eyes and pretend I’m holding Mama’s hand. I want to remember what it feels like forever, like it had the night she was in labor. I’d compared her fingers to mine. Hers were slender and feminine and a little dainty, her nails chipped and jagged, showing life’s cruel sneer, but they were warm. Always they were warm.

I press my nails against the palm of my hand now, wanting to remember the strength of Mama’s flesh, wishing she was there, wishing I could make her appear out of nowhere. I want her to hold me and never let me go.

A crack in the concrete causes me to stumble. I open my eyes. Another large brick building looms before me. This one has darker red bricks than the doskey dom where we left Natalia. The windows are open, and curtains hang out of one of them. They’re flapping in the breeze. Music comes from one of the windows. It’s a kind of music I’ve never heard before. It’s sad.

As we get closer to the building, I drop my hand from Mama’s imaginary one.

A group of girls walk up the cracked mortar steps beside us. They look me up and down—like they’re inspecting my clothes, shoes, and body. None of them smile. They whisper to one another and burst out laughing.

One girl, who walks with a limp, trails behind the others. She glares at me so intently that my eyes shift toward the door to block her gaze. All the girls wear T-shirts under their unzipped jackets. A few wear long skirts, and others wear dark slacks. The girl with the limp wears two different shoes. One is black with a missing buckle and larger than the other, and makes a clumping noise as she walks on the steps.

As Ludmila and I enter the building, the girls stand outside the director's office and watch us enter. I smell a stale odor like that of an old person's breath with rotting teeth. The floor shines, showing the dark shadow of my reflection.

A stocky old lady rises from behind a dark wooden desk to greet us. "How can I help you?" Her voice sounds like a child's—high-pitched and meek. I can't help but stare at her mouth.

Ludmila clears her throat. "I need to leave my niece here."

The lady stands and comes around to the front of the desk, reaching for my hand. "My name is Vera Myasha. What is your name?"

"Oksana." I refuse to put my hand in her crooked, bony one.

She retracts her hand. "Oh, that's such a lovely name. It's the same as my granddaughter's. Come in and have a seat here, please." She motions for us to sit in the metal chairs across from her desk.

As she's closing the door, the girl with the limp snickers and mouths so only I can hear, "Don't believe a word she says." Her words pierce my thoughts.

Mrs. Myasha's wrinkled hands, mottled brown with age spots, reach up to straighten her glasses that are taped in one corner, making them crooked on her nose. The green veins in her hands squiggle, as if they're crawling under her loose flesh.

Ludmila reaches inside her coat and pulls out several papers. "These are from Oksana's mother. She was too sick to come. She went to the police and filled out the forms yesterday."

"You're a liar," I say.

She unfolds the papers and hands them to Mrs. Myasha. "Here."

The director reaches to take the papers, but I seize them first, scanning them. One is my birth document and the other is a form with the police's stamped address at the top, the official form. It's in Ludmila's handwriting with Mama's signature. *No!* The room spins.

Ludmila snatches the papers out of my hands and shoves them into Mrs. Myasha's.

"That isn't Mama's handwriting." I glare at my aunt. "You filled it out."

"Yes, but your mama signed the paper." She glowers at me, her eyes merely slits. "She can't keep you, Oksana. She's sick with the drink, and you know it. When was the last time she fed you?"

Mrs. Myasha tilts her head to look out of her bifocals, reads the paper, then nods at me. "This is the proper paper, and it looks like the signature is in a different handwriting."

I fold my arms. Yes, it's Mama's signature, but Ludmila probably made her sign. But it's my word against Ludmila's. I'll never win. Someday I will get back at my aunt. I close my eyes and see myself kicking her, biting her, throwing stones at her. Tears threaten to spill, wadding in a ball at the back of my throat.

Mrs. Myasha returns to her seat, opens a drawer, and takes out papers. She clasps them to a clipboard and hands them to Ludmila.

I push the hood off my head, feeling heat rise in my cheeks from the anger simmering inside me.

Mrs. Myasha stares at my hair.

My eyes shift to the plaques that adorn her walls—not to read them, but only to focus on something different than her stares and the tears that want to tumble out of my eyes. How many others have sat in this same room and stared at these walls, desperate at their situation, unable to control their fate? How many other children were here with their mama and never saw her again?

The stagnant air suffocates me. There's a smell of fear here, but it's no use waving it away because it's in the walls, in the wooden door—forever emitting an unforgettable stench that can never be erased. It smells like rotting flesh—the kind that starts in the soul, where you can't see the burn, and decays from the inside out. Maybe it's from the other children who were left here too, abandoned by their mama.

Tears break loose and trickle down my face as Ludmila completes the forms. Mrs. Myasha glances at me, pity in her eyes.

"I'm sure your family will come to see you, maybe bring you back home when things get better. It isn't so bad here. Really. You will make friends. There are twenty-two girls and seventeen boys who live here. They are all near your age."

She turns to Ludmila, then points to a place on one of the

forms. “Be sure to fill out this part. We need a way to reach you, a forwarding address. We work with a church in the United States that facilitates adoptions, and if this isn’t filled out”—she pauses to glance at me—“well, we wouldn’t have a way to get in touch with you . . .” She lets her sentence trail.

“I am only here until Mama gets well.”

My aunt pats my hand and leans toward Mrs. Myasha. “We don’t know where we will be. I will have to let you know, call you with our forwarding information.”

“Please, don’t leave me here.” I clench my hands in my lap.

Ludmila ignores me.

I turn to Mrs. Myasha. “Can I leave to visit my mama?”

Ludmila unbuttons her coat. “I already told you. We have to move, we don’t know where we’ll be. You must stay here.”

Mrs. Myasha glances at Ludmila again. “Please read the bottom of the second form—the part where it says what could happen if we don’t have contact from you for three months.”

I look over Ludmila’s shoulder at the papers, but she turns her back. I can’t read the form.

Mrs. Myasha says, “Our goal is to reunite Oksana with her family, but if that’s not possible . . .”

“What will happen?” I stare at my aunt. “I don’t want to go anywhere else. I want to be with Mama. Please bring her—tomorrow. Please! I won’t be any trouble. I’ll go to work.” I hate myself for begging.

She faces Mrs. Myasha. “We may not come to visit for a while. We have to find work first.” Then she turns toward me. “Don’t make that face. I know what’s best for you. You don’t understand. You’re just a child.”

I grab her pen, but she snatches it back. Tears fall like the hope in my heart and spill onto my cheeks, my chin, and into my mouth, where I can taste their saltiness and feel their sting on my lips. A cramp forms in my chest, my shoulders shake, and I hiccup with sobs. “Mama won’t”—my words are staccato-like—“want you to do this. She’ll be . . . mad at you!”

“Your mama knows what I’m doing. She agreed.”

“I don’t believe you. If she did, it was only because you are an evil woman!”

Ludmila raises her hand to strike me, but Mrs. Myasha places a box of tissues at the edge of her desk and says, “Stop. Is this true about her mother? Why isn't she here now?"

"She is ill, sick with the drink. She gave me permission to bring Oksana. It's right there on the paper." Ludmila points to my papers and waves her hand like she's dismissing the director.

Mrs. Myasha gives me another pitiful stare and places my papers in a folder. "Why don't I tell you a little about our place here?"

I swipe the tears with the back of my hand and turn my back to Ludmila. "What about my clothes, my books, and my other things? What will I wear? I didn't bring anything."

Mrs. Myasha says, "We have a donation box from the church stored in the basement. I'll let one of the girls show you where it is." She pauses. "You will wake every day at eight thirty, make your bed, dress, eat, and go to school. There you will study math, science, and history. There is an hour of free time before supper. You will be assigned a cleaning job that you will be responsible for. You'll also do your part to keep your room clean, and on Saturday mornings everyone works together to dust, wash floors, and work in the kitchen."

The room spins again. She talks to me like this is an ordinary day, like I'm simply another book on the shelf, someone without feelings. I glance at her photos of children on her desk. I doubt she'd leave them here. Nausea rises up from the pit of my gut, burning my throat. I swallow and gag. "Tell Mama I love her and to come back soon. I need to tell her something important."

Ludmila stares at the form, avoiding me. I know she can't wait for me to leave.

A low drone fills my ears. Everything feels like it's in slow motion, like this is a dream, like it's not happening. I whisper between clenched teeth to my aunt, "He'll never want you because he'll always want someone younger and more beautiful. He only pretends he likes you." I stand to go, so I'm out of her reach.

Out of the corner of my eye I see her turn and glare at me. She knows who I'm talking about.

"Who would want you? You're nothing but a fat cow," I add.

I think if I was closer, she'd pull my hair, but Mrs. Myasha opens the door and hollers out to a girl in the hall. "Ruzina, come here."

I wipe my face and straighten my back, jut my chin, and tighten my lower lip.

A petite red-haired girl approaches. Her eyes are a steel gray, and her skin is the color of milk. She doesn't look at me the same way the other girls did. Her rounded shoulders slouch forward shyly. Sadness surrounds her like an imaginary friend. She holds up a hand for a second. "*Privyet.*" Her voice is so quiet I can't see her lips move.

Mrs. Myasha says, "This is Oksana. She will be sleeping in the empty bed next to you. Oksana, this is Ruzina. She is new to our home too. She will show you around. Take her to the kitchen and ask cook to give her some kasha. Then take her to the donation box to see if she can find clothes that will fit her."

I look back toward the office and Ludmila stands, smiling. I turn and leave with Ruzina. My heart sinks into a pit of darkness, deep in a valley, a place where I've never been. For a second, the world seems to swallow me. My heart is racing like a scared rabbit, and I don't think I'll ever forget the stale smells of this building. I'm certain they'll follow me like a dark shadow for the rest of my life.

I take a deep breath to steady myself. Someday soon I will leave here and find my way back to Mama.

Chapter Eight

Ruzina walks with me down the tiled hallway and up a flight of stairs, giving me the tour of my new home. The shiny floors smell like wax. The stain on the wooden stair railing is faded from the light shining through the big windows at the landing. I take in the green and gold colors from the trees outside, blocking my view of the building where Natalia's living. A few people walk on the cracked sidewalks. I will make a plan to visit my sister soon, maybe steal her away with me.

"Our bedroom is on the second floor."

We climb the stairs, and I follow her into a room. There are eight beds—two rows of four. Each bed is about six feet from the one next to it.

"We keep our belongings under the bed. The bathroom is across the hall."

The walls had been painted beige, but not recently. Scuffs and etch marks mar the paint in the wooden headboards. There is one small open window with no screen. Flies buzz in the sunlight. I look out and see my aunt walking away from the building. I recognize the back side of her head and the way she wiggles as she walks—plump and pear-shaped. Tears lodge in the back of my throat, pinching like when I ate the apples with Hannah, but this doesn't taste good.

Ruzina is talking to me, but I don't hear her. I fight back tears because if I give in to them, I won't be able to stop. I watch Ludmila until she disappears behind the trees.

"What did you say?" I ask.

"Don't look beneath any of the beds or at anyone else's belongings because you could get blamed for stealing, and if you're caught, you'll get the switch."

"What's that?"

"That's when Olga comes and takes you to the basement and beats you."

"Who is she?"

"She is the day keeper. You'll meet her later. I'll show you the washroom."

She takes me to a room across the hall.

"Have you ever gotten the switch?" I follow her.

She shakes her head. "Let's go to the kitchen."

"What's this place like?"

She only shrugs.

"If I put something private under my bed, does that mean no one will look there?"

Ruzina answers, "Nothing is private here. If you try to hide something, someone will find it. They will sneak a peek when no one is around."

I touch the envelope with the photo in the pocket of my pants. Where will I hide it?

The building we are in is old and worn down. The inside is cleaner and starker than where Mama and I have lived. I inhale deeply, trying not to cry, not to think of Mama. Even though I saw her yesterday, it feels like weeks ago.

We pass other girls on our way to the kitchen. Most of them keep to themselves and don't look up. Just outside the kitchen door, there is a two-inch black cockroach crawling on the wall.

"What are you girls doing here?" a bald man asks.

"Mrs. Myasha told me to show this new girl to the kitchen for a bowl of kasha."

"She did, did she? Well she didn't tell me anything of the sort." He reaches for the wall telephone and we hear him mumble. The kitchen is hot, and there are two ladies clanging pots in and out of the cupboards. Buckets of water sit along one side of the wall.

"What are those buckets of water for?" I ask in a whisper.

"There is something wrong with the well pump, and there is no money to fix it. We have no running water. We have to take turns going to the well and bringing water back for them to boil. Some of it is kept in the refrigerator for drinking, and some is for our baths, the wash, and for cooking. You'll have to take your turn too. Everyone does.

"When do we get to bathe?"

"When it's your turn. I don't know when that will be. We get one a week and must wear the same clothes throughout that time. Most of us only have one set of clothes. We wear T-shirts and shorts when we wash out our clothing. Sometimes we stay in our night clothes all day while the clean ones are drying—especially in the winter when it is so cold it takes a very long time for them to dry.

"We wash our clothes in the laundry room downstairs on Tuesdays and Thursdays. You will be assigned a day. Make sure you do it on that day too. If you forget, then your clothes will stink, and they will call you a ming."

I look at her clothes. Her dress is a faded blue color, dirty and plain. Her shoes are brown and scuffed. One has a buckle and the other does not. She wears yellowed socks.

Her head drops and she looks at the floor. "Tomorrow will be a week for me. I will get my turn to bathe and wash my clothes then." She turns to go.

"How long have you been here?"

"Two months."

"Where is your family?"

"I have no family."

"Where were you before you came here?"

"At an orphanage for younger children. I grew too old for that one and had to move here."

"How old are you?"

"I will be thirteen at my next birthday."

"Hey," the kitchen cook says. "Here is your kasha. It's cold, but it's what we have left from this morning. Go. Eat it in the dining room."

"It's over there." Ruzina motions and I follow.

The room is large. The walls here are butter yellow, and the tile is dark brown. Long rectangular tables sit side by side in rows. We sit at a table and she watches me eat. My kasha tastes bland, and it's sticky and lumpy. I don't share any, but I doubt she expects me to. I'm so hungry that I eat too fast and my stomach cramps.

"It isn't good, but it's all we get for breakfast. You will feel fuller if you eat slower and make it last longer."

I know.

Next, Ruzina says, “We will go to the laundry room in the basement.” Our feet echo back at us on the concrete stairs. Ruzina cannot keep her buckle-less shoe from clunking as it slips off her heel. Footsteps approach from somewhere below, and deep voices and snickering ring out. One’s voice is loud and deep. The other is quieter.

“Did you see her chest?” the one asks.

“Yeah, voom-voom,” he says, and they both laugh.

I want to backtrack up the stairs, but we can’t outrun them. They are too close. Before long we are face-to-face with them.

The one loud-voiced boy whistles at me. I look at him for only an instant and see that he is older and much bigger than we are. He has wavy brown hair and dimples in his cheeks, the type most girls like. I turn my face away.

“Check out that hair! Is it real? It looks dyed. Can I touch it?” he says.

We keep walking. They stop with their backs to the wall as we brush past them. The one boy holds out his hand and reaches his fingers toward my hair. I recoil and bat at his hand.

“Hey, she’s got spunk too. What’s your name?”

Ruzina and I continue toward the laundry room, leaving space between us.

“It doesn’t matter,” he shouts back to me. “I’ll find out soon enough.”

After we’re a good distance away from them, I realize I’m holding my breath. I exhale. “Who was that?”

“His name is Nicholas. All the girls like him. You will too, in time.”

“No, I won’t. I don’t want anything to do with boys.”

We turn in to a hot, steamy room where sheets and clothing are laundered. There is a thin lady whose back is hunched over a dryer. She’s standing, but her back is deformed. Her chin almost rests on her chest. She looks up at us with beady eyes. Ruzina mumbles and tells her that I’m a new girl, and that I’m supposed to look through the clothes. The woman tells me that I only get two pairs of socks, a dress, and a pair of pants, a shirt, and two T-shirts. She points to a metal door and says, “In there.”

Ruzina opens the door and we go inside. It’s damp and smells like soap. She points to a large laundry basket. “There they are. Pick from them.”

The clothes are thrown in the hamper, unfolded. They look like rags. There are dark slacks and light ones with yellow stains. Some have holes. There are mismatched socks of all different colors, and shoes with holes in the bottom. There is one pair of bright pink sandals that must have come from America, but they are far too small for my feet.

Ruzina watches as I rummage through everything. I hold up one faded navy shirt that looks like it'll fit and a few pair of socks and a green-striped dress. I hold it up in front of me. It looks like it'll hang to my knees.

"You can try it on." Ruzina turns her back to me.

I slip it on over my clothes. "What do you think?"

She turns. Her eyes skate over me and she shrugs.

Maybe it's her way not to say how bad it looks, but I don't have too many choices. I slip it over my head and try on a pair of pants. Nothing is worth taking, but I know I must have a few pieces of clothing. I take a few T-shirts to sleep in. They all smell moldy and are almost thread-bare. I jump when I see a little gray mouse at the bottom of the basket scurry under a torn sock. I hold my hand over my mouth to stifle my scream. It's not that I haven't seen a mouse before; it's just that this one startled me. I shake out any other pesky critters from the clothing in my hand.

"Don't you want to look?"

Ruzina says, "I'm not allowed."

On the way back up the stairs, Ruzina nods toward the bent-over lady and says quietly, "That's Elena. Don't go down here alone."

Elena gives us a sideways glance, but pauses as if she's checking me out. She stares at me long and hard. The hair on my arms prickles.

"Why?"

Ruzina only shrugs again.

Pain reflects in Ruzina's eyes. I don't want to know what Elena has done. I believe Ruzina and will stay away from this woman.

Chapter Nine

It doesn't take me long to meet Nicholas. He sits across from me at dinner, but I ignore him and his friends. They're doing some stupid boy thing where they put their hands under their armpits and move their hands so it makes a bathroom sound.

"Hey, what's your name, new girl?" he asks.

Pretending not to hear his question, I eat my soup and cooked cabbage, its pungent smell filling the room, and look past the other tables to the window, where leaves swirl in chaotic wisps and tree limbs shiver in the wind. Nicholas wants me to notice him because all the girls notice him, and he loves the attention, but that's exactly why I don't look at him.

Ruzina sits beside me, watching him and giggling. She whispers, "He keeps looking at you." I feel his stare boring into me as if he's trying to memorize every little flaw on my chin, my elbow, and my mind. It only makes me sit taller and prouder.

One of his friends says, "She's too good to talk to you, Nicholas. Maybe this is one who isn't interested." He laughs, and out of the corner of my eye I see Nicholas jab him between the eyes. When I get up from the table to dispose of my garbage, I slip a serrated knife into my shirtsleeve. The girl with the limp tries to trip me, but I see her clumsy foot and walk around it.

Not all the other girls are cruel. Some smile and seem to want to make friends, but I'm not interested in making friends, except for Ruzina. She's different, like me, content to be alone.

Ruzina nudges my elbow. "There's Olga, the day keeper."

Sitting at a table in the front of the room is a large woman with dark hair. Her arm flab hangs over the tabletop, flapping with her movements as she shovels food into her mouth. It's hard to imagine that she can walk. She must sense that I'm looking at her because she meets my eyes and scowls. I don't want to mess with her.

Ruzina and I exit the dining hall, and she whispers, "The night worker left her job. She wasn't paid enough. Olga has to stay overnight until they find a replacement, and she's not happy. It's happened before. She reads in the dining hall and falls asleep. Her snores are so loud they could wake the dead. She's too large to climb the stairs to check on us, so there's been talk that the boys will play a trick on her or cause trouble."

The knife's blade feels good against my skin. I will hide it under my pillow.

At night, I lie in my bed next to Ruzina's and stare up at the ceiling. My bed is closest to the door. The boys sleep on another floor and on the other side of the stairwell. My mind drifts to Mama. Where is she? What's she doing? I hope she's getting better and thinking of me. I think about Natalia and of a plan to get away to see her.

When the lights go out and we're supposed to be sleeping, bedsheets and blankets rustle, and the box springs on a mattress creak. I listen to the giggles and the sounds of groping and hard breathing. I don't know who they are. I don't care. I try to block the sounds out of my mind and pretend to sleep.

Then I sense someone close to my bed. I feel the person breathing, and the hairs on my arms stand straight up like a cat's when it's approached by a threatening dog. The person smells musky of body odor, and I think it's a boy

Ruzina breathes like she's already dreaming. Even if she were awake, she couldn't help me. She said here we all look out for ourselves. If I pretend to sleep, maybe whoever is looking over me will leave, but I'm not that lucky.

His sour breath heats my neck. He fingers my hair. Always, it's my hair. Slowly, I move my hand under the pillow, faking a stretch, and grip the knife. Just as he begins to crawl under my blanket, I turn toward him and stab his arm with the tip of the blade. He gasps, flinches at the gash, and swears. Then he smiles and twists my wrist, loosening my grip on the knife. In the shadows of the hall light, I see his dimpled cheeks and wavy hair. Nicholas.

He snickers, his hands around my wrists, pinning them down. His breath is in my ear, hot and raspy. "You're a feisty one. I like that."

I spit in his eye and twist my body side to side. His knee comes up between my thighs, and I scream. It's a short scream and no one says anything, but I hear beds creak and footsteps hurrying out of the room. Maybe it's the other boys worried they'll get caught. The girls are probably awake, but they don't say anything.

"Shut up," he says.

When his lips come down on mine, I bite them hard and taste his blood. He swears again. I fling my head, but my strength is no match for his. I feel dizzy and think I'll suffocate from the weight of his body on top of mine. I can't breathe.

He lets my left hand loose to unbutton his pants, and I pull his hair. He laughs.

A tall, dark shadow looms above him, and a silhouette against the hall light strikes the back of Nicholas's head. There's a smack like something hitting bone, and Nicholas's limp body crushes onto mine, knocking the wind out of me. I gasp and push him off and onto the floor. My heartbeat thunders. I gasp for breath.

The shadow takes Nicholas by the feet. It's a pimple-faced boy with red hair and crooked spectacles. I've seen him before but don't know his name. He meets my eyes for only a second, but I can't read them. I roll off the bed and onto the floor, reaching for the knife, breathing hard, but the boy drags Nicholas out of the room without a backward glance.

Will the boy return for his turn? What does this mean? Am I indebted to him now? He probably wants something. I grasp the knife in a tight fist and wait, sitting on the floor, leaning against my bed and facing the hall. My heart races. There's nowhere to go unless I hide somewhere. But where? I vow to inspect the building tomorrow to find a hideout.

Ruzina lifts her head off the pillow. "Are you okay?"

I nod and she closes her eyes.

Several other girls are sitting up in their beds, looking my way. One says, "You're lucky this time. He usually gets what he wants."

It isn't until the morning light filters in through our window that I climb back into my bed and doze.

When I wake, the room is empty, but I hear the girls in the hallway, making their way down to breakfast. I take the knife to the bathroom, stand in front of the mirror, and chop my hair in sections, watching as the pieces fall into the sink. I cut my strands almost down to the scalp. Short pieces stick straight up on my head. Some are longer than others. My hair looks like fringe, giving me a freakish appearance. Unfortunately, it only makes my eyes look bigger, bolder, and more aqua then before.

Ruzina walks in just as I'm scooping my hair out of the sink. She stops, arches her brows, shakes her head, and moves to a stall. "I liked your hair the other way."

Nicholas isn't at breakfast, and there's talk that he's still sleeping and will be in trouble for not waking up on time. My rescuer with the red hair sits across from me at breakfast. His name is Alex.

I say, "Thank you for helping me, but I can take care of myself. I don't want your help or your attention, and I certainly don't want to owe you anything."

"I didn't do it to help you, so don't think I did. It was a payback. It had nothing to do with you. You just happened to be the one who diverted his attention." Then he gets up and walks away.

I shiver. Nicholas will be back. I must be ready.

Chapter Ten

I go to the orphanage school that week in a fog. The rumor is that Nicholas is at the hospital, but no one talks about him, and they avoid me. I don't meet their eyes, and my short hair labels me a freak.

A week later I have a plan. I will go back to our apartment. After my chores are complete, we are free to leave the building. I bundle up in my coat and head out the front door. Flurries float from the gray sky as I make my way back to where we used to live. I must find Mama and tell her what I've done and where Ludmila took me.

I pass Natalia's orphanage, resisting the tug in my heart to look through the window, to lift her from her bed and take her back to Mama, but first I must make sure Mama is there. Then I will come back for my sister.

With each step, my heart pounds louder. The chilly air breathes down my neck and up my pant legs, giving me shivers like a warning.

What if Mama isn't there?

She'll be there. I know she will.

But what if Ludmila is there too? What if Mama doesn't want me?

No, she'll be happy to see me. If Ludmila is there I'll wait outside until she leaves.

People pass me on the sidewalk, but no one looks familiar. Cars honk and race in the street, their engines sputtering, and the smell of sewers wafts up from the ground.

But the closer I get to our apartment, the deeper my doubt spreads like black ooze seeping into my veins. Finally, I'm standing in front of our building. I pause, take a deep breath, and reach for the door handle that leads to the steps. I yank it, but it doesn't budge. The door won't open.

"You can't go in there. It's been condemned." An old man with wrinkled graying skin sits with his back against the building, his deep-shadowed eyes on mine. "The police made everyone vacate."

"Where did they go?" My voice cracks.

He shrugs and looks away. "To the next hellhole."

Heat burns my ears. Tears sting my cheeks. A passerby smoking a cigarette reminds me of Ludmila's friend, but it's not him. I look up one street and down the other. Everything looks dirty. No one looks familiar.

I run, heading toward Pastor Kostia's church. I want to see Hannah, to tell her where I'm living. Maybe she can help me find Mama. I pass people on the streets as I run like a scared deer, breathless and bumping shoulders. The strangers stare at me and curse me. The beat of my heart pounds in my ears, keeping rhythm with my footsteps, but when I see the church, I pause, my tears turning to sobs, suddenly needing to be in Hannah's arms. I pound on the side door, the one I've used before.

There's no answer.

I pound again, my cold fists clenched and burning.

Finally, someone opens the door, someone I've never seen before. She has a scarf around her head and a mop in her hand. "Yes, what can I do for you?" Her voice is gentle.

"I need to see Hannah . . ." I pant, leaning on the doorjamb. "See Pastor. Where are they?"

"I'm sorry, but they went to Moscow and then to America."

"America?" I brush the tears off my face.

"How long will they be gone?"

She shrugs. "I don't know."

My heart thunders in my ears, then tumbles to my toes. Now what?

The lady looks puzzled and a little frightened. My hood has fallen off my head. She stares at the wild wisps of my hair and at the snot dripping from my nose and hastens to shut the door. "I'm sorry."

The door closes, and there's a final click like she's turned the dead bolt.

I fall in a heap and sob into my hands. Who might know where Mama is? There is no one. Mama's only friend Maria has been gone for years, scrounging on the streets of despair, maybe dead by now.

There is no one left in my life.

#

Time lapses slowly before I can finally stand and wander back toward the orphanage. The sights of old buildings and strange faces fill me with deep loneliness. I find myself in front of my sister's orphanage, longing to see her.

A lady dressed in white approaches the gate where I'm standing, seeming to bounce as she walks. "Hello. Are you looking for someone?" She smiles. She's younger than Mama, but older than me and has tiny facial features.

"My sister lives here." My voice is barely audible.

"Oh, what's her name?"

"Natalia."

"Oh, the little one with the peach-colored hair, right?"

I nod.

"Such a good baby." She turns to open the gate and waves. "Come on in. She'll love to see you."

I hesitate. "Really?"

"I don't see why not, just as long as you don't get in the way."

I follow the kind lady in through the front door. A warm gush of air greets me. The building seems quiet, too quiet for a home filled with babies.

The lady unwraps the scarf from around her head and unbuttons her coat. She leads me down a long tiled hallway, her white rubber-soled shoes not making a sound. "She's in with the newborns in this room." She points to a door and glances at her watch. "It might be feeding time. What's your name?"

"Oksana."

"I'm Dominka."

I nod as she opens the door to the nursery, to the room I saw from the window outside. This room smells of dirty diapers and sour milk. Cribs line one wall. One baby fusses, but most lie in their beds, the room eerily quiet.

The large red-haired woman with thick eyebrows, who stared at me before, now sits on a chair feeding a baby. She scowls at me. “Who’s this?”

Dominka doesn’t seem fazed by the other woman’s harsh tone. “This is Oksana.” She turns to me. “Oksana, this is Veronika. She works here more than any other person, guarding these children.” She turns to Veronika. “Natalia is Oksana’s sister. She came to see her. Is it time for her to eat? Maybe she can feed her for you.” Dominka hangs her coat on a hook and reaches to take mine.

When I hand it to her, she glances at my hair. “Cute haircut.” She smiles.

A grin creases my face.

The other woman says, “Did you get approval for her to be here? How do you know she’s not lying?”

Dominka waves her off. “Oh pooh, she’s harmless. Who would lie about having a sister here?” She glances at the cribs and points. “Your sister sleeps over in this bed.”

I follow her and stop when I see Natalia, her eyes wide open, her legs kicking and arms jerking. She stares at the ceiling until she notices us. Her eyes lock on to Dominka’s, and she smiles. I gasp and cover my mouth. She looks like Mama. I must have startled her because her smile fades, but only for a second. Tears fill my eyes, and I reach into the crib for her, then pull her to my breast, cradling her in my arms and gazing into her eyes. The sounds in the room turn mute as she smiles up at me and coos.

Veronika says, “You can feed her, but you have to stay over here in this chair where I can watch you.” She squints her beady eyes and nods to the chair next to her.

I do as she instructs and spend the next hour holding, feeding, and changing my sister’s diaper. The warmth of her body spreads through me, replacing the black ooze of despair with a color of hope, hope that somehow staying with Natalia and seeing her will make me feel closer to Mama, and maybe bring us all back together again.

Chapter Eleven

When I return to the orphanage after seeing Natalia, my despair returns. It's dark and dinnertime, but I'm not hungry, just tired. So tired. I lie on my bed and sink into a deep sleep, dreaming that I'm falling in a tunnel, dropping down a dark hole. The bile in my stomach rises to burn my throat, the bottom of the hole nowhere in sight. I fall deeper and deeper until I'm so hot I can't breathe. I'm suffocating.

I lie in a bed, shivering with body aches and fever. I sleep off and on and can't raise my head off the pillow. I dream that Mama comes to see me and Ludmila pulls her by the hair, dragging her away. I cry and try to follow her, but I can't move. I don't have the strength to get up, and then I wake with a start, trembling.

Light slices into the room from the window, telling me it's daytime. I've slept through the night and past breakfast. My clothing is drenched in sweat, but my body quakes with shivers.

Ruzina stands over me. "You're sick. It's going around. I'm going to get help."

The next time I wake, I'm in a different room, lying in a corner on a narrow bed, alone. The room smells of bleach and antiseptic. The overhead lights are so bright, I see dark spots when I close my eyes.

"Mama, where are you?" I think I've uttered the words, but I don't hear their sound. Maybe I only thought them. "Water." My throat burns and my lips sting. I try to lick them, but can't seem to make saliva. Finally, my tongue moistens, and I taste blood from my cracked lips.

Nurses and doctors come and go. No one talks to me or tells me what's happening. There's no one to hold my hand or sing to me or to tell me I'll be okay. I don't understand.

I think I'm going to die, and I don't care.

Finally, I wake and realize I'm in a hospital. I don't want to be here because I've heard stories of how they leave children here to die. My heartbeat sprints, but then thoughts of Mama, the empty building, and the clogged streets with rusted cars come rushing back. I crimp my eyes shut. Maybe I'll die. I don't care. Maybe it will be better if I do.

Sometime later I wake again to a sound. Someone says my name.

"Oksana."

The voice sounds far away but familiar. My eyelids feel like they're glued shut. I want to open them, but they're too heavy. It's easier to keep them closed.

Then there's a warm petite hand on my arm. "Oksana. Wake up."

Mama? My eyes flutter open. No, it's Ruzina. She washes the nightmares from my sleep, standing over me, holding something. What is it? It's green. An apple? A green apple.

"How are you doing?" she says.

"How long have I been here?"

"Three days."

"Three days? How can that be?" I clutch my dry throat and lean on my elbows, trying to sit, but am overcome with dizziness.

"You were really sick, but your fever has broke. I brought you two of these." She hands me one apple and reaches into her coat for the other.

I take them. "Thank you. Where did you get them?"

She smiles.

"You stole them, didn't you?" Something inside me awakens, makes me giggle. I can't believe she cares enough about me to risk stealing.

"You need to eat. They aren't feeding you much. Olga said the only food you get here is your portion from the doskey dom, so you need to get better and get out of here." She reaches for a bag I hadn't noticed before, sitting on a chair. She pulls out several plates of food, setting them on the bed. "It's cold, but it's all there is." Then she reaches for a cup on my table, fills it with water, and tells me to drink.

"Thank you." Sipping the water, I let it swirl in my mouth before it slides down my throat. It soothes and refreshes me like Ruzina.

#

When I return to the orphanage from the hospital a week later, I'm weak and keep to myself. The others look at me strangely, like they'll get sick if they get too close, but they already suffer from what I have. It's called loneliness.

Every day starts the same. The only change is the weather outside. It's colder and snowier. The weather doesn't affect me though. What does it matter? It doesn't change where I am, what I'm doing, or who I am. I stay here because there is no other choice. I sleep often and don't go out to see Nat because I don't have boots, and she reminds me too much of Mama.

I lie in bed some mornings and stare at the walls and the tiled floor. The floor is old, and many of the corners are chipped. Some days when I don't pay attention to where I'm walking, my bare feet snag a corner and rip a little piece of my toe skin. When I want to fall asleep, I stare at the ceiling and count the tiles. There are exactly twenty-two, but some are cut in half.

Mama never comes, and as the weeks tumble by, my hope of seeing her again diminishes. Most of the kids here don't have visitors. Many of them have siblings but rarely get to see them because they're far away—too far to walk. At least I can visit Natalia. If I want.

I become the quiet girl—only existing—going to school, doing my chores, and keeping to myself. I talk to Ruzina but no one else. Since I've returned from the hospital, I have turned in to myself. The others think of me as a freak, and that works fine with me.

On my fourteenth birthday, no one wishes me a happy birthday because no one knows it's my day. Dasha turned sixteen yesterday and had to leave—to live on the streets—because she has no family. Sixteen is the age limit—which means I have two more years. Then, like Dasha, I must find a way to live. Dasha cried when she said good-bye to her friends. Her fingers had trembled with nails bitten down to nothing.

Three months after I return from the hospital, I still feel tired, but spring arrives and makes me want to go outside to see Natalia. The air is still cold, but since we are free to come and go after school, I decide to visit her before supper. No one knows where I'm going except Ruzina. Sometimes it's easier to keep things to myself.

As I walk toward the orphanage, the sun shines brightly, and the breezy air smells of springtime. Purple flowers push out of the ground, showing their faces. It reminds me of when Sergey and Mama fell in love and how we moved into our apartment, happy and together.

I wear a new jacket donated by the people from a church in America. Mine is blue and has a hood. I keep my brown coat under my bed with the envelope hidden in the pocket. This jacket is too large, and the sleeves hang below my hands, but it's warm. I make a fist and shrink into the sleeves and cover my hair with the hood. Even though my hair has grown some, the wisps are still in shaggy sweeps.

As I approach the doskey dom, I hear soft music through the shut windows. I walk off the sidewalk and let myself in through the gate and step onto the grass next to the building. I peer into the windows, where I'll be hidden from the street and passersby. On my tiptoes, I cup the glass with my hands and stick my nose on the windowpane. The lights are on in the room.

I want to make sure Dominka is there. She said she works on Thursdays and today is Thursday, but what if she quit? I don't like Veronika.

Dominka sees me through the glass and smiles, motioning for me to come inside. I hurry into the building and through the door that leads to the nursery.

When I open the door, the familiar dirty diaper smell greets me. There are more cribs and babies here than there were the last time. Veronika is on the other side of the room, bathing one. Many of the infants lie awake in their cribs, sucking their fingers but not crying.

Dominka says, "Hello, come and see how your sister has grown." She points to a crib behind her.

Natalia's lying on her back, kicking her bare legs and sucking her middle fingers. Her hair, still the color of a peach, has grown long enough to curl. She drools on her fingers and stares at the ceiling. Oh, how she looks like Mama. Even the shape of her head and her ivory skin resembles Mama's, making me miss her more.

Tears fill my eyes.

I lift my sister and hold her, running my finger along her cheek and feeling the silky smoothness. Her body stiffens like she's not used to feeling my touches, like she's going to cry.

"It's me, Oksana, your sister."

I've been gone too long. She doesn't recognize me. Tears fall faster, dripping down my face. I'm angry for not coming more often.

She turns toward my finger, her pale eyelashes fluttering and staring into my eyes, but when I meet hers, she quickly looks away, gazing at the ceiling.

I cluck my tongue and she turns to look at me again, but only for a fleeting moment. She doesn't know who I am. I must keep coming to see her.

Dominka interrupts. "Go ahead and feed her. The bottles are in the cooler." She nods toward a fridge. "Where have you been?"

I shrug and go to the cooler to get the bottle, sit in a chair, and feed her. Her mouth latches on to the nipple hungrily, but she stares off at something other than me. She smells like the sour feeling gripping my gut. Already she's learning to survive in a world without love.

#

I visit Natalia three more Thursdays, and finally she seems to recognize me a little more, smiling, keeping her eyes on mine. But then something happens the following Thursday. Like always, I peer through the window first, to see if Dominka is there. This time a lady in a white uniform walks into the room and asks Veronika a question. Veronika hands the lady a baby with peach-colored curls like my sister, but she's too far away for me to know for sure if the baby is Nat. Dominka isn't in the room.

Where is the lady taking the baby?

I run to another window—one that I haven't looked through before—and I see an office filled with people. I jump back, certain that they've seen me, but no one says anything, so I steal another glance.

It is Nat! The lady in white gives Nat to another lady, who cries and holds Nat close, like my sister is her baby. A bald-headed man, who stands at the lady's side and looks like her husband, holds Nat's tiny fist.

They're talking and smiling while everyone is looking on. Dominka is in the room, holding something up near her face, maybe a camera.

There's a gray-haired man, another woman, and the orphanage caretaker. Who are they? What are they doing with Nat? The couple lean over the table like they're signing papers. My heart races. Are they taking my sister?

I move from the window and run toward the front door of the building. When I enter, the front hall is empty. I follow muffled voices down a hallway and past an office, pursuing the voices. I'm in the open doorway. I look in. Natalia is still in the woman's arms.

"You can't take her! I won't let you!" I leap across the room and grab my sister from the woman's arms, clutching her tight.

The lady's mouth drops open, and she says something I don't understand. The man next to her places his hand on her arm. For a second everyone goes silent, and they stare at me.

The man with the gray hair crosses the room and grabs my arm. "Who let you in here?"

"This is my sister." I hug Natalia to my body. "No one is going to take her." I glare at the lady with the pink beads and the perfect hair, then at the man with the shiny head and pleated pants. They shake their heads like they don't understand.

"Mama is coming back for us," I shout at them.

Dominka crosses the room and places her hand on my arm. "Oksana, these people have come to adopt your sister and take her to America." She speaks in her soft voice.

"No! I won't let them." Tears roll down my cheeks. I turn toward the door to leave with Nat in my arms, but the gray-haired man crosses in front of me and closes the door, blocking my path. I can't leave.

Natalia is crying like she's frightened.

The lady with the perfect hair stands and says something to me. She's crying, talking in a different language I don't understand.

The gray-haired man tells me to sit down so he can explain. He takes Nat from my arms, but I don't want to hear what he has to say. I know what is going to happen. They will take Natalia and I will be alone. Forever. Just like Mama, I will never see Natalia again.

I throw open the door and race down the hall, my footsteps clomping on the tile like my heartbeat pounding in my ears. Outside, tears drip off my nose as I run. My sister is going to America. I will be alone and forgotten forever.

I run past an elderly lady on the sidewalk, bumping her shoulder and practically knocking her down. I'm sobbing. People turn to stare at me. I slip on a bit of ice and crash onto the cold concrete, my skin burning like the hope that stings inside me. Now I'm bleeding on the outside and the inside too.

When I get to the orphanage, I sprint up the stairs and go to my room, diving into my bed, facedown. I stay there until my pillowcase is tear-sodden.

I should have taken Nat away before. But where would I have gone? Mama is gone, and Pastor and Hannah have probably gone back to America for good.

I sink into a deep sleep and wish for my life to end.

Chapter Twelve

Several mornings later, I wake to Mrs. Myasha's hideous voice. She rarely comes upstairs. Most of the girls are sleeping. "Oksana, I need you to get dressed and come down to my office."

The other girls wake. They tease me. "What did you do? Are you in trouble?"

Maybe Mama is here!

I gather my things, hurry into the bathroom, and dress. My heart thunders. Maybe today will be the day I leave here. After brushing what's left of my hair, I stare at myself in the mirror. My hair stands on end. I wet it down, but it doesn't help. I look pitiful! My dress is faded like the yellowed walls in the dining room, and my legs are like skinny poles except for the red patch on my knee. I pinch my pale cheeks. They flush for an instant, but I can't erase their milkiness.

I run down the two flights of stairs, taking two at a time, my heels clunking on the tile. Within minutes I knock on Mrs. Myasha's door, out of breath.

"Enter."

I open the door. Mama isn't here. The other people are—the ones who came to take Nat. What are they doing here? Why are they here?

My sister sits on the lady's lap, smiling and playing with her necklace. Natalia is wearing a pink dress with ruffles along the bottom, tights, and black shiny shoes. She has a pink bow in her hair too. I barely recognize her. The sight of her in another woman's arms brings tears to my eyes.

Nat clings to the lady. I run to her, and pull her away from the stranger, holding her to my body. She cries and reaches for the lady with the perfect hair. She'd rather go to a stranger than to me. Then it dawns on me. I'm a stranger to her. In the six months of her life, I've only seen her maybe six times.

I'm the only stranger in the room. A sick feeling fills my gut. I brush the tears off my face with the back of my hand and inhale. I will not cry.

Natalia's eyes narrow like she's not sure if she should trust me, watching me out of the corner of her eye, stiff in my arms. I should hand her back to the lady, but I can't.

Mrs. Myasha takes my arm and pulls me to a chair. "Oksana, please sit down. This is Jack and Katie Engle from the United States. They've come to adopt Natalia."

I glare at them and sit on the edge of the seat, Nat still in my arms. "I know. I don't want them to take my sister. What if Mama returns and finds her gone?"

Mrs. Myasha rests her hand on my arm and frowns. "Your mama is not coming back."

My body feels heavy. "You don't know that."

She says, "We have not heard from her. We have no forwarding address." She licks her lips and sighs. "There is a registry, a list of orphans. We are required to search for your family. Your name has been on the registry for five months, and we have not heard from anyone."

"Mama doesn't read. How is she supposed to know?"

Mrs. Myasha shakes her head. "These people didn't know about you until they saw you at Natalia's orphanage two days ago. They've been working with the authorities on all the paperwork to adopt you too."

Me, leave Russia? I turn my gaze to Katie and her husband. They're smiling at me. Katie has tears in her eyes like she pities me. Jack squeezes her shoulder. His fingers are long and thick with clean nails—like Sergey's.

"No, what if Mama returns? There's something I must tell her. I have to wait for her."

Mrs. Myasha pats my arm. "This is a chance for you to go with Natalia to America, where people will love you and make you a part of their family. Don't you want to stay with your sister?" Her voice sounds more gentle than usual. “You don’t want to be on the streets when you’re sixteen like Dasha, do you?”

No, I don’t, but I don’t trust her or these strangers either. They look like lovers—the kind that never last.

The Katie lady turns to another woman in the room. She has curly hair and says something in English I don’t understand.

Mrs. Myasha says, “Oksana, this is Polina, the translator. She’ll tell the Engles anything you want them to know or ask, but be careful what you say. Can you stay calm?”

Nobody says anything. They’re watching me, waiting for me to say something. Natalia puts her two fingers in her mouth. She’s drooling and looking at me out of the corner of her eye.

Tears well in my eyes. I can’t stop them now. They fall down my cheeks, drip onto Nat’s clothes, and then onto my lap. I don’t like my choices. I don’t want my sister to leave, but I don’t want to leave Mama either. If I go to America I’ll never see her again, never get the chance to tell her what I did. But if Natalia leaves without me, I’ll never see her again.

Katie smiles and holds out her hand for mine. She says hello in Russian. I look away.

Mrs. Myasha scowls at me and pushes her glasses up on her nose. She hands me a tissue.

I wipe my eyes and swallow hard, willing the tears to stop. ”Where do they live?”

“In a state called Michigan,” Polina interprets.

Katie pulls out a book from a bag on the floor next to her. She hands it to me. Inside are photographs of a house and people I don’t know. Natalia pats the book, her wet fingers on the picture of the gray house with a white picket fence and thick green grass. A black shaggy dog sits on the porch with its pink tongue hanging out. A view of the lake shows blue skies and modern boats. I turn the pages, see more smiling strangers. The last page shows kids riding different-colored horses. I stare at them and then at Katie, pointing.

Polina translates Katie’s words. “Those are horses. My sister, Laura, owns them. She has a ranch.”

I look at the pictures. What would it be like to sit on a horse like the little girl in the photograph? I hand the book back to Katie. “Why do they want to adopt us?” I ask Polina, who translates.

Katie answers. “We love children and can’t have any of our own.”

Jack, who has a goofy, crooked smile with a brown mustache says, "It's true." His bald head reflects the light. He seems uncomfortable that I'm staring at him because he wiggles in his seat.

I turn away and look down at my shoes.

Jack says to Polina, who translates, "Perhaps this is all too sudden for Oksana. Maybe we could take her and Natalia for a ride in the city, maybe stop for ice cream somewhere. Would you like that?"

I agree.

Before we leave, the director hands me a bag. "They brought you these clothes to wear. Go change. Bring the clothes you're wearing back here to me."

I open the bag and look inside, the strange scent from the new clothes filling my nostrils.

Katie says, and Polina translates, "I hope they fit. We guessed your size, and now I can see that the shoes we brought are much too small. You're tall. We'll find you a pair when we go into the city. Would that be okay?"

I nod.

I hand Natalia back to Katie, leave the room, and run up the stairs with the bag of new clothes, hurrying into the bathroom. I lift the clothes out of the bag and inhale their scent again, reveling in their newness. Are they trying to bribe me into going with them? The jeans are too short, but the sweater and the zippered jacket fit well.

I go back to my room. It's empty. The girls are either having breakfast or at school. I decide to leave my old coat under the bed. I'm hopeful I'll be able to return, that this isn't a trick.

I wish I could tell Ruzina where I'm going, but I'll be back, probably tonight. I'll explain then and see what she says. I'm hungry but too nervous to care.

Chapter Thirteen

We stop to eat breakfast at a little restaurant. The waitress stacks my plate full of meat sausage, fruit, and cakes. There's juice and milk to drink. It's so much more food than the meager kasha in the orphanage. I want to eat every bite, but my stomach cramps full. Maybe in America I would never be hungry.

We shop in Kazak with Polina, who continues to translate. We look through store windows for shoes. I'm asked which I like, but I don't know, don't care. I'm new at making decisions on style. Finally, Katie chooses a pair for me, and the saleslady measures my foot and returns with a few different sizes. I'm uncomfortable with this attention.

Jack and Katie watch me like I'm a new species. They tell me to walk around, so I stand and pace, feeling like I'm on springs. The sneakers are bouncy. I make a circle and sit back down again.

I nod yes, they fit.

Katie chooses a few pairs of socks, and while she pays the person at the counter, Nat fusses.

Jack, who's holding Natalia, talks baby talk to her and makes silly faces like he's trying to get her to stop. Natalia pauses and smiles. Then she coos.

I scowl and take her from Jack's arms.

He digs into the bag draped on his shoulder and pulls out a bottle for me to feed her. He smiles.

I don't smile back. I sit in a chair and feed my sister, who shuts her eyes and falls asleep. Jack, Katie, and Polina watch and wait.

Once Nat is sleeping, I wrap her in a blanket and we leave the store.

I don't like being with these strangers, but I like being with Natalia and knowing she's safe.

While we walk the streets, I look into the faces of the people, hoping to see someone I know—Mama or Ludmila or one of her male friends—but they don't come to this part of town. This is the richer part of the city, the section I dreamed of living in someday, the streets where I've never roamed. We are far from the poor section and Hannah and Pastor.

A knot lodges in the back of my throat when I think of them. Something tells me they're gone for good. I swallow the ache.

Katie and Jack point to buildings and ask Polina questions. Jack holds Katie's hand and helps her across the street, showing her kindness.

Polina answers their questions, maybe telling them about the city. They ask if Nat is getting heavy, but I shake my head. I want to carry her. They ask if I want ice cream. What is my favorite flavor? I've only had a few flavors in my life, so how would I know? We stop at an ice cream store, and I look at the flavors through the glass. There are so many different colors, but I don't want to try anything new, so I order the chocolate. Katie has something with chunks of nuts and Jack has chocolate like me.

They tell me that they'll buy me more clothes in America, where there are more styles and better prices. They assume I am going. My stomach somersaults at leaving, living with people I don't know in a strange, new place.

What would it be like living with these people? They seem nice to Nat, and Jack seems kind to Katie, but maybe it's a show. Sergey used to be nice too.

Katie insists on buying me a few more things—underwear, sweatshirts, jeans, and tops. I let her choose and shrug with indifference, but a part of me is excited. No one has ever taken me shopping like this before. The clothes I've worn have been hand-me-downs and rags. The fabrics and styles of these new clothes make me look different, like I'm not skinny and sickly. Maybe people won't look at me with pity in their eyes when I wear them.

I turn sideways in front of the full-length mirror, staring at my reflection, admiring myself in a pink sweater and faded jeans that are finally long enough to cover my legs and my feet. The person I see looks different—cold and harsh. I've never thought of myself in this way, but now it's like I'm seeing what other people see when they look at me. A freak. I don't like it. I smile to soften my face. There. Now I don't look so haunting.

Katie smiles in the mirror at me.

Jutting my chin forward, I turn away. It's like she knows my private thoughts, and I don't want to let her in.

What would Mama think if she saw me now? Would she be proud? If I go to America will she think I've abandoned her?

No, she's the one who left me. She's the one who never returned.

I hurry into the fitting room to change my clothes, my fists clenched, angry and hurting inside, like a blister is forming in my heart. I squeeze my eyes shut, wishing I could fly away, wishing Mama was standing here beside me instead of Katie.

I will not cry.

I will go to America because I don't want to be separated from Natalia. I will go, and someday I will return to find Mama and tell her. Even though I say this in my mind, I'm scared to leave my country, but the fear of staying and never having anyone is greater.

When we've finished shopping, Polina goes home for the evening but tells me she'll be back in the morning. I'm going to stay with the Engles in a hotel room in Kazak. The building is clean with fancy lights, and our room has running water, a tub, and big beds. They take Nat into the bathroom to bathe her. When she hears the bath water running, she cries. I go in to see what they're doing, but they're only filling the tub. Nat is sitting on Katie's lap on the stool, but she's hysterical.

She reaches for me to take her out of the room, so I take her from Katie and bring her into the room with the beds. I stay there until she's quiet and the water has stopped running. Slowly, I make my way back to the bathroom, soothing her.

Jack sits on the side of the tub, and Katie kneels on the floor, reaching for Natalia. I hand her to Katie, watching, ready to pull her hair and wrestle her for my sister if she does anything to harm her. Katie dangles Nat's feet in the water, one toe at a time. Nat flaps her arms like she's excited. She's probably never had a bath like this before. In the orphanage they give them sponge baths, rinsing them with rags soaked in water.

Katie laughs and splashes more water on Nat until she laughs too. Eventually, Katie immerses most of Nat's body, and once she's in the water, she relaxes.

Jack tickles Nat's feet and talks baby talk to her again. I don't know what he's saying, but he changes the sound of his voice. He and Katie laugh like they're having fun. I turn and go to lie on the bed. It's soft and warm, so I curl up under the covers with my clothes on and run my hand over the smooth cotton sheets, smell their clean scent, and fall asleep.

The next day, Polina returns and tells me that we have to go back to the orphanage for the Engles to finish the paperwork for my adoption, and then both Nat and I have to see the doctor there. Good, because I want to say good-bye to Ruzina.

This is final; I'll be leaving for good. Suddenly, I'm warm all over. A dull pain settles in my stomach.

"Why do we need to see a doctor?" I ask.

"This is procedure. You must obey," Polina says.

Polina pulls our car up to the orphanage. Students are outside walking to school. Ruzina sees me and waves. I hurry out of the car and go to her. We stand on the steps of the orphanage.

She smiles. "Where were you?"

"With a family who's adopting me and my sister. I'm going to America."

Her thin smile fades. "This is good for you. You will be happy. Make a good life." She turns to go.

I touch her arm. "Wait." Moving in closer, I lower my voice. "Come with me to the room for a minute. There's something I want to give you."

"What?"

"You'll see."

She follows me up the stairs and into our bedroom, where I kneel on the floor and collect my old coat. She watches as I pull the envelope out of the pocket, open it, and take out the photo. I leave the money in there but flash it so she can see. "You keep this. And my coat." It's all I have to give her, and I don't want to keep the money. It makes me too ashamed of what I did. I scrunch my eyes and take one long sniff of the coat—the smell reminding me of Mama—and shove it back under the bed. I zip the photograph into the pocket of my new jacket.

She smiles. "Thank you."

Together we descend the steps, she before me, as if she'll find a way to go on and maybe forget me.

She waves one last time at the curb outside and walks away. Her shoulders slump, and her head bends so low that her hair covers her tiny face. Something tugs and turns inside me. I want to cry for her. Even though I feel bad about leaving Mama, at least I remember my mama, and I have a sister. Ruzina has no one. What must she feel right now?

I understand why she doesn't hug me. Getting too close to anyone only hurts more later.

#

We follow Mrs. Myasha to a room down the hall from her office that has been converted into an exam room. I'm asked to sit on the table and let the doctor look at me.

He shines a light into my ears, eyes, and throat and places the stethoscope on my back. "Breathe deep."

Jack and Katie watch. Polina tells me I need several immunizations because it looks like I haven't had the ones I need to go to America. The doctor wheels a cart from a closet and pulls out several syringes and needles. They're lined up in a row.

My eyes widen and my heart thumps faster. I've had shots before, but are the ones for America different? "Will they hurt?"

"Just a little," Polina says. "But you must have them and the proof that you've had them before you can enter the United States."

The room spins. I feel hot. My breathing gets fast.

"Don't watch; it'll help if you don't," Polina says. "Look at me or across the room."

Katie stands at my side and places her hand on my shoulder. I flinch. I don't need her help. She looks surprised, but I don't care.

What if this is a trick and they are drugging me? Then it's better if I take my turn first before Nat. If I start to feel funny, I can latch on to Nat and run. But if they're telling the truth, then I must let this happen. I squeeze my eyes shut and smell the alcohol the doctor wipes on my arm.

"This is going to sting. Relax," he says.

I can't. He does this three times, but nothing changes in my head to make me feel funny. He lays me on my back and presses on my abdomen.

"Everything is good," he says, and sits me up.

Next is Nat's turn, but I can't watch. I leave the room and stand outside the door, my arms folded across my chest. The hallway is empty now. Nat cries, and I want to burst into the room and stop the doctor, but I know I can't, so I put my fingers in my ears and hum.

Jack steps outside as if he's looking for me. When he realizes I'm just outside the door, he reaches out like he's going to pat my arm, like he pities me, but I move out of his reach. I don't want him to touch me. Ever. I've seen how men touch women, use them, and leave them.

Chapter Fourteen

The next few days fly by in a blur. We travel to the Kazaksky Railway Station, a place I'd never seen. It's nighttime when we arrive. The building's lights throw shadows in the crevices of its grand architecture, illuminating a tall steeple like that on a church. Outside, the building glows like a warm ember, but inside the structure feels cold and unwelcoming. The ceilings are tall and arched—so open that I feel lost and cold.

I stay close to Katie's side as we sit on a hard bench to wait for the train. Before we board, we use the bathroom. Inside, we must squat at the troughs to relieve ourselves.

We ride the train for fifteen hours into Moscow, where the adoption will be finalized. Polina travels with us. Her home is in Moscow. She stays in the sleeping car next to ours. Our green train car has four beds, but the space is only about four meters square. In between the beds is a little table, and down the hall is the toilet that splashes out onto the tracks. The train is loud and smells of burning coal. The ride is rickety and jarring, which helps rock us to sleep. I have the top bunk across from Jack.

We wake in the morning from the train's more frequent stops, the rhythm of the continuous flow broken. Finally, the train stops in Moscow, where we gather our suitcases and join in line to exit.

Moscow's buildings are more crowded together than in Kazak, their architecture older and less angular too. Airplanes soar overhead. Cars flood the streets, weaving in and out, honking their horns and squealing their brakes, emitting the scent of rubber from their tires. Dust floats in the air, tasting like dirt. Throngs of people rush by on the sidewalks like they're all late for something.

Polina hails a cab. Once inside, Katie grips Jack's hand like she fears for her safety. Nat sits on my lap, sucking her fingers.

#

We stay at a hotel for two nights while we wait for more paperwork at the US Embassy. Our hotel is unlike any I've seen. The ceiling lights have little pieces of glass that clink and turn, casting a reflection of rainbow colors on the walls. The rooms are large and clean, the hallways long and wide.

To pass the time, I watch television, and Nat plays with little toys that the Engles brought. The television in the orphanage rarely worked, and Mama never owned one, so now I'm fascinated with the silliness in a show called *Nickelodeon*. There's a small yellow square cartoon person who wears pants and has a hideous laugh.

Jack and Katie try to talk to me by pointing to things like the TV and reciting the English way to say it. I don't want to play the game. I keep silent and look away. Jack frowns like he's annoyed at me, but Katie soothes him. She strokes his arm and rubs his shoulders and plays peek-a-boo with Nat, who smiles and blows bubbles when she laughs.

Nat's happier than I've ever seen her. Her mouth makes a funny shape—one I haven't seen—when she smiles. It's as if she's learning how to smile for the first time, and the muscles aren't working right.

Finally, it's our day to go to the US Embassy. Polina parks the car in front of a wide gold-colored building with arched doorways. People loiter in front, but I don't know why. Some must be waiting at a bus stop.

We go through the entrance and sit on old metal chairs in a stark room filled with other people, many of whom are adopting children. A man calls us back to an office and asks questions. Katie wears a serious face and licks her lips like she's nervous.

The man speaks to me in Russian and smiles. "You will have a good life there in America, no?" He reminds me of a snake, a slithering creature who can strike at any moment without warning. When he finally stamps the papers, Katie winces.

We go to another building, where someone snaps Natalia's and my photo and slaps each in a small blue book. Polina calls the books a United States passport. It looks official. I'm going to America, leaving behind the scattered pieces of my life. Like the links to Sergey's cheap bracelet lying in the filth of the streets, Mama will forever be separated from me and bound by poverty.

Chapter Fifteen

Later that afternoon, we arrive at the airport in Moscow. At the curb, Polina explains that we will fly for almost a day—twelve hours—and stop at a city called Chicago. Then we will travel another hour to a smaller airport.

She says good-bye. My world goes silent except for those people in the airport or on the plane who speak Russian. Mobs of people get in and out of cars at the curbside. The dusty air still smells of car exhaust, but now there's a foul body odor too. My hands tremble at all the commotion, and a thin film of sweat trickles down my back.

Jack empties the trunk, and I carry Nat so Katie can take the smaller bags. Jack motions for me to stay close to them, and he's careful not to lose me in the crowd, but I feel dizzy. I grip Katie's coat sleeve.

When we finally get on the plane, I'm tired and think I will throw up. This is it. Good-bye, Russia. Good-bye, Mama. We will be at opposite sides of the world, scattered and isolated.

I've never been on a plane before so I'm not sure what to expect, and going to another country scares me more. Katie sits at the window, Nat's seat is between us, and I'm on the end. Jack sits across the aisle. Nat is in Katie's lap.

When the plane begins to move, I shut my eyes and lock my hands on the armrests. Here we go, Mama! I'm leaving you. Tears fall as I pretend to hold her strong hands again. I feel their warmth, pretend she's with me. Our jet slowly moves forward but not up yet, and already my stomach turns cartwheels. I open my eyes. Katie points to the window and asks if I want to switch seats with her by pointing to me and then at her seat. I shake my head and close my eyes again.

The plane increases speed and the engine roars louder, and when I think it can't go any faster, I feel it pull up into the sky. The motion shudders my body and my bag on the floor. How is it possible for such a heavy piece of metal to stay up in the air? The plane rattles again, and I think it'll explode, but when I open my eyes and see the faces of the other passengers, they show no fear. This noise and motion must be typical because some people read their books like they're sitting on a bench at the park, but no one is holding on to their armrests, fearing for their life. Except me.

I release my hands from the seat dividers and look over at Katie. She smiles and puts her thumb up in the air. I guess that means everything is good.

A plump girl sits in front of Jack. She looks my age and speaks English. She has long hair tied back in a ponytail that she twirls over and over again. She's holding something rectangular and pushes buttons on it when she's not twirling. It holds her attention. Is it a game, and what is it that makes her jump in her seat and giggle? What is her life like? Has she ever been hungry? I doubt it. She has rolls of fat around her middle.

Katie hands me a book with pictures. English words are written under little photos of cars, birds, cats, household items, buildings, food, etc. The words and letters don't mean anything, so I close my eyes again. The hum of the plane's engine hypnotizes me into dreamland.

I wake with a strange feeling in my ears. The plane is louder now, and the sky is black except for a little light on the wing that flashes. I put my fingers in my ears and shake my head. Jack motions for me to drink a soda that's on his tray table. I drink and my ears clear. Katie hands me a piece of gum and motions for me to chew and swallow. A few minutes later, I feel a pop in my ears again, but I swallow and it goes away.

Natalia cries. Maybe her ears feel the same way. Katie feeds her a bottle, and she settles down. A uniformed lady asks me if I want to have a snack, and Jack motions for me to go ahead. I take three snack bags, open one, and hide the other two in my backpack.

It's early morning when the plane lands with a thud. I grip the seat dividers again and think we'll all die, but then the plane coasts, and I realize we're safe. I sigh.

Jack points to a map in the seat holder in front of him. He says we are here and holds up one finger and points to another place on the map. He calls it Michigan. I think he means we have one more plane ride to Michigan.

We stand and move toward the front of the plane. I'm sandwiched between Katie and Jack. When we step out into the airport, people run and walk in all different directions. No one looks me in the eye. Some are in a hurry and others sit on chairs, waiting.

Everything around me looks shiny, new, and clean, and the noises are loud. A cart beeps, someone sneezes, a baby cries, and an announcer says something over a loudspeaker. I don't understand what anyone is saying. There are signs above, which have symbols and letters I don't recognize. Stores are lined in a row. Some sell candy and books. Strange new smells, clean smells, fill my nostrils. The change is overwhelming, and I latch on to Katie's sleeve again. She hands Nat to Jack and walks with her arm around me. Nat's eyes are bright and roaming on her surroundings too.

I see golden arches and recognize this as McDonald's. It's the one thing I know even though the menu looks frighteningly strange. People waiting in line have rolls of fat on their arms and middle sections.

We're walking fast and step onto a floor that moves. All we have to do is stand on it with our luggage, and it takes us closer to where we're going. A light show dances on the ceiling, and eerie music plays. I'm tired, but suddenly I don't feel strong anymore.

Tears roll down my cheeks. I can't stop them. I'm sobbing with my hands on my ears. People stare at me and move away from me like I'm crazy. As soon as the moving floor ends, Katie pulls me into the women's bathroom, where the sinks and floor are spotlessly clean. Katie runs paper linens under the cold faucet and holds them to my face. She talks to me, but it doesn't help. I don't understand her.

I see my face in the mirror next to hers. I'm already taller than she is. Katie's nothing like Mama, but I tell myself, no, don't think like that. Be brave. You must keep going. But all the days since I'd last seen Mama come rushing into my thoughts like water pouring into the basin. I shouldn't be here. I should have never left.

What if these people are only pretending to be kind but will sell my body parts? I think I'm going to vomit. I rush into a stall and stand there with the door open, Katie's hand resting on my shoulder. I gag over the toilet, but nothing comes out. I'm shaking, and I only see black in front of me. I begin to fall. Katie squeals and grabs me from under my arms, dragging me out of the stall and onto the floor, my back against the wall. She guides my head between my knees, my head that's as limp as a wilted weed.

Katie places more wet compresses on my neck and face. A few minutes go by, and she helps me stand. We need to get to our next plane but we have time to stop, so Jack stops and buys me lunch. We sit together and they watch me as I eat. They must think I'm crazy because they keep staring at me like I'm a foreign specimen. I wave my hand to tell them to quit staring! They look away, but they still have wrinkled foreheads.

The next plane we board is much smaller and louder, but I'm okay because I know what to expect. I look through a magazine that Jack bought for me at the other airport. There are pictures of teen movie stars who I've never seen before. The style of their clothing is bizarre. When I'm done browsing, I doze and wake when I feel the plane going down.

This time I look out the window. This city looks smaller than the last airport. It's like we're going to drop into a paved field of green grass. There are no tall buildings—just fields, rows of something growing, and a few lakes. The sun is straight up in the blue sky.

Shortly after the plane lands, we gather our stuff and exit. When we get in the building, there are swarms of people gathered. They hold balloons and signs. Cameras flash at us, taking my picture. A few people run to Jack and Katie, someone takes Nat, and someone else embraces me.

I stiffen. Who are these people?

The lady who hugs me looks about Katie's age; maybe she's her sister, but they don't look alike. The lady doesn't notice I'm uncomfortable. She kisses my cheeks and says, "Hello," like I'm across the room. I want to say, "I'm right here." Her voice is so loud. She's wearing jeans, brown boots, a plaid shirt, and a red jacket. She looks like cowgirls I've seen in magazines and smells like something I've never smelled before. It's not totally unpleasant, just different.

"Welcome, welcome!" they all chant.

People who aren't with them stop to watch us and smile. Someone says, "Congratulations!" I feel like Nat and I are some kind of prize. The room spins, and I'm hot again. I need to sit down. Katie is too busy greeting her relatives to notice. I swoon and the plaid-shirted lady notices, takes my arm, and leads me to a chair. She's shorter than me but thick and strong. My legs go limp like noodles in water, but cowgirl lifts me to a chair. I hear her shout orders to someone, and before I know it, I'm sipping Coke again.

Jack's at my side now and says something to the crowd, and they look away, give me space.

Cowgirl points to me and says, "Oksana." Then she points to herself and says, "Laura." She repeats it so many times I think she's crazy.

Just to get her to stop saying her name, I say, "Laura."

She jumps up and holds her hand up to mine. I look at it. She laughs and takes a hold of my hand and slaps hers to mine. She says something about "high five." I have no idea what she's saying, but she seems happy, and her laugh is so loud it's kind of infectious, so I laugh too.

Chapter Sixteen

Jack stops at a big white car and unlocks the doors. The other people at the airport go in their cars. Katie places Natalia in the back in a blue seat with little straps that's built just for a little person. She buckles her in. How strange. I sit next to Natalia, and Jack and Katie sit in the front. The seats are softer than my bed used to be.

I stare out the window. The world is so much more open here—full of sky and deep- green grass and flat land where wide, dark cattle roam in the fields. The first time I saw a scene similar to this was when we were on the train to Moscow, but those lands looked desolate with only brown grass and dandelions. Here, the grass is greener, speckled with flowers that dance in the wind like the rich paintings I've seen in books.

There are no tall, dark buildings crowding next to each other like in Russia. The ones here are shorter and more horizontal. The roads are all neat and clean with bright-white lane lines—not like in Russia where cars weave in and out of colorless lanes. Multicolored signs stand on stilts on both sides of the road, some further back off the road and others over the road.

I accidentally nudge a button with my elbow and my window opens. I jump. I touch the button again and my window goes up. I touch it again and it goes all the way down. I hold it there, and when it doesn't move anymore, I stick my head out to feel the breeze and smell the air. Even the air smells different, cleaner, not like dirt. This air makes me sleepy and reminds me that I'm so far from Mama now.

Jack turns in his seat, looks at me, says something I don't understand, and then my window goes up again. He must have a way to control it from the front. It's like magic—something I've never seen before.

After a long while, we turn off the wide road and onto a smaller one, where large houses line the streets in rows. My mouth opens wide. The houses remind me of the homes I've seen on TV, so rich and wide. Do people on this street share their home with other families? They all must be so rich.

Our car slows. Kids are running on the sidewalks, riding bikes, and standing on little boards with wheels, weaving up and down walks. They laugh and scream and stop to watch our car pass. They meet my eyes and smile, and some wave.

We pull in front of the yellow house with the picket fence I saw in Katie's photo album, but the house looks bigger in real life. There's a large paper sign with colored letters draped over the door. We climb out of the car as some of the other people from the airport drive up behind us. A long row of cars are parked in the street. Jack opens the trunk, and Laura helps him carry the suitcases to the front door. Katie carries Nat.

Someone inside opens the door and holds it for us. There are so many people. It's like they have been waiting for us. They say hello and congratulations. Do they all live here? Katie seems surprised because she cries and hugs a few of them. A man and woman smile and lean toward me like they're going to hug me, but I look away.

Food smells waft around me, reminding me how hungry I am, pulling me toward their scent. I follow my nose into a brightly lit kitchen, where red, blue, and glass platters of food cover a long table. I've never seen so many things to eat on one table at one time. It's so colorful. There's something bright red, cut in squares, on a plate. I reach for one, and it jiggles under my touch. Weird. I throw it into my mouth. It's smooth and sweet. I take a plate and spoon each item onto it, sampling those from each container. Next, I fill my pockets with little round candies.

A bells rings, and Katie calls my name.

I set my plate down and follow her voice to the front door. A group of kids—some my age, some younger—stand on the porch, looking at me. They're wearing brightly colored clothes—nothing like at the doskey dom. They wave and say hi. I wave back. They inch their way in through the door and closer to me—so close that I can smell their sweaty necks and armpits. I feel like I'm a freak on display. They look at my hair, shoes, clothes—everything.

Then one little freckled girl with long braids takes my hand and pulls me out the door. Laura must see the terror in my eyes because she says something and the girl nods, backs off, and waves goodbye. Laura points to the kitchen and puts an imaginary spoon in her mouth, and I get it. It's time to eat. I'm grateful because I have no idea what those kids wanted with me. They were probably going to make me stand on those boards or push me off of one.

The mention of food makes my stomach growl. I'm ready to eat and retreat once again to the kitchen, leaving the others in the front room talking and laughing. I scoop another handful of candy and stuff them into my back pockets.

Laura calls my name and footsteps follow. She stands in the doorway.

I sit at a table by myself, eating the items that are stacked high on my plate. The flavors are sweet and sour and rich—all at the same time. My stomach grumbles with eat bite.

"There you are," Laura says.

I nod.

She crosses the room to me, her hand on her hip, smiling and talking. I don't understand her. Reaching for a cup on the counter, Laura fills it with something and sets it in front of me, watching me eat and drink.

She chuckles and takes a plate for herself, sits across from me again, and we eat in silence. In two minutes, I'm finished. Laura still has food on her plate, but when I stand to get more, she holds up a finger, stands, and motions for me to follow her. I guess she's going to leave her food behind.

We wander from room to room. The ceilings are high, and the walls are painted with bright colors. One room has the largest television I've ever seen. Opposite it is a brown lumpy L-shaped sofa. I plunk down into it and sink because it's so squishy. Mama would love this room.

Laura crosses the room, smiles, and takes my arm, leading me to another part of the house. She waves her hand in front of a pink room and says, "Natalia's." Stuffed monkeys and giraffes sit in the crib. There's a rocking chair, a small bed, and a table with diapers in the room.

I open the closet door to rows of little baby clothes on hangers.

"Oh!" I exhale a loud sigh and touch the fabrics. There are ruffled dresses in pink and red, fancy hats, and frilly sweaters. Natalia has never had so many nice clothes. How will she ever wear them all?

Laura winds up a toy that hangs over the crib, and we listen to soft twinkling music, but soon there's a ruckus in the kitchen, and we hurry into the hallway to see why.

Jack's voice booms at a large white fluffy dog.

I peer around the corner as the white ball of fur rushes across the floor, sliding into people and jumping up and down. My eyes lock on his, and he sees me and makes a beeline right for me. I scream and jump up on the rocking chair, because it's the closest getaway place. The house quiets. Katie runs toward me, and Nat cries. The beast jumps up on his hind legs and almost reaches my knees. If I were standing, he'd probably be as tall as my shoulders. The chair is rocking because that's what it's made to do, so it looks like I'm dancing. I scream again.

Laura says something to the dog, and Jack drags him to the other side of the room.

Katie rushes to my side and gives me her hand. She says, "Jasper."

I don't care what his name is. I've seen a dog before but have never been attacked by one. Quickly, I jump down off the chair, ready to bolt again if I need to. A crowd has gathered at the door. Everyone stares at me like I'm some kind of lunatic, but what do they expect? The animal was going to knock me down.

Jack laughs and pats the dog and strokes his ears. Jasper's tongue slurps out and licks his hand. All I see is his pointed teeth. Jack encourages me to pet him. Is he crazy? No way.

Laura holds Nat and brings her closer to the creature, bending down for the dog to sniff her. I watch in horror, ready to grab Nat in a second, but I don't have to. The dog licks Nat's face, and she laughs and flaps her arms.

After Laura gives Nat to Katie, she takes my arm and leads me out, past the crowd at the door and into another room. She points and says, "Oksana's."

This must be my room, my *own* room. The walls are plain white but cleaner than the doskey dom. There's a window above the bed, overlooking the lake. I look outside and see the water lapping at the beach. The sun reflects off the waves and glistens. There's a walkway that leads into the water. I don't know the names of all these things because I've never seen anything like them. I stare at the boats docked by long ropes and the people standing on flat boards in the water. What are they doing?

Laura lifts something off the chest of drawers and looks through it. She adjusts the ring on top and then hands it to me. She says, "Binoculars."

Huh? I take it and look through it like she did.

I'm amazed at this magical lens. How is it that something far away can look so close? I watch a man with a pole and a string, sitting on a chair on a faraway wooden plank. A child sits on something that looks like a big bubble in the water. He's laughing. I want to look everywhere with these things. I look at Laura, but I have to look away because she's suddenly too large. She laughs, and surprisingly I laugh too. It's strange to hear the happy sound come from my lips. I haven't heard it in a long time.

Chapter Seventeen

My new world is like a canvas full of bright colors—oranges, pinks, purples, reds, and bright blues, rather than the browns, grays, taupes, and blacks of Russia. The colors here bring hope, liveliness, creativity, and energy. I feel like I've walked into a colored television set after living in a black-and-white one all my life. Sometimes the colors are too bright—they distract me, making it hard to breathe. When I feel overwhelmed, I run laps around the house. The first time I leave the house and run, the Engles look at me with puzzled expressions. They don't understand, but how could they?

Communicating with them is like pulling these new and random colors from the sky. They're beyond my reach—I can't grip them. Jack purchases discs to put into a computer, books on English, and Katie hires a college girl, Anna, to teach me English. Anna is from Moscow but is studying in the states. She comes to the house three times a week and translates for Katie.

Finally, I'm able to understand a little of what the Engles are trying to say, but I like pretending I don't know. It's easier for me to ignore them that way. Katie likes to boss me into doing what she wants me to do.

For several days, I try to adjust and take many laps around the house. The Engles point to pictures in books. Sometimes they draw pictures, but I can't recognize what they're drawing, and I'm not an artist—nor are they. When I get frustrated and overwhelmed, I go to my room and shut my eyes just so I can see black again.

A few weeks later, Anna translates, "You and Natalia will go to the doctor's office today to get your immunizations and have a physical."

"Why? We did this in Russia. We don't need to see a doctor." I think she's lying. This is when they'll take our body parts.

"The doctors here are different from those in Russia. Here you have to establish a relationship with the doctor for him to care for you. The immunization laws are different too. Katie and Jack need to make sure you're up to date with your shots before you can attend school."

"How many are there?"

"It depends on how many you've already had."

"I've had them all. I don't need any more." I get up and go to the bathroom and lock myself in. I can hear Anna and Katie talking. Who knows what they're saying?

Several minutes go by, and Katie knocks at the door. "Are you okay? Come out and we'll play a game."

It takes me a few minutes, but I do. Katie takes my hand, but I pull it away.

She says, "We won't let the doctor hurt you. We'll just go and talk to her. Would it make you feel better if Anna went too?"

"No."

"Well, let's play a memory game while Natalia naps."

Anna, Katie, and I sit at the kitchen table, and Katie takes a deck of cards and sorts through them, making a pile of twenty matching cards. She turns them over so we can't see them and mixes them up. Anna explains that we have to find two cards that are the same. As we turn them over, they say the numbers and encourage me to say them too. Katie says that it's her made-up game and that it isn't the real way to play cards, but she feels better knowing that she's teaching me something. She wants me to go to school soon, but I'm not ready to meet a bunch of kids I can't understand. I want to learn this language first. Or do I? Maybe I don't.

We play the game three times. I win every game even though Katie adds more pairs to make it harder. They're discovering I don't forget.

Natalia wakes and Anna leaves, so I go to get Natalia. I love to feed her and play with her and dress her. I feel closer to Mama when I'm with her. But Katie points to herself, suggesting that she take care of Natalia. She shows me to my room, where she's laid out the clothes she wants me to wear today, but I have something else in mind. Katie leaves my room to get Natalia dressed, and I pull out a pair of jeans from my closet and a long, tight shirt. I find scissors and cut the bottom of the shirt in shredded points. I like that look better. It's not all perfect and prissy like Katie. Besides, I don't want her to think she can boss me around.

Katie gasps when she sees me and points to the bottom of my shirt. She storms back to my closet and takes out another shirt and hands it to me. I shake my head, and she throws up her arms. She's angry now. She won't look at me.

We drive to the doctor's office in silence, which suits me fine, but Katie stews. She looks in the rearview mirror at me. I can feel her eyes, but I don't look until she's looking the other way. I play with Natalia, and she squeals with glee.

After Katie parks the car, we head toward the doctor's office. A slight breeze catches a strand of hair, tickling my cheek. I don't need a coat because it's warm today.

We wait in the waiting room. There are other mothers there with their children. They look at us. One woman must know Katie because she hugs her, smiles at me, and holds Natalia. The lady's daughter looks different from her mama. She's dark and her eyes are slanted. Is she from another country too? The girl is a few years younger than me, but a lot shorter. Katie introduces her as Zoe. She smiles and I wave.

There are magazines on a table, and one draws my attention; it's one with a young girl on a horse. I pick up the magazine and study the pictures inside. There are different-colored horses with riders who are dressed in peculiar ways. Red ribbons hang around the horse's necks. Did they win a prize? How?

A young lady dressed in white slacks and a baggy shirt calls our names. She chomps on gum as she leads us to a room with an examining table. She says something to Katie, and Katie takes Natalia's clothes off—all except her diaper—and then the lady carries Nat out to a metal scale and sits her on it. Nat's eyes skate across the room. She smiles, seeming to trust everyone.

Not me.

The lady writes something on a piece of paper, and then asks me to step on a scale. She gets my weight and height. Katie asks another question, then points to us and then to pink graphs in our file folders. The nurse places the two charts on the exam table. She points to me, then at a spot on the chart; then to Nat and a spot on the other chart. I think it has to do with how tall we are because the lady looks at the top of my head.

The doctor enters and I want to laugh. She's short and doesn't have a waist. Her pants are all the way up under her large breasts. She must have trouble hearing because she talks really loud. Does she think we can't hear her?

Her dark-gray hair is pulled back into a tight bun, making her eyes bulge. Her glasses are so thick that if I look her in her eyes I see magnified eyelashes, so I look away. She introduces herself, but she's difficult to understand. Her accent is different from the ones I've heard, and she speaks fast.

Nat is sitting on the exam table, and the doctor tickles her toes and lets her play with a little wooden stick. She examines us similar to the way the doctor did in Russia. When she lays Nat on her back Nat gets annoyed and whimpers. I move closer to the table. The doctor taps on her stomach and opens her diaper to examine what's inside. Nat's frightened now and screams. I push between the doctor and Katie, pick her up, and clutch her into my arms. Nobody is going to hurt my sister. I grab Nat's clothes, glare at the doctor, and then look at the door.

Katie must know what I'm thinking because she stands at the door and blocks my exit, motioning for me to stay and says something I don't understand.

She wants me to believe that everything is okay, but how am I supposed to believe her? What if they're examining her body parts to sell? What other explanation could there be? There's nothing wrong with my sister, and I don't need a doctor to tell me.

The doctor doesn't fight me. She holds her hands up as if to say she won't touch my sister if I don't want her to. She takes Katie's arm and pulls her into the corner of the room, where they stand and talk. After Katie helps me dress Nat, the doctor sits on a stool and continues her conversation with Katie. I keep Nat in my arms.

When the doctor smiles and turns to go, I sigh. We must not need any more shots. Maybe they won't hurt us after all. At least not today.

Chapter Eighteen

On our way out of the doctor's office, Katie says Laura's name and motions like she's driving a car. I think she means we're going to Laura's house.

I climb in the backseat with Nat and look at Katie in the rearview mirror. The wrinkles between her eyebrows are deeper. Nat dozes. I like the silence and the sun of the summer day. The green leaves are bushy and thick, and flowers sprout from gardens. We pass open fields of green grass and houses that are still being built and some completed new homes with dirt-covered yards, waiting to be filled with furniture, people, and lives unlike any I've seen in Russia. Oh, how Mama would be amazed at such luxury!

I remember that Laura lives with horses because of the photos I've seen, and I want to see such a place. We turn down a small rock road off the main one and come to a gate. Katie gets out and opens it, gets back in the car, drives forward, and gets out to close the gate.

Trees line both sides of the road, shading our path, and I feel like I'm in a tunnel. Then I realize that this road is actually a driveway. Dust follows our car as we bounce off the little white stones. Nat's head bobs, but she doesn't wake.

The driveway is long and narrow, and after we turn the corner, the trees stop. Ahead are a large red barn, a white house, and several rolling green pastures. Horses bend their heads eating grass until they see us. Then they run to the fence toward our car.

A large black dog runs out of the barn, barking and jumping. I've never seen a dog this big. I'm thankful for the window between us. His teeth are pointed and large.

Katie shouts at the dog and motions for him to move.

Laura waves from the barn entrance. She's got the cowgirl look going again, except this time there's dust on her jeans and hay in her hair. She smiles and calls to the dog. He runs to her side, and she closes him behind the gate near the house.

A wooden picnic table covered with a red-checkered cloth sits outside the barn underneath a pine tree. Laura has set out food and drinks. She hugs me tight, burying my nose into her shoulder, where I smell her strange scent again. Now I know they're ranch smells—hay and horses. She carries Nat to the table, swings her up on her hip, and pours me a pale-colored drink.

"Lem-on-ade," she says slowly.

I say "lemonade" to myself, take a sip, and shiver. It's sour and sweet at the same time. I make a face and Laura laughs. The drink makes me feel cool, so I take several more sips before I decide I like it. But when I reach for a sandwich on a plate, Laura knits her hands together and says, "Pray."

Nat sits in Katie's lap. Laura reaches for Katie's hand and mine across the table. We all hold hands, and Laura bows her head and says something about God. The only words I recognize are our names: Oksana and Natalia. The prayer reminds me of Pastor and his kindness. When Laura's done, she looks up and into my eyes. I mean *really* into my eyes—like she can see what I'm thinking, which is that I like Laura, but I'm not sure why. I look away.

A gray horse with light spots makes a throaty noise from the fence. Laura says this is called a nicker and takes my hand, pulling me over to her. I grab a sandwich and follow.

"Star," she says, and pats the horse's head. It nickers again.

Laura puts my hand on the horse. I stroke its neck. It feels hot and sweaty, but the skin is soft. The horse's nose turns into my hand, but then other horses in the field come running, and it sounds like they'll crash through the fence. One screeches loudly—so loud I back away. He's the largest and darkest, and he bites Star in the butt. I don't like him. He has one white leg, one blue eye, and one brown one. His ears are pinned back, and to me he looks evil, like one of Ludmila's friends. Laura calls him Jet.

"Treat." She points to the sandwich in my hand and then at the horse.

I'm not going to share. I take another bite.

"Come." She waves for Katie and me to follow her into the barn. Her boots clunk on the dusty dirt floor. The smells here are new to me, but I like them. I think it's from the hay and the horse poo. The stall doors are open—all except one.

Inside the closed door is a dirty and emaciated white horse. Its back is to us and its head hangs down in the corner of the stall. It looks weak and injured, but I don't know enough about horses to understand what's wrong. Laura tells us about the horse, but I don't understand her words. All I can do is watch her expression and see that she is sad.

It looks like he's dying, like someone hurt him. His rib bones protrude from his skin, and it looks like they'll pop right through one of the crusted sores on his back. Mud cakes the bottoms of his hooves. From the corner of the stall, he watches us with one eye. He doesn't trust us. I can tell.

Laura reaches for an ointment tube, a comb, and a brush that sit on a shelf outside his door. She opens the stall and takes my hand.

I hesitate. Me? I don't know anything about these animals.

She nods. She wants me to go inside the tiny box with that huge thing? I pull away, and she lets go and leaves the door ajar, maybe so I can watch from the opening. Katie stands beside me holding Nat.

Laura says hello to him and approaches from the front. She touches the side of his neck in a swirling motion, and talks to him in a low, soothing voice. His eyes close when she applies the ointment and moves the brush gently along the parts of his healthy skin. She combs the long hair down his back and turns to me. "Mane."

I repeat, "Mane."

She motions for me to come closer, and I do because he doesn't look like he could hurt anyone. He's too weak to care. There's something in his eyes that I understand. It's that look that says nothing matters, that he's been beaten, that he doesn't care anymore.

I ask Laura, *"Kak teba zobut?"*

She doesn't understand, so I point my finger at myself and say, "Oksana," and I point to her and say, "Laura," and then I point to the horse and say, "Kak teba zobut?"

She gets it. She shrugs and shakes her head like she doesn't know and points to me. "Oksana name him."

I think about this for a few minutes and say, "Boris." This name means warrior, and I know this horse will have to fight to survive. I recognize the distrust in his eyes too and want to make him my friend.

Katie watches from outside the stall door, still holding Nat.

I move a little closer to Boris, and Laura shows me his different body parts. She scratches above the long hairs at the base of his neck and says, “Withers.”

He moves away like he thinks we might hurt him. When Laura talks in a soft voice, his eyes close again like he enjoys the comfort of this affection, like maybe he could trust her for a moment. He’s ready to bolt if he has to, but he can’t because he’s too weak.

Laura rubs his chest, and I move toward him to rub his withers. He opens his eyes and trembles. His legs shake and he shudders. I jump back, afraid of this sudden movement.

Laura says, “Whoa.”

But he collapses to the ground with a thud. Dust flies, and I bolt for the door. Katie motions for me to join her. Nat squirms in her arms.

Laura’s eyebrows wrinkle together, and her forehead creases. “No!” She lies on the ground in the dirt next to him, stroking his stomach and talking to him. His nostrils flare and he snorts. I think he wants to get up, but he’s not strong enough. His eyes close.

Has he lost his will to live?

It reminds me of the time when Mama and Ludmila left me alone. It was night, and I was supposed to be sleeping. Bright flashes of lightning woke me, and thunder rattled the windows. Rain hurled in through the broken window next to my bed. I curled up in a ball pretending to be somewhere else. I thought I was going to die, and then I didn’t care if I did because then I wouldn’t have to think about being safe.

I recognize that same fear in Boris’s eyes—only this is worse. He wants to die. I kneel in front of him and stroke his face. Sorrow sits on my chest like it’s causing a cramp, and a lump forms in my throat.

Boris lifts his head, watching me. I slide my legs under his head and hold it in my lap, forgetting that anyone is nearby.

Tears spill down my face. At first they trickle, but when Boris closes his eyes, and I feel him withdraw, the tears get caught in my throat in one big lump. I snort, suck air, and my shoulders shudder as the lump breaks free. I weep loud and hard—so hard that I think I scare Boris because he opens his eyes and looks at me with wide eyes.

Laura wraps her arm around me.

I cry because I miss Mama and my home and because this horse makes me remember the hurt inside me. He's broken and beaten like me.

He lifts his head again, and his legs scramble as if trying to grip the earth. They shuffle in the dirt, and slowly he stands.

"Thatta boy." Laura stands, encourages him, and pats his back.

Boris drops his head, nudging me where I still sit on the ground.

I stand beside him and wipe the tears with the back of my hand. Laura rubs my back. Boris puts his head on my shoulder. It kind of tickles and makes me laugh.

Laura hollers and it sounds like, "Who-hoo!"

Katie meets my eyes. There are tears in hers.

I turn away. I didn't want her to see me cry.

Laura leaves the stall for a few seconds and returns with a bag of carrots. She shows me how to feed him by making my hand flat. In a few minutes, he tickles my hand with his wiggling lips and crunches on the carrot. I laugh and forget about the tears still damp on my face.

Laura wraps her arm around me again, then points to Boris, then at me, and hugs herself. I think she's trying to tell me that he likes me. I smile. Maybe he does.

Natalia fusses and Katie says, "Eat."

I understand that word now, but I wave them on because I don't want to leave Boris. Laura brings me my sandwich, and I eat while Boris finishes his carrots.

I'm singing to him, when a boy about my age and height taps on the stall door. He startles me and I jump. Boris turns to look at him. The boy holds up a hand and says hello, but his voice sounds odd. It's different from any I've heard. He grunts his words and reminds me of Nicholas with his wavy dark hair, and my stomach does one of those flips that signals a warning.

He opens the stall door and asks me a question, and moves his hands and fingers in all different ways.

"Go away," I say in Russian.

His brows crease like he's puzzled.

"Go away."

Laura runs to the stall, her mouth full of food. She turns to the boy and uses her fingers and hands like the boy did, as if she's talking with her hands. He moves his fingers back at her.

Laura turns to me and points to her ears and shakes her head. I understand now. This boy can't hear, but I don't care. I still don't trust him. What does he want? He shrugs and leaves the stall, shaking his head.

Laura points to him and says, "Bryce."

Katie approaches. Nat is fussing again, so Katie tells me it's time to go.

I don't want to go. I want to stay with Boris. I shake my head and pat the horse.

Laura and Katie speak back and forth. Laura wants me to stay, but Katie says no.

I'm not happy, but I get in the car. As we drive off, I watch Bryce throw a ball to the black dog. The dog catches the ball in his mouth and brings it back. The deaf boy turns to wave good-bye, and I look away.

I hope Boris stays well until I return.

Chapter Nineteen

For the rest of the summer and early fall, I work with Anna on my English even though I'd rather be with Boris. But if I work hard, Katie says I can go. I'm getting better at learning American words, but the ones I find most confusing are the idioms. They're silly. I mean, how can someone be wet between the ears, and how can you crack up and live to talk about it? Anna says that English is "all Greek to me." What am I learning—English or Greek? And one more thing—do dogs eat dogs?

One day, I notice Anna writing a letter. "Who are you writing?"

"My family in Moscow."

I nod, wishing I could send Mama a letter. "How do you know where to send it?"

She points to an envelope and explains that she puts the address on the front. Then she types on the computer at the desk in my room, and a large map appears. She points to where her family lives and where we are now. Then she shows me the envelope with the address in Moscow.

"Where's Kapaz?" I nod toward the screen, sitting beside her at the desk.

She shows me. It's east of Moscow. "Is that where your family lives?"

I shrug. "I don't know where they live now."

"Oh, I'm sorry. Maybe you could journal, pretend to write to them. Do you want me to see if I can find them?"

"How?" I lean forward in my chair.

"I'll type in your mom's name and see if it comes up."

I give her Mama's name and I hold my breath. Could Anna really find her?

She types the name in an empty space and presses a key.

Words fill the screen, but I don't know how to read them. Photos of women with Mama's first name appear, but none of them are Mama. Anna moves her fingers and clicks on something else, her eyes pasted to the screen. But then she turns to me. "None have her first and last name."

I'm disappointed, but I'm not surprised. I want to show Anna the photo from Pastor and the writing on the back, but she'll ask too many questions, and she'll probably tell the Engles. I can't tell her. Or can I?

Jasper bursts into the room, his paws muddy. He pants and drools on my hand. I'm not as afraid of him now, but am surprised the Engles let the dirty animal in their home. He gets more food than we did in the orphanage.

Katie follows him in, takes hold of his collar, and drags him out, but by then I've lost the courage I almost had to show Anna the photo.

#

When I return to Laura's one Thursday, the dog—whose name is Duke—greets me first. He's the ranch doorbell. The first few times I go, he knocks me down and licks my face, which makes me scream and spooks the horses. He's like a monster creature—big and black with fangs and slimy drool. I'm so terrified of him that he's in my nightmares.

Lately, I've learned to outwit him. When I see him coming I grab his ball, jump up on this chair that looks like a cowboy lap because it has no head or upper torso—it's just a wooden replica of the lower half of a man—and throw him his ball. If I throw it enough times, he pants and eventually leaves me alone.

Laura teaches me horse stuff. She shows me how to approach a horse, the different parts of the horse, and the different tools used to ride them: a halter, saddle, lead line, lunge line, and bit. I whisper them to her, embarrassed I'm saying them wrong, but she doesn't laugh. She claps.

I work side by side with her, watching her feed grain and hay to the horses, muck the stalls, and shine the saddles. But most of the time I talk to Boris.

Laura says Boris likes me better than any of the other kids and helpers on the ranch. She says this with serious eyes, like she means it. She says I'm a horse whisperer. I don't know what this means, but Boris lets only me feed him carrots or take him on walks in the arena. He shies away from other kids. I'm the only one he lets put salve on his wounds, but they've healed now, and he's getting fatter.

It's like he gets better for me—like he's taking care of me instead of the other way around.

Laura teaches kids with problems and gives them rides on the horses. Some kids walk funny, others are hyper and can't stand still, and one girl, Megan, is blind. She comes on Tuesdays and Thursdays.

The first time I meet her, she holds on to her mama's arm and takes short steps. Her milky eyes stare past me, and I look over my shoulder to see what she's looking at before I realize she can't see. She's blind, but she's going to ride a horse? Before she saddles up, Laura introduces us.

"Megan, there's somebody here I want you to meet."

"Who?"

"This is my niece, Oksana. My sister, Katie, adopted her and her sister from Russia, so her English isn't the best yet."

"Hi, Oksana. Welcome to America," she says, and holds out her hand for me to shake. "Call me Meg." She's a tiny thing with tiny features, but she looks like she's my age, maybe a little older.

I say hello and shake her hand.

"Can I look at you?" she asks.

What? How can she look at me if she can't see? But Laura leads her toward me, and Meg holds out her arms. She places her hands on my face and uses her fingers to trace the outline of my forehead, eyes, cheekbones, chin, and nose. She asks me what color my hair is, and Laura tells her it's almost as white and bright as the snow.

She smiles and steps back. "You're beautiful."

I'm silent. No one has ever told me that.

"I embarrassed you, didn't I? I'm sorry."

She must have felt my face turn red. I can't even hide that from a blind person.

"No one has ever looked at you that way before, have they?"

She laughs, and it makes me laugh.

"No."

She smiles as Laura leads her to the barn. I follow them.

Laura says, "How would you like to ride Rose today? She hasn't been ridden for a few days, and I think she'd like to spend time with you."

How does a blind person ride?

Meg says, "Okay, I will, but why can't I ride Firefly? Has he been bad?"

"No. He lost a shoe, and I'm waiting for the farrier to come and fix it. He'll be here later. Next week you should be able to ride him."

What is a farrier*?* There are still so many words I don't understand.

"Could I stop and see him first?"

They stop to see Firefly, and Meg holds out her hand for him to nuzzle. He nickers. Laura leads her hand up to his withers, and she gives it a deep rub. She talks to him for a while, and then Laura leads her to Rose's stall. Meg puts her hand in Rose's water trough.

I say, "I gave her water."

Meg smiles.

Laura hands her the currycomb and brush and tells her about the weather and the blue sky.

Meg looks in my direction. "Do you miss Russia?"

"Yes."

"America must be very strange to you, but the Engles are great people. I'm glad you are here."

"Thank you." She doesn't know me, but she is kind. She acts like being blind is no big deal, like there's nothing wrong with her. I don't think I would feel that way.

With Laura's help, Meg saddles Rose and leads her into the outdoor arena, boosts up onto the mare, and trots around the arena in circles.

I sit on the outside of the fence and watch her ride. Meg sits straight, totally relaxed. She makes riding look easy. Laura tells her when to squeeze her legs, how to move the reins, and where to put her hands. There's so much to think about, but if Meg can ride I think I can too.

Duke barks at Bryce, who is riding his bicycle up the driveway.

Laura shouts over to me, "Why don't you give Boris a bath?

Bryce will help you." She motions for Bryce to come to her and talks to him with her hands.

He looks at me and shakes his head, shrugs, and says, "Okay, okay, I'll try," in his queer voice. But his shoulders slump like he really doesn't want to help me.

Bryce grabs a halter, and we go into Boris's stall. He slips it over Boris's nose, but Boris pins his ears back and walks to the corner.

"Me," I say, and take the halter.

I inch my way closer to Boris and talk to him in Russian, soothing him, telling him he's a good boy, and slowly I lift the halter and place it on his head. Laura showed me how to do it. Once it's there, Boris lets Bryce show me how to pull his ears through and buckle it. Then Bryce hands me the lead line and shows me the way to the wash rack. I lead and Boris follows.

Bryce hooks Boris to the wall on one side and then the other. The horse stares at the hose and tries to back up but can't. When Bryce turns on the water, he loses the handle grip, and water shoots out and all around like a wild rocket. Cold water sprays my face. I scream, and Boris's front legs come up off the ground. Bryce grabs hold of the faucet head and pulls me into his arms, shielding me from Boris's hooves.

My nose is pressed against Bryce's neck. I smell dirt and sweat, and for a second I freeze. I shudder. Boris could have killed me. One stomp with his leg and I could have died. Why would he hurt me?

Laura runs in from the arena. "What happened?"

She sees me trembling in Bryce's arms. Her eyes widen.

I push away from Bryce and run into the bathroom next to the tack room, shut the door, and cry in the dark. I thought Boris was my friend, but he's not. He's just a stupid animal. Tears drip until I fall asleep in the dark. I don't want to see Boris again.

I dream I'm in the basement at the orphanage, and the hunched-back lady with the switch is glaring at me with red eyes. She chases me in one direction, then another, blocking every way out, showing me her crooked teeth. I can't escape her. Then Mama's face replaces the wicked lady's. She's scowling at me like she knows what I did. I scream and wake with a start.

Laura is standing over me. She nudges my shoulder. "Hey, Oksy, you okay?"

She's the only one who calls me Oksy. My eyes squint,

adjusting to the light coming in through the door. I nod.

"You gonna sleep all day?" She holds a plate of cookies. I take one. It's warm and melts in my mouth. "How long have I slept?"

"For an hour."

I stand and Laura leads me out. She points to Boris in his stall and says, "Come."

I follow her to Boris's stall, wanting to see him, embarrassed I reacted the way I did. Boris only spooked, but he scared me. He could have killed me.

Laura takes my hand and leads me into his stall. His head is in the corner, drooping like he's sleeping. His legs are clean now, which means Bryce must have finished his bath. The horse looks sad. Laura hands me a brush. I pause, a little tentative.

Boris sees me and saunters to my side, then hangs his head on my shoulder. I think this is a horse-hug. My hands are shaking. I'm scared, but maybe he's trying to tell me he's sorry.

I accept his apology.

Chapter Twenty

Jack and Katie say if I'm studying idioms I must be ready for school. Even though it started five weeks ago, they didn't make me start, but now it's time. Katie puts clothes on the bed that she wants me to wear. Is she off her rocker? I learned that one yesterday. It looks like something she'd wear: bright pinks, beaded jewelry, puffy sleeves, and a long skirt. Yuk! It's totally wrong. I want to wear something more like boots, jeans, and a plaid shirt, like Laura.

Laura gave me an old pair of boots that someone had left behind at the barn. I put those on now with my dusty jeans and plaid shirt and make my way to the kitchen.

Katie's forehead creases. She puts her hands on her hips, opens her mouth, throws her hands up in the air, and says, "Oh well."

On our way to school, my stomach feels like autumn's dead leaves twirling on the ground in the chilly air. We pull up to the bricked school with its neatly manicured lawn and acres of football fields. Katie says this is a Christian school, where teachers and students believe in God. There are sixth-graders up to twelfth-graders. I pull Natalia out of her car seat, but Katie takes her from me. I guess I can't hide behind her today.

When we open the front door of the school, the familiar smell of floor wax takes me back to the orphanage. I fight a wave of nausea. This is not the time to get sick.

We walk to the office, where Katie introduces me to a lady wearing a lime-green headband. Katie tells her we're here to register me for school. Katie promised me, with the help of Anna's interpretation, that I wouldn't have to stay the entire day if I didn't feel comfortable, so I'm only here to check it out.

A tall, dark curly-haired man with big brown eyes and a big white-toothed smile walks toward us from down the hall. He stops and introduces himself as Principal Harry Recker. His voice sounds as big as he is tall. Harry is a good name for him too because he has hair everywhere—on his arms and curling out of the top of his V-neck shirt.

Katie explains that I was recently adopted from Russia, and he says, "We have several students who were also adopted—one from China and another one from Russia, but she's a senior and only here half days, otherwise I'd have her show Oksana around. What grade are you in?"

I look at Katie, who says to Mr. Recker, "She's fourteen, and normally she'd be a freshman, but could we start her in the eighth grade since we're not sure how far she got with her studies?"

"We could start her there and see how she does. Testing her would be difficult, as I'm sure there's a language barrier and cultural differences. She looks taller than most of the eighth-graders though." He turns to me and asks, "Would you like to meet that class? You could shadow someone for the rest of the day."

I shrug. I'm not sure what he means by shadow. I don't want to be here at all. I want to go to the barn.

"Follow me. I know the perfect teacher and classroom for you. It's a great group of students, and you'll like Mrs. Stine."

He knocks on the door and interrupts Mrs. Stine. She's at the chalkboard, writing numbers, most of which I recognize from the card game I've played with Anna. As we walk into the classroom I feel naked. Everyone looks at me. No single person in the room wears hard leather boots. So what? I don't care about them anyway. I cross my arms.

Mr. Recker motions for the teacher to come to the door. He whispers to her, "This is Oksana. She's new and just moved here from Russia. Would you choose someone she can shadow for the day?"

Mrs. Stine smiles and turns to me. "Welcome, Oksana. It's a pleasure to meet you."

I give her the nice-to-meet-you pinch of a smile I'm supposed to give her. She's wearing a sweater over a collared shirt, slacks, and shoes with shiny pennies staring out of them. Her blond hair flips up on the ends.

Principal Recker turns to me. “We’ll have Mom pay for lunch today, and Mrs. Stine will assign someone here to show you the ropes. If you need anything, you can ask her. Does that sound good?”

Katie nods.

I think, no. Why do we need ropes? I shrug.

The principal and Katie turn to go, and Katie blows me a kiss. I think I’ll die. A few of the kids laugh. Who blows kisses?

Natalia waves, and in her baby talk says, “Bye-bye.”

A few girls say, “Aw, isn’t she cute?”

After they leave, Mrs. Stine introduces me.

“Hi, Oksana.” Two boys near the back of the room whistle, and I feel my face flush.

Suddenly warm, I slip out of my jacket.

Mrs. Stine says, “Why don’t you take this empty seat here next to Crissy? You can shadow her today.” The teacher points to a seat near a short, heavy girl with a round face who must be Crissy.

She smiles.

Mrs. Stine puts a math book on my desk and tells me to turn to page seventy-eight, but I have to think about that page. A seven and an eight. Crissy leans over and shuffles the pages for me. I watch the board, but my eyes get heavy and my mind wanders to Boris. I wonder how he’s doing. I wish I was with him.

Just before my head nods to dreamland, kids start fidgeting in their seats, and Mrs. Stine says it’s time for lunch. Crissy gets up with the rest of the kids, and I grab my jacket and follow her into the cafeteria. We take a tray, and ladies with hairnets serve us. One of the whistling boys tries to squeeze in next to me. He has light hair, but not as white as mine. A lady, who looks like she’s standing guard, shoos him to the back of the line.

Crissy giggles. “Nice try, Nate.”

I eat everything on my plate except for a cookie in a wrapper that I hide in my pocket. Kids around me laugh, joke, and ask me questions, but I pretend not to understand. I have nothing in common with any of them. I don’t care about them. But then I hear them whisper and know what they’re saying. Someone says something about Russia, living here, being adopted, how white my hair is, and if it’s true that all the people in Russia drink vodka. I wish I could disappear.

I tell Crissy I'm going to the bathroom. When she stands to follow me, I say, "I'll go alone." I think she is trying to be nice, but I don't want her to follow me, and I don't want her to be my friend.

I walk past the bathroom and out the front door of the school, slipping on my jacket. I know my way to Laura's from here. Katie said I didn't have to stay in school the whole day, so I'm not going to.

Chapter Twenty-One

Along my way to the barn, the sun shines, but a cold breeze reminds me that winter will press its icy fingers into my life soon. I walk faster to get warmer, and I shove my hands into my jacket sleeves. Brittle leaves scatter the grass. A few early snowflakes fall. Cars flash by, but no one stops. I pass cows along fence lines and rusted pop cans on the shoulder of the road. I hum to myself, and before long Laura's ranch is within view.

I go directly to Boris's stall. He stands in the corner, his tail swishing at a few hardy flies buzzing around him. He's sleeping again standing up. How does he do that? He hears me and turns. His left eye finds me, and he ambles to my side and pushes his nose into my pocket.

"You're always looking for a treat, aren't you? You can't have my cookie. It's mine."

I grab the comb and brush from outside his door and comb his mane. I rub his withers until he pulls up long at the neck and his bottom lip dangles along with some dribble. "You like that, don't you?"

There's a noise outside his stall. Boris turns and cowers in the corner, pinning his ears back.

"What is it?"

I turn. A gray-haired man with a beard stands outside Boris's stall. His eyes are as blue as a dark sky at night and his skin is tan, giving him a movie star look. But when he scowls I see a different man, the man on the inside, who's different than the one with good looks.

"What are you looking at?" His eyes dart from Boris to me, then he enters Boris's stall with a wheelbarrow, ready to rake the manure. Boris stays in the corner.

"I do this." I reach for the rake.

"No, it's my job." He snatches the rake.

"Who are you?"

Laura enters the barn, sees me, and stops short. "Oksy, what are you doing here?"

I nod at Boris.

"How did you get here?"

"I walked."

"Does Katie know you're here?"

I shake my head. "She said I didn't have to stay in school all day."

"You just left?"

I look at the man in the stall and shudder. "Who is he?"

"Mr. Blackwell, this is my niece." Then she turns to me and says, "He came looking for work, and I offered to pay him to help out until he can get on his feet."

I look at his feet. There doesn't seem to be anything the matter with them. "I don't want him to come in here. Get him out."

Laura asks Mr. Blackwell to muck the other stalls first. He's not happy, but he leaves. Her cell phone rings, and she doesn't see the way he looks at me. The hair on my neck prickles. He reminds me of one of Ludmila's friends—snakelike.

"Hi, Katie," Laura says. Her eyes meet mine. "Yes, she's here."

"What?" Katie says this loud enough for me to hear. I can't make out the words that follow, but there's anger in her tone, unlike Laura, who keeps her voice calm.

"It's okay if she stays with me today." She pauses to listen. "Why don't you wait until Nat wakes from her nap?" Laura listens again, disconnects, then turns to me. "She's coming to get you as soon as Nat wakes. You shouldn't have left school. They didn't know what happened to you. People were worried."

I don't know why they're so upset. In Russia, I could come and go and no one asked or cared where I went.

Boris inches his way back to me now that Mr. Blackwell is out of his stall.

Laura stands at my side and sighs. "Boris likes you. I

understand why you like to come here. He's comfortable around you. See how he makes his mouth look like he's chewing?" She mimics him. "That means he's content."

This word *content* I do not know, but I can tell that he likes me to touch him. "What happened to him?"

"I don't know. I got a call from a rancher who'd gotten my name from a friend who knew I rescued horses. They found Boris in a field, surrounded by dead horses, and brought him to me. Sometimes people are stupid and don't take care of their horses." She pats his side.

Boris lifts his head. His sores have healed, but the scars are still visible.

She says, "Do you want to walk him around the arena outside?"

I nod.

Laura puts on his halter, clips the lead rope to it, and opens the door. She tells me to stay on his left side and demonstrates. She puts the lead rope in my hand, and together we walk him to the arena.

"Lead him slowly."

She opens the gate to the arena, and he follows me in circles. I stop. He stops. He trusts me. His ribs still protrude from his hide, but he's slightly fatter. Is he too weak to go?

Laura reassures me that it's okay, that he's healed.

We make several more circles, and I turn to Laura, who's standing at the fence. "He's hungry. Do we have carrots?"

She brings a bag and lets me feed him. The sun makes his white coat look transparent, and I can't help but stare at the scars. I hate who did this to him.

"He loves you, girl. He really does!" Laura says.

I smile. Her words make me feel good inside, like when she gave me the warm cookies.

Duke barks, and I look up to see Bryce getting off his bike. I haven't seen him since the wash incident. He waves at us, and I look away.

Laura says, "He won't hurt you, you know. He's a good boy."

#

When Katie arrives, she's still angry. I'm watering the horses and overhear her and Laura talking. They can't see me. I'm in Firefly's stall at the other end of the barn.

Laura says, “Maybe she’s not ready for school yet.”

“The longer she doesn’t go, the more difficult it’s going to be,” Katie says.

“Why are you trying to rush this? What are you really afraid of?”

“I don’t know what you’re talking about.”

“How did you think this was supposed to go? You’re expecting no problems, but Oksana didn’t have the kind of life American children have. Parenting her the American way isn’t going to be enough. Loving her isn’t going to be enough. Can’t you see that? Maybe you’re in a hurry to get back to your job. Is that what this is about?”

Katie stammers. “She doesn’t talk to us. She’ll barely look at me. How are we supposed to help her if she keeps walking away? Besides, we didn’t go to Russia to adopt her. We didn’t even know she existed until we met Natalia.”

Laura’s voice gets lower like she’s talking between her teeth. “So that’s it? Now you’re thinking that you don’t want her?”

“No! Of course we want her . . . it’s just difficult to go from no children to having two—and one who doesn’t seem to like us, need us, or want to have anything to do with us.” Katie’s voice cracks like she’s crying.

Laura makes her voice softer. “She needs you, trust me. She just doesn’t know she needs you.”

I stand frozen, spinning in the stall, whirling inside like a top out of control. The air turns thick, pressing into my chest. I need air. I know they only wanted Nat, yet it hurts to hear the words. A tang fills my stomach, like a blade twisting my insides, and a bulge forms in my throat.

When Katie and Laura are out of sight, I run to Boris out in the pasture, opening my coat to feel the cold sting of the air invading my skin, and to hide the salty tears trailing down my cheeks and into my mouth. I bury my face in Boris’s neck and wrap my arms around him, taking solace in the safest place I know, muffling my wretched sobs into the tissue of his healed scars. “You are the only one who understands.”

Chapter Twenty-Two

The next morning at breakfast, Katie and Jack tell me they've talked it over and will let me wait until January to start school because they think I'll feel more confident if I have more time with Anna to work on my English. I am thankful because I don't want to go, but I don't say that to them.

Jack says, "You have to study here though. None of this going to the barn and hanging out there all day long. Anna will show you the Internet, so when she's not here you can work on things right here at home."

I tell them what they want to hear—that I'll work at home with Anna, but only because I have to do that to go to Laura's barn. That's all I really want. I don't want to be with them.

Anna teaches me about the computer. I'm slow at working the keys and knowing the alphabet. It takes so much time. Anna comes on her days off of school and sits with me. She brings her work and studies while I find my way through computer movies that teach. I want to learn as fast as I can so I can look up the letters on the back of the photo, but I don't talk to Anna about the picture.

She shows me maps on the computer again and how far we are from Russia. It feels like there's a heavy coat on my heart, one I can't take off. How will I ever get back to Mama?

#

Several days later when I'm at Laura's, a silver truck and trailer pull into the driveway. The driver gets out and talks to my aunt and together they open the back door of the trailer. There are two horses—one large one and one small, a baby.

A high-pitched screech, unlike any whinny I've ever heard, rings through the air. Laura goes in the front and halters the mama before the man unfastens a chain near her backside. Slowly, the man leads the mama out. "Come on, girl," he says.

"Stand aside, Oksana. I don't know what the little colt is going to do," Laura warns.

This baby is called a colt?

The mama backs down out of the trailer as if every step will kill her. She's slow, emaciated, and has sores like Boris did. She looks like she's sleepwalking, except I've never seen a horse sleepwalk. The baby neighs and follows his mama, kicking and squealing. The man jumps back, away from the colt. "Let him go. He won't go far," he says.

We watch as his thin, awkward body dances and kicks in circles. His mama watches him from the corner of her eye, but stands still. The man leads her into the open fenced pasture, and the colt follows. Laura shuts the gate behind them.

The colt darts in different directions before he finally calms down and nurses from his mama. He slurps and sucks, but he seems frustrated. It's as if his mama doesn't have anything to give him.

It reminds me of Natalia in Russia when she would scream for food, but Mama wasn't there, and I couldn't feed her. I spin, dizzy, and reach to hold the fence.

Laura says the baby is hungry and dehydrated.

I know.

The colt screeches again and pulls away from his mama. He's wild. Laura shakes the man's hand and he drives off. I glare at him. Why didn't he take better care of these horses?

Laura seems to know what I'm thinking. She says, "He didn't do this. Someone else did. He only rescued them. Come, we need to feed them."

I no longer feel dizzy. Unlike in Russia, I can help the baby here.

Laura and I go into the barn for hay. We fill two buckets with water, and I carry them out to the pasture. Laura brings a flake of hay. Boris watches from the other pasture and nickers as I go by.

I lay the hay in the field, and Laura places the buckets in front of the mama and the other one close to her. The colt watches, but he keeps his distance. He comes closer and then runs away. We leave the pasture and watch from the fence. The colt walks to the bucket, sniffs, jumps back, sniffs again, and drinks.

Mama drinks from her bucket and eats the hay. Laura tells me it's too soon to feed them grain because they may not have had anything to eat in a long time, and it'll make them sick. I remember the first night in American at Katie's and how I ate so many plates of different foods and had to sleep on the floor in the bathroom because my stomach hurt so badly.

Standing at the fence, I watch the mama and her baby. I'm sad for them.

"Can I brush the mama?" I ask Laura.

"No, not yet. Wait for the vet to come to examine them first."

#

The Baker Boys, Matt and Tyler, arrive for their lesson. They're busy in that they can't stop moving. Laura makes them run laps in the empty arena a few times. They kick up dirt and shout, and afterward they seem calmer. She tells them to put on their helmets, and with the help of the boys' mother, they get up on their horses and in the arena. Laura leads Matt, the oldest, and his mother leads Tyler. They play a game of stopping and starting, and they're all laughing.

I look away and watch the emaciated mama with her baby. The mama can't give him what he wants, just like Mama with me when I was little. I feel a lump in my throat but swallow it down.

I remember when Ludmila was gone, and I was hungry and Mama was sleeping. I woke her and said, "I'm hungry, Mama." She opened her eyes and said, "I'm sorry. I'm so, so sorry." Then she fell back to sleep. I was angry. How could she do this—sleep all the time? Didn't she care? I don't remember how old I was, but from that moment on, I learned to find food for myself because I couldn't rely on anyone else.

The colt knows how I feel. His head is bent, and he's chewing on every blade of grass he can find.

I hear a neigh from the barn and see Boris's head bobbing at me as it hangs out his window. I laugh. Is he jealous? I go to his stall and he greets me. Gathering the brushes, I go inside.

Mr. Blackwell hauls the wheelbarrow to Star's stall across from Boris's. The man chews something like a wad of gum, but it's not gum. I'm not sure what it is. He spits it out and it's brown. He's disgusting!

I stay with Boris for an hour and talk to him in Russian, and he listens. I pick the dirt off his legs, comb his tail, and spray him with fly spray. I play games with him. I go to one corner and stand still like a statue. I don't move until he comes to me, and when he does, I rub his withers and laugh. I tell him, "Good boy!" Then I move to another corner and start the game again. Eventually he gets faster at playing it and follows me everywhere. He's smart, and I can tell he's having fun, but then his mood changes.

Mr. Blackwell opens the stall. Boris pins his ears back.

I glare at the man. "Go away."

He spits, enters the stall, turns his back, and rakes the manure. Boris crosses in front of me and bites Mr. Blackwell in the arm. The man curses, flings around, and strikes Boris in the face with his fist. Boris screeches.

How dare he! A force inside me erupts. It gives me strength. I kick Mr. Blackwell in the shins, and he curses, then lifts his arm to strike me. I duck and he sways off balance. I push him into the wheelbarrow in the doorway and kick it over. He falls with a thud, As he scrambles, I lock Boris's stall, the door rattling on its hinges before I turn to run. But Mr. Blackwell lunges toward me and grabs my ankle.

I scream, kicking his face, and run past Laura and the Baker boys, who are bringing their horses into the barn.

"What's going on?" Laura says.

My heart beats fast like the hooves of the colt. I run down the gravel driveway toward the gate, past where the trees dangle over and shade the path.

"Come back," my aunt yells. "Where are you going?"

Tears stream down my face. I can't stop running. I hate Mr. Blackwell. How could Laura invite him to help? Is she blinded by his good looks and his phony smile? Why can't she see what type of man he is on the inside? I get to the gate and hear Laura's truck barreling down after me. She's yelling out the window. "Oksy, wait!"

I pause.

Laura stops the truck, gets out, and comes to me. She gazes into my tear-filled eyes and wraps me in her arms. "What happened?"

I shake my head and push her away. She won't believe me. Mama never did.

She touches my arm. "Please, get in the truck and talk to me."

Slowly, with crossed arms, I follow her to the truck.

She climbs in and turns the truck around, but instead of heading to the barn, she heads down a dirt path that circles the pond on the outskirts of her land and stops.

"Please talk to me."

I stare out the window. "Mr. Blackwell struck Boris with his fist. He's an evil man. Boris doesn't like him."

"Boris may not like any man because someone in his life may have abused him, but that doesn't mean Mr. Blackwell deserves to be treated like the abuser. However, if he hit Boris, then I need to speak to him."

"He's bad . . . I know." *She won't believe me, so why am I bothering to explain? His good looks trapped her.*

Laura turns the engine off, gets out of the truck, and motions for me to swap places with her.

"Me? Drive?" Why is she doing this?

"Drive," she says.

I get out of the truck. The Bakers drive by, leaving the ranch. The boys wave at me. Laura turns and waves good-bye too.

My heart skips a beat that I get to drive. My tears stop. I have never driven a car but am excited to learn how. I climb up into the ripped front seat, close the creaking door, and hold the steering wheel. Laura shows me how to turn the key.

I turn it like I've seen Katie do. The engine rumbles. I smile. Laura shows me how to adjust the seat and put the truck in Drive while keeping my foot on the brake. I do, and the truck jerks forward. Next, Laura shows me where the pedal is that's called the accelerator. I don't try to say this word. I know I can't.

I press the Go pedal and squeal. This is way better than running. I take it slow at first to get the feel of it, then gradually I press the foot pedal harder, and we go faster. Laura points to a rectangular mirror and tells me it's called a rearview mirror, and when I look into it, I can see the dust from the dirt path we've left behind.

Laura says, "Yeeeee-haaaa!" and buckles her seat belt.

I laugh and laugh. I drive in circles around the pond at least six times, but the first time is much slower than the last. At first I press the Go pedal slowly, and when I take the turn, I press the brake too hard. I think Laura will hit the dashboard, but she doesn't. She only laughs. When I turn and overcorrect, I feel like we're teetering, but Laura doesn't seem worried. She tells me I'll get it, to keep trying. Eventually I get better, and I'm able to even out the intensity of my fasts and slows. I don't go too fast though because I don't want to end up in the pond.

The sixth time around, I see Katie pulling in through the gate. Laura tells me to follow her down to the barn. I drive past Firefly, Star, and the new mama and her colt grazing in the pasture and pull up next to Katie. Laura and I are laughing.

Katie sees that I'm driving and looks angry. She gets out of her car with her makeup on and her clothes neatly pressed. She dresses so proper, unlike Laura, who looks more natural.

Katie says to Laura, "Are you crazy?"

"Oh, Katie. It's okay. Oksana knows not to drive anywhere except on the ranch. This is harmless."

How can these two be sisters? They look and act so different.

"I don't think so, and I'm her mother. I would appreciate it if you would consult me first about something like this." Her back stiffens, and her eyes squint at Laura.

Laura shakes her head. "It's really no big deal."

"It is to me." Katie's voice gets a little louder. "Oksana, get in the car. We have to go. Nat isn't feeling well."

"I want to stay here."

"This isn't your home." Katie glares at Laura, like Katie wishes I was laughing with her instead of Laura.

Laura turns to me. "Go now so you can come back soon. Let's not ruin a good thing."

I climb in the backseat with Nat, who's crying, and I want to see why. She smiles through her tears when she sees me, but her face is pale.

As Katie pulls away, Mr. Blackwell leans against the barn, smiles, and shows his brown rotted teeth. Laura approaches him with her arms crossed. Maybe she'll fire him. What does she see in him anyway? She's smart about kids and horses, but not about men.

Chapter Twenty-Three

I'm in my bedroom at my computer, but I can hear Jack and Katie in the kitchen. They talk like they don't think I understand, or can hear.

"Maybe we should adopt a kitten for her," Katie says.

"We already have a dog," Jack says.

"It's not the same. Jasper is our dog—not Oksana's. He comes to you. He's primarily bonded to you. She needs something that bonds to only her that she has to take care of and be responsible for."

The newspaper rattles, and I picture Jack sipping his coffee and listening to Katie as he reads the paper. "Where would you find one?"

"I thought I'd take her to the animal shelter and check out what they have. You know, rescue an animal. Do you want to go? We could wait until Saturday."

"No, you go ahead. Caring for another animal will be more work for you than me. Are you sure you're up for this?"

Katie hesitates. "If it helps Oksana, I'm all for it."

What does she mean, if it helps me? I don't need help, and I don't want a cat. But after Jack leaves for work and we clean the kitchen, we go to the animal shelter.

When we pull into the parking lot, I hear dogs barking—many of them. Some have deep barks and others have yappy ones. Katie takes Nat out of her car seat.

The lady at the front desk gives us a tour. We pass through one door that leads to a hallway and then to several other rooms. Everything is concrete, which makes the dogs' barks loud and frightening. Nat holds on to Laura with a firm grip.

The building smells like bleach and the bathrooms in Russia.

In one large room, cages of cats and kittens line the walls. They're at eye level, and I see one gray kitten with blue eyes pawing at its door and meowing. Each crate has at least one animal in it. Some have two. In each crate there's a litter box, food, and a water bowl. Some bowls are empty because they've been knocked over. This room smells like pee. Our guide explains that if we'd like to take a cat out and play with it, we can go into a bonding room designed for adoption considerations.

What's *bonding* and *considerations*? She talks in big words. I hate seeing the animals locked in cages.

The next room is filled with the smaller dogs. When we enter the room they stand up and bark, each one fighting for our attention, scratching at their metal doors. Some have messes in the corner of their cages. All have a blanket, a bowl of water, and sad eyes. Their tails wag. One wire-haired dog doesn't get up. He lies on his side looking out at us as his tail slowly thumps the metal floor of his crate. He has goop oozing from the corner of his eyes. He sneezes. Poor thing.

"You can take one out if you'd like. The leashes are on the wall over there." She points to a wall with a dozen different leashes hung on nail pegs.

Katie and I are silent.

The guide turns to leave the room, and the small dogs whine and bark louder, more desperate. I want to let them all go. Animals were made to be free.

The room for larger dogs has bigger cages lined up on the floor. There must be fifteen cages on the right and as many cages on the left. All of them are filled. Again, when we enter the concrete-floored room, they bark, and the noise echoes off the walls, increasing the volume. Some jump up and down, and others pace back and forth. Big brown-eyed dogs stare and beg for us to take them. Each has a pink or blue paper attached to their crate, indicating their sex. The paper includes their names and breed types.

"How long have they been here?" I ask.

"Some have been here longer than others." The guide says.

"Why do you keep them in these cages?"

"We can't let them run loose in the building. They'd fight. They're safer this way."

"Do they get out of their cages?"

"When volunteers come and walk them. But some days they don't get out."

"Where do they go to the bathroom?"

"Unfortunately many times they have to go in their crates."

Why does she call them crates? They're cages.

Genka, a girl in the orphanage who slept next to Ruzina, used to wet her bed. It would dry during the day because she wasn't allowed to clean the sheets except once a week, and even if she could, she was afraid to tell anyone, but the stench remained, and she'd have to sleep in it again and again. I hated lying in bed, smelling the pee, but Genka had it the worse because she'd have to sleep in it. No one would get next to her during the day because she always smelled. The kids called her Skunk.

The dogs make me think of her and how she had to lie in her stink.

"Have you seen any you'd like to walk?" Katie asks me.

I shrug. No, they're pitiful, but I don't say that.

"There are more outside, but they can't be adopted yet. They are the recent ones that are isolated so we can determine their temperaments. Sometimes a family has lost them and comes here to claim them."

"How often does that happen?" Katie asks.

"Not too often, maybe three percent of the time. If they're found abandoned, it's because their owners don't care enough to keep them safe and contained," the guide says.

They're all orphans without a home. Their faces stare at me through the bars, unable to escape to freedom. Some look angry and growl. They look like wolves. Aren't dogs like wolves? Couldn't they survive on their own? I don't think so, but still, I want them to be free.

I walk on the bleached concrete and look through each wire cage. There's Jackson, Tucker, Suzie, Eddie, Angel, and others. "Who named them?"

"We do. Most of them come to us without names, so we get the privilege of naming them."

"How do they come here?"

"They're picked up off the street. Sometimes an owner will

leave one chained to a door or a fence overnight with a water dish. They're abandoned."

Like me.

They all need to be saved. Just like in Russia.

I stand outside the cage of a golden-colored dog. "How come he doesn't bark like all the others?"

"He's older. Maybe that's why. He's been here a long time, and no one has adopted him."

"Why not?"

"He's aggressive toward other dogs, so he's been difficult to place."

"Why is he like that?"

She sighs like she's annoyed at my questions. "Some just are. We're not sure what causes them to be one way or another."

I remember the kids from the orphanage who would steal and hurt others. Then they'd lie with a straight face. Sometimes they stole for food or simply because someone looked at them a certain way. They were unpredictable.

I move away from the old dog. Even though there's wire between us, I don't trust him. One black shiny dog named Shylee cowers back in her cage. Her tail wags, but her ears are drooping and she's crouching low.

"What is she afraid of?"

"Us, maybe. It's possible someone abused her when she was little. She doesn't trust us because of how she used to be treated."

"Can I walk her?" I look at Katie.

Katie turns to me. "We have a dog, so she wouldn't work for us. I'd rather you adopt a kitten."

"I just want to walk her."

The guide glances at Katie.

Katie nods okay.

The lady hands me a leash and opens the cage door. Shylee cowers more and backs away from me. I stoop so I'm at her level. "It's okay, girl. Let's go for a walk."

As I get closer, she wags her tail and rolls onto her back with her feet in the air. I pet her stomach. She's so excited she jumps on me, and her nails scratch my legs. I screech, which makes her run to the back of her cage again.

I rub the burn from the scratches on my legs. "It's okay," I say to her, again moving forward. This time when she rolls over I put the clasp on her collar. “Come on, girl.”

She doesn’t get up. Instead she lies with her tummy on the ground and lets me slide her out. “Can I carry her out?”

“Sure,” the guide says. “She’s still a puppy and probably hasn’t been on a leash very often.”

Katie says again, “I don’t think another dog will work for us, Oksana.”

“I just want to play with her.” She weighs maybe fifteen pounds. I lift her, and she squirms in my arms, but I get her outside the building, where she’s free to jump and run and play in the grass. She crouches, doing a tummy crawl. I sit in the grass, and in one second she leaps into my lap, licks my face, and paws at my arms. I try to pet her, but she wiggles onto her back and kicks her legs in the air. She squirms all over the place. I think if dogs could giggle, she’d be giggling.

Katie’s cell phone rings. She answers it and says to me, “I’ll be in the car. I need to take this call.”

A man in a red pickup truck pulls up and starts unloading boxes from his car. The guide says to me, “Go ahead and play with her all you like. I have to take care of this customer’s donation.”

I play with Smilin’ Shylee, proud that I haven’t run scared. I like her name. Maybe I’m getting used to dogs because of Duke and Jasper. I try to walk Shylee around the building, but she won’t let me lead her. I pick her up and carry her back inside the building to her crate. A sadness stabs at my insides because I can’t take her home. At least in the orphanage I wasn’t locked away. I don’t want to close her in the cage.

The other dogs watch me, clawing at their cages, barking, whining. I know what I must do.

First, I start with the large dogs because I think they’ll lead the way for the smaller ones. I open the back door of the building and set a rock in front of it to hold it open. Then I move fast, unlocking each cage and opening each gate.

“Go!” I tell them. “Run!” I shoo them away with my arms, waving them toward the back door. They wag their tails and some jump on me, like they’re thanking me. They bark, but once they realize they are free to go, they jet toward the back door and out into the great big world, free from their cages and the pee stench. They’re like one big wild pack.

I smile, holding back a giggle. They look happy. Maybe for a few days they'll love being free.

When all the large cages are empty, I run into the small dog room and unlock their cages. One by one, I set them on the floor and shoo them out the back door. That's when I hear our guide.

"What's going on here?" She chases after the dogs, trying to herd them at the back door.

While she runs to the back, I hurry out the front. Katie's still on the phone in the car, but says good-bye to the person when she sees me. I climb in next to Nat, who's playing with a doll.

I say, "I'm done. I don't want to adopt a kitten."

Katie seems distracted. She starts the car and pulls away before she sees our guide running out the door shaking her fist at us.

Chapter Twenty-Four

The next morning, while Katie, Jack, Nat, and I are having breakfast at the kitchen table, Jack reads the morning paper as usual, trying to verse me on current events. He does this every morning, trying to get my attention about the government and what America needs, like he's trying to find something to talk to me about, but he's trying too hard. My disinterest makes him sigh and causes lines in his forehead. I'm not like Katie. I'm not going to soothe his temper. His frustration often makes him lash out at me, like he wants to punish me, or get back at me for ignoring him.

Today, he looks up from reading the front page of the paper, and says to Katie, "Didn't you go to the shelter yesterday?"

She pours milk into a cup for Nat. "Yes, we went, but it was awful. Those poor animals."

"Did you see what happened there?" Jack shows Katie the newspaper.

"What does it say?" Katie takes a quick glance at the paper while feeding Nat.

Jack says, "Someone let all the dogs go. What time were you there?"

Katie pauses and stares at me, then at the paper, then back at me. "Did you do this?"

I shift my eyes downward to my cereal bowl.

Jack says, "It says here that many of them were found, but one was hit and killed by a car."

I look up and gasp. "Which one?" I hope it wasn't Shylee.

"Oh, my!" Katie covers her mouth. "Oksana, what did you do?"

I can feel their eyes on me, but I stare out the window, and set my jaw. I'm still glad I let them go, even if it was for a little while. I'm not happy one died, but he's probably better off anyway.

"Oksana!" Jack pounds his fist on the table. "Look at us when we're talking to you. Did you do this?"

Nat startles and bursts out crying.

Katie glares at Jack, lifts my sister and hugs her, and looks my way. "I'm sure you thought you had all the right reasons for doing what you did, but what you did was wrong."

He's always mad at me. It doesn't matter what I do. "You don't understand."

Katie says, "These dogs can't live in the wild like some animals can. They need someone to feed them and care for them. Besides, they're not there forever. People adopt them every day."

Jack's face is red, his bottom lip stiff. "She'll have to go back to apologize and hope that they won't press charges."

"I'll take her," Katie says, her voice low.

I pick up my cereal bowl and set it in the sink, the ceramic clinking against the porcelain.

"Get back here," Jack says, "We're not done talking to you!"

I run to my room, slam the door, and lock it. Jack is mean—just like other men.

A few hours later, after I hear Jack leave for work, Katie makes a phone call. She's mumbling, but I don't know who she's talking to. I'm writing a letter to Mama that I'll never send, when there's a knock at the door. I close my journal pad.

"What?"

From the other side of the door, Katie says, "We're going to go to the Animal Welfare League in an hour so you can apologize in person."

I don't want to go back to that place. "If I go will you take me to see Boris?"

"Your father says you can't go until Saturday."

He is not my father! I look at the calendar on the wall next to my bed. I don't have the days memorized yet. I get confused with Saturday and Sunday. I count. That's five days away! I kick the desk and fold my arms across my chest. I want to run away.

Chapter Twenty-Five

I'm at the animal shelter with Katie, standing at the desk where the pimply-face lady, who was our guide, sits. Her cheeks flash red when she sees me. I find a place on the wall above her head and stare. The dogs are barking, and the pee smell makes me want to puke.

"I'm sorry for letting the dogs go free," I say.

"Do you realize what you did?" she says, her voice louder than it needs to be.

"Yes, she does," Katie says. "She didn't think it through. She wouldn't purposely kill an animal."

Old pimple face glares at Katie. I turn to go. No one says a word as I leave.

On the way home, Katie tells me that Nat and I are spending the night at Laura's Saturday because she and Jack have a dinner to go to for Jack's work. Finally, I'll get to see Boris.

It takes forever for Saturday to come. It's definitely not a *New York minute*. So I stay in my room and study more idioms like sick as a dog, smell a rat, scot-free, water under the bridge, and when it rains it pours. I shiver, reaching for a hoodie in my closet to *take the chill off*.

On Saturday, I take Boris into the arena and walk with him for almost forty-five minutes. He's stronger now. I whisper a secret in his ear. "I'm going to ride you tonight." I want to show Laura that I can ride like the other kids, but I want it to be a surprise. She's asked me if I wanted to learn, but I said no. I was too scared, but not anymore. Now I'm excited. I figure if the others can ride, especially Megan, then I should be able to too.

Before it's time to eat supper, I help Laura peel potatoes. It reminds me of when I helped Hannah peel the apples. I think of Pastor and what I did, what I never told Mama. Tears threaten to sting my eyes, but I hurry and think of something else. I'm getting better on the computer, so soon I'll be able to type the numbers and letters from the back of the photo into the space bar and understand what I see.

After we eat, I get to help with Nat because Laura lets me, unlike Katie who says I help too much, that I need to let her be the mom. Laura lets me bathe, dress, and feed Nat a bottle. My sister looks more like Mama every day, especially as her hair grows, but she's still tiny for nine months.

When it's ten o'clock, I say good night to Laura and pretend to go to bed, but instead, I get under the covers with my clothes on and wait for her light to go out. I hear her in the bathroom and the click when she turns out the light. Soon she's snoring, and I tiptoe in the hallway, grab the flashlight off the hook in the garage, put my on mud-covered boots and my heavy coat, and head out to the barn.

My heart is racing. I'm going to ride Boris! Won't I surprise everyone?

It's a cloudless, crisp night. I see my breath in the air. The ground is covered with light snow, and there's a full moon that guides my path. I turn on my flashlight in the barn. The horses are quiet, but some nicker as I walk by their stalls.

"Shhh."

Reaching for the halter on the hook, I enter Boris's stall. He comes to me right away. I put on the halter, first upside down and then right-side up. It takes me longer than it should to figure out the buckle, but maybe it's because my hands are shaking from the cold.

I walk Boris out to the cross ties, brush him, and put a blanket on his back. I go to the tack room to find a saddle. Which one should I use? They all look the same now that no one is here to tell me which one works best. I lift a saddle and think it looks perfect, and carry it to Boris. The saddle is heavy and I bump into him, but he doesn't budge. I'm ready to buckle the girth, when I realize I've put his saddle on backward. Laughing, I get a stool to stand on and flip the saddle around. I climb down off the stool and tighten the girth again. This time it works.

Getting him to open his mouth for the bit is a challenge, but he wiggles his tongue, and the bit clanks into place. I walk him outside through the barn door and position him in front of a step stool that Laura uses for her shorter students. A large overhead light illuminates the yard and the arena where I plan to ride him. I bring the reins around and climb the stool stairs, put my foot in the stirrup, and fling my other leg around, but the stirrups are too short. Shoot! I'd forgotten to adjust them.

I climb off and adjust the stirrup straps. It takes forever because the leather is stiff. I'm sweating underneath my jacket. When I remount Boris, my legs feel more comfortable. I put my feet in the stirrups, trembling at how high I am. But before I can get my balance, Duke darts from the other side of the barn, barking and charging at Boris like he's an intruder.

Boris startles and bolts.

I pull the reins, but Boris trots forward. He won't stop. He's moving fast.

"Whoa!" I jerk backward, and the reins slip out of my hands.

Boris canters away from the arena toward the long driveway. I holler, "Whoa!" again, but he doesn't stop. Squeezing my legs and holding on to the horn, I reach for the reins, finally getting hold of them.

I pull and scream, but Boris keeps going. I'm bouncing like a rock in a wheelbarrow, thumping against the saddle. I don't know how much longer I can hold on.

Boris heads down the driveway, his ears pinned back. I pull harder on the reins, and his head bucks up, making me teeter in the saddle. I'm so unsteady. It takes everything I have to stay in the saddle.

"Stop!" I yell.

Boris races past the pond, down the tunnel of trees, and toward the gate. Is the gate shut? It has to be. I see it. It's closed. Certainly Boris won't try to run through the gate, will he?

Headlights from an oncoming car illuminate the road to my right. I see the beams out of the corner of my eye. Boris stops dead at the gate, and I can't hang on. I fly over the top, scream, and land in the dirt road in front of the path of the car.

My head hits something sharp, and my arms and legs scrape across the rocks. The driver screeches to a halt. Then everything goes still and black.

A car door opens. Footsteps follow. A guy's voice sounds. "Holy crap! Are you okay?"

I open my eyes. I'm lying in the road. The lights from the car are shining into my eyes, blinding me. I can't see the man's face, only his cowboy boots. I shield my eyes from the light and look up at his face. His hair is almost as light as mine, and he's the cutest boy I've ever seen.

"I could have killed you!" he says. "Are you crazy? You like . . . came out of nowhere . . . like some kind of flying girl."

A warm fluid oozes down the collar of my coat. I close my eyes, feeling dizzy.

He kneels beside me. "Talk to me—are you okay?"

I try to sit. "Does it look like I'm okay?" My head hurts. I forgot to wear a helmet. That's one of Laura's strict rules. How could I have forgotten? I'm stunned.

The guy reaches into his belt clip for his phone. "I'm calling 911." He opens his cell and is ready to punch numbers, so I grab it from him.

"No, don't call. I'm okay."

"Are you sure?"

I hand him back his phone. "Look, I can talk to you, can't I? My aunt is inside. She'll take care of me. Where's Boris?" I manage to sit up and put my hand to my head, but when I pull my hand away and see the blood, it brings back memories of Mama's delivery. I close my eyes and swoon.

"Who's Boris?"

"My horse." I feel dizzy.

"Hey, you're bleeding."

I turn and spit, feeling like I'm going to vomit. Acid burns my throat. I spit again.

He takes off his coat and then his T-shirt, which he wads up and puts behind my head where I'm bleeding. He's naked from the waist up, and he's close enough that I see the ripples of his stomach muscles and smell his deodorant. He puts on his coat, zips it up, and kneels in front of me.

"Here, let me help you up. Can you hold my shirt to your head?"

I hold the shirt in place, still sitting.

"Try to apply pressure." He slips his arms underneath me and lifts me into his arms.

"What are you doing?"

"You're a little unstable to walk. Just relax."

I'm uncomfortable, not only because my head hurts, but this boy is way too close. But I don't have the strength to fight him even though I want to.

"Is your aunt home?" He nods toward Laura's house.

"I don't want her to see me like this. She's going to be disappointed." I exhale loudly. "Is Boris okay?" I try to look around but feel dizzy again.

"Stay still. I'll get you up to the house, then find your horse. Just keep applying pressure to your head."

He takes short, large puffs as he opens the gate and carries me up the driveway. Halfway there, I hear Laura running toward us and crying, "Oksy?"

The guy says, "We're here, Miss Laura."

He knows my aunt?

"Luke, thank God!" She looks at me. "I thought I heard you scream. What have you done, child?"

"I wanted to surprise you and ride Boris, but he spooked, and I forgot to wear a helmet."

"I was driving by . . . when I saw her get . . . flung over your gate," Luke says between pants.

"Thank you, thank you. Can you carry her to the house?"

"I think so." He grunts.

Laura keeps saying, "Oh my. Oh my. Why didn't you tell me you were ready to learn how to ride? There's more to it than you realize."

"Where is Boris? Can you see him?" I ask.

She says, "He's around here somewhere. We'll find him. He can't go anywhere. There's a fence around the perimeter. Don't worry about him right now."

Tears fill my eyes. "Why did he do that? I thought he liked me."

"He does like you," she says as she holds my arm and walks beside Luke. "But he's still an animal, unpredictable. Besides, you said he got spooked. How?"

"Duke."

The dog hears his name and runs to Laura's side. She hits herself in the head with her palm. "I forgot to put him in the kennel before I went to bed." She pushes the hair out of my eyes. "Riding

Boris is going to take time. Something happened to him before he came here. We have to give him time to heal from those wounds."

Laura opens the door for Luke, and he places me gently on the sofa. He exhales and steps back, watching me, his eyes wide like he's worried. His pale lashes curl longer than the lashes of most girls I know. He shoves his hands into his back pockets and rocks on the balls of his feet.

I feel like an idiot.

Laura hands me a few tissues and runs into the kitchen. She gets a cold washrag, a bag of ice, and returns. She examines my head and tells me I have a goose egg, but she doesn't think I need to have it sewn up. She examines the rest of my body.

"I'm okay," I say. I don't want Luke to think I'm weak.

"Do you hurt anywhere else?" she asks.

"No, no, I just want to find Boris." I sit up, but feel dizzy again and lie back down.

"I'll go find him and put him in his stall," Luke says. "I have to move my truck out of the road anyway. Which stall does the horse go in?"

Laura gives him instructions. "Thank you for your help. Oksy was lucky you were driving by."

He smiles at me. "Glad I could help." Then he turns to leave.

Laura has tears in her eyes when she turns to me. "Oh my, oh my. Maybe I should take you to the emergency room." She looks at my eyes and says my pupils look okay.

I think they should. I didn't get poked in the eye.

She gives me a pill for pain and makes me drink water. She takes care of me like I'm her daughter, in a way no one ever has before, not even Mama. I wish Laura was my mama instead of Katie because she likes animals and doesn't try to boss me around.

Luke returns almost a half hour later, looking tired. Laura and I are sitting on the sofa watching TV. She doesn't want me to fall asleep yet. I don't want to because I need to know Boris is safe first. When I see Luke, I sit up.

He says, "I don't know where he went. I'm sorry, I can't find him."

"What?" Tears well in my eyes. "I can find him. I know he'll come to me." I turn to Laura. "Please let me go find him."

She bites her lip like she doesn't want me to go, but she understands. "I don't want you to go alone, but I can't leave Nat.

Luke, can you stay a little longer and help Oksy? You can take my red truck out there."

"Let me call home first. I'm past curfew." He takes his cell phone out of his pocket and punches a few numbers.

Laura says, "I'll talk to your mom if you think it'll help."

Luke nods and hands her the phone.

While Laura works out the details with Luke's mom, I stand with the bag of ice on my head and slowly walk to the door. Luke walks beside me.

"Do you need me to hold you? Just in case?" He places his hand on my elbow, and I let him because I need to find Boris, and I'm still a little dizzy. His touch doesn't feel bad; rather, it feels protective.

I take slow, short steps to Laura's truck. Luke boosts me up into the seat, climbs in the driver's side, and shines the truck's lights. He scans the pastures, the pond, and the nearby woods. We drive slowly and watch for any movement.

I squint my eyes, searching. "He had the lead rope attached to him. Maybe it wrapped itself around a tree and he's caught. Let's go closer to the trees."

Luke drives around the pond to the back of the property. At the edge of the woods, I ask him to stop, and I get out. He jumps out and takes my arm, leading me to the edge of the woods. I bat at a mosquito buzzing in my ear.

"Boris, here boy."

Leaves rustle. He nickers. He's not far, but I can't see him.

"Come here." I cluck and hold out my arm out like I do when we play the game, but he doesn't come. Maybe it's because Luke is standing beside me. "Luke, you have to go back to the truck or he won't come."

"What about you? Are you okay?" He's as tall as me, eye-to-blue-eye, and he's so close I can smell his breath. It smells like peppermint gum.

"I'll be okay, yes. I'll lean against this tree until he comes close enough for me to grab his lead." I point to the closest tree and move there.

Luke goes back to the truck and waits.

I stand against the tree, hoping it doesn't take long. "Come on, boy."

Hooves crunch in the brush. I don't move. I'm still playing

statue, but my eyes are roaming, searching for his white hide in the dark.

Boris finally saunters to my side. I sigh, take the reins, and pet his back. “It’s okay. I’m okay. I know you didn’t mean to hurt me.”

He lays his head on my shoulder like he’s apologizing. Even though he’s only an animal, like Laura says, he understands me, and I’m glad he’s calm now.

Chapter Twenty-Six

The next day, Nat wakes with a fever and I have a headache. Jack and Katie arrive in time for breakfast, but things don't go well with Jack and Katie.

Katie says to Laura, "You didn't hear her go out?"

"No, I was asleep. I never thought she'd try to ride on her own. I woke as soon as I heard her scream."

She's defending herself as if Jack and Katie are the bosses of her too. Why couldn't she have made something up? I cross my arms and squint my eyes at her, feeling betrayed.

She squeezes my shoulder, maybe to give me a sign she's on my side. I'm not sure.

"She's okay now, though, aren't you? Today is a new day."

Jack looks over at me and shakes his head like he's disappointed. Of course.

When it's time to go home, I get in a quiet car because Nat sleeps and Jack and Katie seem angry. We head home, and I go to my room and listen to Katie on the phone. She talks to the nurse, getting instructions about my head and what to give Nat for her fever. Then she comes to talk to me.

"How do you feel?"

I shrug. "My head right here is sore, but I'll be okay." I touch the back where the bump is.

"Are you still dizzy?"

"No… not since last night."

Jack enters my room. He rarely comes here. There's no place

for him to sit, so he stands. It's like he's the king looking down at me.

"Katie and I have decided that you aren't allowed to go to the barn for a while. What you did was wrong, and there have to be consequences. You'll stay here until you can prove you're responsible. There are chores that need to be done here, but it's time for you to go back to school too, so you'll need to concentrate on that. You will obey our rules."

His voice is firm. I shudder and turn my back to him, facing the corner of my room and crossing my arms over my chest. He's like Ludmila. Always trying to be the boss of me.

They leave, and I lie on my bed and cry. I don't understand. It's not like I wanted to fall off of Boris. I thought I would make them proud. I trusted Boris.

An hour later the doorbell rings, and I hear Laura's voice. She's talking to Katie. I open my door a few inches to listen.

Laura says, "Keeping her away from the barn won't help. Doesn't Jack see that?"

"No, he doesn't. He thinks we need to channel Oksana's interests in another direction, give her boundaries and make her earn privileges."

"How?"

"What do you mean?"

Laura says, "How do you stop anyone from doing what God has called them to do? What if we told you that you couldn't pursue your design interests and made you go to an accounting job where you had to work with numbers all day?"

"You're being melodramatic. Oksana is a child. We don't know anything about what her gifts are yet."

"You're wrong. I've seen the way Boris responds to her. He's healing her and she's healing him. Somehow it's working. They understand each other. It's her gift—the way she connects with animals. Shutting her here in this room or within your boundaries is only leaving her in the dark again. She'll never make progress this way." She pauses. "You can't force her to love you, Katie."

Katie makes a sound like "humpgh." Her heels click on the tile, and I picture her moving away from Laura. "How absurd. I'm not *forcing* her to love me, but rules are rules. How will she be able to live in society if she can't obey the rules?"

There's a long pause, and Laura's voice grows quiet. "Will you let me see her?"

"Sure, she's in her room."

Quickly, I shut my door so Laura doesn't think I've been listening. I sit at my desk and pretend to do research on my computer.

Laura knocks.

"What?" I say.

Laura enters. "Hey, cowgirl. What's happenin'?"

I shrug, my back to her.

"How's your head?"

"Okay." I stay turned away so I can't see her. So the lump in my throat won't plop out and dislodge the tears.

"What are you researching there?" She sits on the edge of my bed and looks over my shoulder at the computer screen. The search bar is empty.

"A blank page, eh?" She takes my chin and turns my head toward her, meeting my eyes. "I'm sorry. This is really bad news, isn't it—you not being allowed to come to the ranch?"

I can't look at her. I turn away.

She reaches for my hand. "Look at me, Oksy."

I look at her again, then look away.

She waits until I meet her eyes before she says, "I'm not mad at you."

Tears fill my eyes. "I'm sorry for what I did. I wanted to surprise you."

"You did that, all right!" She chuckles.

"No, I wanted you to be proud of me."

"I am proud of you. More than you'll ever know." She squeezes my arm.

"I don't understand why Boris did that to me."

"Boris spooked, just like you said. It wasn't your fault. You couldn't have avoided it. Sometimes animals are unpredictable. Boris is still healing. He might look like he's healed on the outside, but on the inside he's still hurting, and sometimes that takes longer. I'm just happy you're both okay. You understand, right?"

I hiccup a sob and nod. "I want to see him."

"Katie said you have to stay away for a while. Give it time, and I'm sure they'll let you return. They love you, Oksy. They want you to be safe, and they think you're safer here."

"They don't understand me." I wipe my tears with the bottom

of my shirt.

"I'm sure that's what it feels like, but they were children once, and they think they know what's best for you."

"They don't know what's best for me. If they did, they'd let me go to the barn."

"I have an idea. Why don't you apologize to them and ask them how you can earn a trip back? Maybe if you show them you're willing to work toward this, and show them in baby steps you can be trusted, they'll allow you to return. I'll teach you how to ride, but we'll start on Firefly. He's more sound. Maybe, in time, you'll be able to ride Boris, but not yet. I know you'll be a quick learner because you're a bright girl." She squeezes my hand. "You have no fear, do you?"

Yes, I do, but I don't tell her that. I fear being alone and never seeing Mama again. "I forgot to wear my helmet."

"Yes, you did."

"Next time I won't."

"You're right. You'll never forget." She squeezes my hand again. "You're going to be an awesome rider someday. Soon. Give it time."

Before she leaves, she makes me promise to think about sucking up to Jack and Katie. I laugh. This is a new idiom—suck up. It means to beg, charm, and do whatever is necessary to get what you want. I will do this.

#

At supper Jack talks to Katie about someone he knew from work who died of a heart attack. I feel invisible. He won't look at me or talk to me. I want to kick him under the table, but I know if I want to see the barn again I have to kiss *bootie.* I don't like it. He makes me mad.

Katie pretends like everything is fine, and good old Nat babbles in between bites of food. The medicine seems to have helped her fever. I wish I could be as happy-go-lucky as my sister. Jack tickles her bare feet and she giggles. He smiles at her, but not at me. He never smiles at me.

I push my peas back and forth on my plate and pierce them with my fork. I become more forceful with each stab and finally I blurt out, "I'm sorry!"

Jack and Katie stop their conversation midstream and stare at me.

"For what?" Jack asks.

"For loving the horses and wanting to ride Boris and for not putting on my helmet."

"What about for sneaking out when you should have been in bed?" he says.

I sit silent. It won't help me to say anything more. I apologized. Isn't that enough?

Katie butts in, "We care about you. We want you to think about the consequences of your actions before you plunge into things."

Jack says, "Look at your mother when she's talking to you!"

"She's not my mama!" I throw back my chair, run out of the room, fling open the garage door, and stand next to the cars in the cold. I don't bother to close the door. Nat cries.

"Now look at what you've done," Katie says.

"What *I've* done?" Jack says. "Why are you blaming this on me?"

Katie follows me into the garage where I'm leaning against the wall with my arms wrapped around myself. It's cold enough to see my breath.

Katie softens her voice. "Oksana, come back, please. Don't go. Running away doesn't help."

She takes my hand and leads me back inside. I run to my room and fling myself on the bed. Nothing is right. Nothing ever will be.

Mama, why did you abandon me?

Chapter Twenty-Seven

The next day Katie takes Nat to the doctor because her fever is back. I don't want to go. My head feels fine; it's just bruised. Jack says I have to go to school tomorrow, but he's giving me this day to recuperate from my fall. I'm raiding the snack pantry when the doorbell rings. I answer it with a mouthful of Cheetos and almost choke when I see Bryce standing there.

"Hi," he says. He's wearing a navy coat, a blue headband, and black gloves.

"Oh, hi." I know he reads lips so I talk to him. But what should I say? Should I invite him in? What does he want?

He blurts out, "How are you? I heard about your accident."

I can tell he's nervous because he's playing with the fingers of his gloves. I smell mints.

"I'm good. I only bumped my head." I turn and point to the spot on the back of my head.

"Does it hurt?"

I shake my head. "Not too bad."

"Do you want to ride over to the barn with me?"

A ride? I look at the driveway and see his bicycle. "Ah . . . on your bike?"

"Yeah . . . on the handlebars."

I can't picture myself on the little handlebars. I'm too tall, and it's a long way to go on a bike too. "I'm not allowed to go."

"Why?"

"Jack and Katie won't let me." I shrug and pause to remember the word I want to say. "I'm grounded."

"I'm sorry. I was hoping I could teach you to ride."

"Thanks, but Laura is going to teach me."

"Oh, okay, well, I'm glad you're doing better."

He signs good-bye and I copy him. He climbs on his bike and I think, *Wow, I can't believe he came to see me.* I didn't think he liked me enough to care.

I go back to the kitchen to finish eating my Cheetos, when the doorbell rings again. I lick the orange cheese powder off of my finger and open the door.

This time Luke is standing there. My stomach somersaults. I can't believe he's here. His blue truck is parked at the curb. He's wearing worn-out jeans, an oversized coat, leather cowboy boots, and a cowboy hat.

He touches the tip of his hat and says, "It's my Stetson." Pieces of his light hair fall across his forehead. His cheeks are flushed from the cold, which only makes his eyes bluer. They're almost the color of a blue bird, the color I can't look away from. I didn't notice before, but his mischievous eyes are in contrast with his shyness. I'm not sure which one to believe. Is he really this awesome—another new word in my vocab—and sincere, or is he like the boys in Russia with one thing on their mind?

"How are you doing?" he asks, and walks into the house.

I hesitate. What would Katie say? What would Jack say? "Uh, maybe we should stay out on the porch. Jack and Katie aren't home, so I can't let you in."

"Oh," he says and steps back onto the porch. He's staring at my lips.

I wipe them with the back of my hand. "I was eating Cheetos."

He laughs. "No wonder your lips are orange." He clears his throat.

"One minute." I go to the closet, get my coat, and return to the porch. I sit on the concrete stoop. He sits next to me.

"You want some Cheetos?"

"No, thanks. How are you doing? Laura told me you weren't allowed to go to the barn."

"Were you there? Did you see Boris?"

"Yeah, actually I did see him."

"Is he good? Did he seem okay to you?"

"He's skinny, but I don't know. I never saw him before to

know if he's better."

"He is better than he was. He was much worse."

Luke tells me he lives on a ranch and has Arabian horses. I don't know this breed or how they're different from Laura's horses. He says they are smaller and prettier. He asks me if I'd like to see them sometime, and I say sure.

Then he asks me, "What do you think of America so far?"

I look to see if he's making fun of me, but he seems serious about his question.

"America is a place where there's lots of color and people who don't worry about running water or food."

Luke's eyes get big. "Wow, you must have had a really different life."

"Yes." I'm quiet now. I don't know what to say. I've never had a conversation with a boy like this. "I have to go to school tomorrow."

"Really? Cool! Which one?"

I tell him. He says he goes to that school too. He acts excited. I wish I felt the same.

Katie pulls into the driveway and doesn't seem to notice us sitting on the porch.

"Should I go?" Luke asks.

"No, it's okay. I'll show you to my sister and Katie." We get up and walk to the garage. Katie is lifting Nat out of her car seat, but Katie is crying. I've never seen mascara dribbling down her face like this.

My hearts thumps fast. "What's wrong?" Nat rests her head on Katie's shoulder.

Katie jumps a little, like we surprised her. "Oh! Oksana. I didn't see you. Who is your friend?" She wipes her tears with a wadded tissue in her hand.

I don't want to answer. I want to know why she's crying. "This is Luke. Luke, this is Katie. Luke is the one who helped me at Laura's."

"Thank you for rescuing Oksana. I don't know what she would have done if you hadn't come along when you did."

Natalia fusses and lifts her head off Katie's shoulder.

"This is my sister, Natalia, but we call her Nat," I tell Luke, then turn to Laura. "What did the doctor say? Is she okay?"

Katie turns to go inside the house. "It was a pleasure to meet you, Luke. I need to get Nat in her bed right now."

"Is something wrong with Nat?"

"No, I'll tell you later," she says as she goes into the house.

My stomach twists in a knot. Something is wrong. Nat looks pale, like the color of my hair.

Luke says he better go too, but invites me to his house tomorrow. "I'll take you after school to meet my horses, if it's okay with your mom . . . er, Katie.

"I will ask. Maybe."

He pulls his phone off his belt. "What's your phone number?"

"I don't know. I never called myself before."

He laughs. "Well, I'll see you at school tomorrow. You can tell me then."

I wave good-bye and go into the kitchen. Katie is standing over the sink, her back to me.

"Why are you crying?" I ask.

"I'm just tired." She wipes her eyes again and puts her tissue in the garbage under the sink.

"You're crying because you're tired?" I move to face her.

She meets my eyes. "The doctor took blood from Nat, and it upset me to see her so upset."

"Why did they take her blood?" I should have gone with them.

She opens the dishwasher and loads a few dishes. "It's probably just a virus. We'll know soon."

"What's a virus? Why do they take blood?"

"They take the blood because it'll give them information about why she's been sick. A virus is an infection that takes about ten days to get over." She sighs. "She'll get better. I'm tired because I didn't sleep well last night." She opens the refrigerator. It's like she doesn't want to look at me. "Are you hungry? Can I get you something to eat?"

"No, I ate snacks before now." I sit at the table and watch her.

"Luke seems like a nice boy. I know his family. His dad is a doctor." She takes two pieces of cheese out of the refrigerator and shuts the door.

Nat cries from her bedroom, and Katie looks scared.

"I'll get her," I say.

Nat's lying in her crib, rubbing her eyes with her little fists and whimpering. Her pale face puckers into a dimpled grapefruit. Perspiration beads along her temples, and a large white bandage covers the top of her little hand. I hadn't noticed it before.

"Shh, Oksana is here; you'll be okay." I pick her up. "Don't you feel well today?"

She opens her eyes and smiles briefly, but drops her head onto my shoulder like she's too weak to keep it up. I lay her back down and scratch her back until she falls asleep, which doesn't take long. Katie stands in the doorway. I think she's crying again, but she turns away so I can't be sure. Does she know something about Nat she isn't telling me? She goes to the kitchen and cuts veggies for supper.

I follow her. "She's really sick, isn't she? She seems too small."

"We just don't know yet. We'll know more when we get the blood results. Let's pray that she gets better soon." Katie reaches for my hand and pulls me toward her into a hug. I stiffen, but I let her hold me because I think she needs to.

She says, "Dear God, thank you for the gift of my children. Please keep them safe and free from harm, and give Nat the strength to fight whatever it is she's fighting. I believe in you and all your goodness. Amen."

Katie squeezes my hand and turns to finish preparing dinner. I know that Katie and Jack pray, but this is the first time Katie has stopped everything and asked me to hold her hand and pray with her. It gives me a funny feeling, a sick feeling in the pit of my heart. I think something is really wrong. Why does she pray to someone she can't see? How is he supposed to help?

I go to my room, sit at my desk, close my eyes, and whisper, "Dear God, will you make my sister better? If Katie is worried, then it must be for a reason. Help me find a way to get home, back to Russia, and help Katie and Jack understand I need to see Boris."

I will see if praying works.

Chapter Twenty-Eight

Nat doesn't smile or play like she usually does that evening. She reminds me of the tree branches outside, the limbs thin and bare like they're cold and sickly and without life. Nat's lost her energy. She is weak and has dark blotches under her eyes.

Jack and Katie are quiet. Katie's eyes are puffy and red like she's been crying again.

When I try to feed Nat, she turns her head and spits out what I shovel in.

Luke calls. He got our number from Laura. He wants to know if I can go over to his house after school, but I say no. "My sister is sick. I don't want to leave her right now." He sounds disappointed, but I don't care. He doesn't understand. I don't want to go to school tomorrow, but Jack says I have to go.

In the morning, I dress in my usual jeans and boots. Nat doesn't seem any better, but she doesn't cry. She slept all night but still seems tired. I kiss her good-bye and she smiles.

Jack drives me to school in silence. I don't have anything to say to him either. He seems awkward in this new role of being my chauffeur. Typically he's at work already, but today he's helping Katie.

He parks the car and walks me to the office. The lady with the green headband has a blue one today. Jack signs some papers, shakes Principal Recker's hand, and leaves for work. Before he goes, he reminds me to take bus #4 home, and since I've never done this before the office lady tells him that she'll make sure I get on. I think I'd rather walk home, but I don't say that because I don't want to make Jack mad. Not now.

Luke is in the cafeteria at lunch. There are different shifts depending on the grade you're in. Luke is a senior, so he eats after me. He stops to talk to me and Chrissy. and her friends are impressed I know him, that he's my friend.

After school, I take the bus home and sit in an empty seat. I don't know anyone, but a dark-haired girl gets on and sits next to me.

She says, "Hi," in a soft voice like Ruzina's and smiles. I think of Ruzina and where she is, what she's doing. My life in the orphanage seems so long ago.

Someone behind me tugs at my ponytail. I turn around and glare at the boy, but he points to the boy next to him. They laugh.

The girl next to me says, "They're so immature." She reaches for her long ponytail and turns it to stream down the front of her shirt.

Mine isn't that long yet, so I pull my hoodie up. Idiots.

Both Katie and Jack are home when the bus drops me off. Jack is never home in the middle of the day, so I know something is wrong. Katie's crying and her trendy hairstyle is flat like she never took time to fix it. She doesn't look like "put-together Katie." Jack has his arm around her, and they're sitting in the living room.

I come in through the front door, throw my book bag on a chair, and sink into a chair.

"What's wrong?" Warning bells ring in my head.

Jack says, "Nat is sick, Oksana. Her test results came back confirming that she has leukemia."

Katie's cries grow louder.

"What's leukemia?" I don't like that Katie is out of control, that she's worried to tears. Is Nat going to die?

"It's cancer in her blood and in the marrow of her bones. It's complicated. It has to do with white blood cells and red blood cells. Her cells aren't working right, and it's causing her body to shut down. That's why she's been getting a fever and why she doesn't have energy."

"Make the doctors fix it." There's a buzzing sound in my ears. My stomach feels like it floated to my throat. I'm dizzy.

Katie wipes her face with a tissue.

Jack says, "There are medicines they can give her that can kill the bad cells, but they're worried she might have had the disease for too long. It might be so far gone that typical treatment won't work. She might need a bone marrow donor."

"What's that?"

Jack explains that there are certain cells in our bones, and if someone's good cells match Nat's, then the doctors can help her better.

"Can I give her my . . . what do you call it . . . bone marrow? She can have some of mine."

Jack smiles and takes my hand. "Thank you. Maybe you can."

I'm uncomfortable, but it'll seem rude to pull my hand away, so I let him hold it, hoping he lets go soon.

Katie's eyes drip with more tears. "Thank you, Oksana."

Jack says, "Typically, siblings have the highest probability of being that match. The doctor explained that Nat's immune cells would attack a donor's cells if they weren't compatible." He motions toward Katie and himself. "Ours are probably not a match."

I don't understand the words *immune, cells,* or *compatible*, but I know she needs something I may have. "I want to give her mine—whatever she needs."

Katie dabs her eyes again. "That means so much, Oksana."

Jack explains that they have to put a needle in my arm and draw out blood, but I don't care if it'll help Nat. "The doctor wants to test your blood to see if you're a match. If you and Nat have different fathers, there's a good chance you won't be."

My heart drops. Nat and I have different fathers. "What if I'm not a match?" I slip my hand out of Jack's and place it with my other one, folding them tightly in my lap.

Jack glances at Katie, and her eyes fill with tears again. He squeezes her hand this time. "We don't want to think about that right now. We're going to think positive that you'll be a match."

"What caused this to happen?" I want to ask if I could have this disease too, but I don't.

"It's nothing anyone has done," Katie says. "No one really knows what causes it." Her voice quivers, and she cocks her head as if reading my mind. "You can't catch it either. It's highly unlikely that you would have it too."

They explain that Nat had a biopsy of her bone marrow that morning. The doctors put a needle in her hip after they numbed it and took fluid out to study it.

Poor Nat. I get up and go to her room and watch her sleep. Katie stands beside me.

We leave Nat's room and I say to Katie, "We have to go now to do that needle thing. We can't wait."

"They scheduled it for tomorrow morning. We have to wait." She places her hand on my shoulder.

I go to my room and turn on my computer like Anna taught me. I type in the word *lukemia.* I don't know how to spell it. The search asks me if I meant *leukemia.* Yes, maybe that's the correct way to spell it. I'm not fast at reading the words, but the disease sounds serious but curable. It says twins have a better *probability* of being a match. I'm not sure what that word means, but Nat has a different father than me, so it must mean I might not be a match. My heart races, and my palms get sweaty.

I lift my mattress and feel for the photo I've kept hidden. I turn it over and read the words Pastor had written on the back and return to my computer. I type the letters and numbers in the search bar and press Enter. Multiple listings appear. One has a phone number. I jot that number on the back, underneath the address. I will call this number. Soon.

Next, I click on the address and a map appears. This place is only 129 miles away—two hours! Wow, that's not far at all. My heart skips, excited I'm so close, but maybe I won't need to know this information right away. Maybe I will be a match and Nat will get better, and I won't have to tell anyone.

But what I'm not a match? I'll have to tell someone then. Who? A sinking feeling fills the pit of my stomach. I don't want anyone to know.

I go to bed, but I don't sleep. I pray to a God I don't really know, because I don't know what else to do. Eventually I fall asleep, but I dream of an old, dark building and hear Mama crying, searching and reaching for me. She's flailing her arms in front of her, but it's so dark she can't find me. She's calling for me, "Oksana, Oksana."

I wake to Katie's voice saying, "It's time to get up."

#

Jack, Katie, Natalia, and I go to the hospital. The sky is cloud-covered gray, like it can't decide if it should show the sun or not. A snow squall floats from the darkest cloud, creating a harsh wind as intrusive as this disease. We hurry into the modern building with large blue windows, turning our backs to the wind's teeth. Jack leads us to an office that looks like a mini hospital. Jack says it's for children with cancer. There's a place in one corner for kids to build blocks, draw pictures, and listen to music. There are a few booths that have TV monitors and electronic games to play.

Several bald-headed children play at the tables, but most sit in their parent's lap. Their heads look queer and unnatural. I'm scared for Nat, but she seems oblivious. We find chairs near the games. Nat sits in Katie's lap, looking at a book. Both Nat and Katie have dark circles under their eyes. I think that Nat is now sicker than a dog, but this is not the time to think of idioms.

A lady wearing an aqua-blue outfit with zoo animals calls my name. She's smiling. She must whiten her teeth because they look whiter than the snow outside, fake. I can't stop staring at them. She puts us in a room. Jack, Katie, and Nat sit across from me on chairs along the wall. The lady takes my blood pressure and pulse and says she'll draw my blood, and then the doctor will be in to speak to us.

The room spins. It's the same feeling I had at the airport. There's a smell here that triggers my fear too. It's a cleaning solution or something. I'm not sure.

My breathing quickens, and the fake teeth lady tells me to lie down and relax. How do I relax? So many questions twirl in my head. What if I'm not a match? How soon will we know? What will happen to Nat if I'm not a match?

The lady sits on a stool on wheels and places a rolling cart next to her. The stool clatters across the floor toward me.

"Look the other way if it helps," she says.

I can't. I watch her instead. She wraps a large red rubber band around the top of my arm. When she takes the needle off her table and pulls the top off, I turn away. She tells me I'll feel a poke. I do. It stings. I cringe. But then the spike of pain ends. She says she's almost done and releases the rubber band. I'm looking the other way and am about to blurt out, just get it over with, when she tells me she's done. I exhale loudly.

Dr. Kaufman enters the room and looks like he just woke from a nap. He's in no hurry. The doctor looks over my chart and smiles, sits on the rolling stool, and introduces himself. "You're a brave girl to want to help your sister. Do you have any questions?"

Yes, a million, but I don't want to talk. I shake my head.

"I'm going to take a little swab of your cheek tissue. It's painless. If your blood type is the same as your sister's, then we'll see if your DNA is a close match too." He takes my hand. "It's highly unlikely that you'll be a match, but we can hope and pray."

I nod, afraid to speak for fear I'll sob. His word *unlikely* wedges in my mind, and I can think of nothing else.

He squeezes my hand. "If you're not a match, don't blame yourself. We'll put her on a donor list. We'll find someone soon."

Jack says, "What are the odds of that?"

Dr. Kaufman looks at the ceiling like he's trying to find the answer up there. "Let's wait and see, okay?"

He's lying. He won't find a match for Nat. I clench my teeth because sometimes that helps keep me from crying.

Later that evening, the phone rings. Jack answers. I know before he hangs up that what I feared the most is true. I am not a match.

I prayed and it did nothing. Guilt stabs me in the heart. Maybe this is my fault. Tears spill down my cheeks. Maybe this God is making me pay for what I did.

Chapter Twenty-Nine

Jack and Katie are talking in hushed voices in the other room. Now I know what I must do to save Nat. I need to make the call first. I read the phone number on the back of the photo and dial from the phone in my room, the one on my desk.

"Hello," a lady says.

"Are you Mrs. Murphy?"

"Yes, who wants to know?" Her voice sounds chipper, bright, like she's a happy person.

"Do you know Pastor Kostia?"

There's a slight pause before she says, "Who is this?"

Katie's voice grows loud outside my door, like she's coming to my room. The door isn't locked. Hurrying, I disconnect the phone with trembling fingers and place it back on the receiver, then face my computer, pretending to work. There's a shadow from her footsteps in the crack under the door. She passes by. I sigh. She isn't going to come to my room.

Should I tell her? No, she wouldn't understand. I could tell Laura, but she'd have to tell Katie, and I don't know for certain if things happened the way I hope they did. In that case, no one needs to know what I did.

Wringing my hands together, I think. Should I call Mrs. Murphy again? Ask her more questions? No, what would I say? She'd think I was crazy. Maybe she'd even call the police. It's better if I go to her house. In person. But how do I get there? I'm torn over what to do.

I click on my computer. The motor whirs. I'll get directions to her house.

The phone rings and I jump, my nerves jittery. I answer it right away, thinking maybe Mrs. Murphy is calling me back. "Hello?"

"Hi, Oksana."

It's Luke.

"Hey, you weren't in school today. How's your sister?"

He sounds like he really wants to know. I don't know him well, but I know he seems kind. "Not good. I had to go to the hospital to have blood tests to see if my bone marrow matches hers."

"Well?"

"It doesn't." I take a deep breath.

"I'm sorry, that sucks. I wish there was something I could do."

"There is." I lower my voice. "Would you help if you could?"

"Sure, but what could I do?"

"I need a ride somewhere, but I can't tell the Engles."

"You mean, like, sneak out?"

"Yeah, I can't tell them anything until I'm sure."

"Sure of what?"

"I think I know how to save Nat."

"How?"

"I can't tell you. You have to trust me. I have to find someone. Don't ask me any more right now, okay? Do you think you could pick me up in two hours—when your parents are asleep?"

He hesitates and blows out a huge gush of air. "I don't know. How long will this take?"

"Look, if you don't want to do it, I understand. It's just that I don't know too many people, and this is Nat's life." My voice cracks. "You're my only hope."

Luke sighs.

"If you don't do it, I'll drive myself."

He says, "You don't have a license, do you?"

"No."

"Okay, yeah, okay, I'll help you."

"Meet me at the end of the driveway at eleven o'clock. They should be asleep by then. I don't want anyone to hear me leave. Oh, and turn your lights down too."

#

In two hours, I hear Jack snoring. It's shortly before eleven o'clock. I put on my winter coat and throw my backpack over my shoulder. It contains the map, snacks, and a change of clothes. I tiptoe into Nat's room, wrap her in her favorite blanket, and lift her into my arms. She cuddles into me and falls back to sleep. She's so light she feels like a rack of bones. I reach for the stocked diaper bag sitting on the chair and go out the kitchen door that leads to the garage. It's the farthest exit from Jack and Katie's bedroom.

I step out into the garage and pull the door shut, turn down the driveway, and wait. The wind takes my hair, and I wish I'd worn a hat. The chill creeps under my pant legs and down the back of my neck. I bundle Nat tighter and drape her blanket loosely over her head.

A truck glides up the street, its yellow parking lights glowing. It's Luke. I hop in the front seat and smell soap, like he just took a shower.

His eyes are wide open like he's worried and shocked. "You're bringing Nat?"

"I have to. If I don't bring her, they won't believe me." I sit Nat in my lap and hold her close, pull the backpack off my back, and set in on the floor in front of me. I wish I had a car seat for Nat, but I couldn't juggle her, the bag, and the car seat too.

"Who won't believe you?"

"Shh, keep your voice down. I don't want to wake her."

He stares at me like I'm crazy.

"Please, just hurry. I don't want anyone to see us. I'll explain everything, I promise."

He puts the truck in Drive and shakes his head. "This is, like, kidnapping. I don't know if I can do this." He runs his long, thick fingers through his hair several times and licks his lips.

"Listen." I take a deep breath so I won't cry. "There's someone who can help Nat. She lives in Indiana. At least, I think she does. I hope she does."

"Indiana! That's hours from here." His voice is loud, and he pulls off to the side of the road.

Nat stirs. "Shh. According to the map, it's two hours, but if she's there it'll be worth it."

"*If* she's there? You mean you're not sure?" He puts the truck in Park and runs his hands through his hair again. "I'm hosed."

I can't fight the knot in my throat. He's not going to take me.

Tears threaten to sting my eyes. If Luke won't do this then . . . "I know," I say, swallowing hard, "This seems crazy to you, but if I don't try, Nat could . . . die."

Luke is quiet. "Can't you just call this person and talk to them?"

I'm losing him. I can feel it. He doesn't understand either. "This isn't the kind of thing someone will believe."

He sighs loudly. "What's the address?"

I pull the paper out of my backpack and hand it to him.

He studies the map.

Nat stirs in my arms. A tear escapes down my cheek, so I look away.

"Looks like the quickest way there is 69 South." He puts the truck in Drive.

"You'll do it?" I swipe the tear with the back of my hand.

He nods and pulls away from the curb, noticing my tear. "Let's go find her. Tell me what you know."

I smile. He is kind, and I will always remember. "I will, but hurry."

Chapter Thirty

We travel south through the cold night. I shift Nat to the backseat because Luke has the radio on. I try not to think about the one person who can help Nat, or if we'll find her, or if her family will be willing to help. I've never chewed my nails before, but I am now.

I explain to Luke that I can't tell him what I know because I'm ashamed of something I did. He doesn't push me.

He talks about his horses and how he wants to be a doctor of animals. I know he's trying to distract me, but it's difficult to listen. I'm worried. Nat whimpers in her sleep. Luke flashes me a worried look. I turn to Nat and place my hand on her arm. She doesn't open her eyes, but relaxes. Her skin feels hot.

Finally, Luke turns off the highway and glances at the directions on my paper. He turns down a few streets. Houses are dark, and only a few cars are out. He slows down the car and says, "Help me look for 1414 on the house."

He looks to his left, and I look to the right. We pass several large homes.

"There it is." Luke points and stops the car at the curb.

It's a red-brick house with a driveway that goes in a circle. This is the house from the photograph. It has a white picket fence and a long porch. The landscaping looks different, but maybe it's because it's dark outside and the trees aren't in bloom. The full moon throws a dim light across the yard, and a soft glow from inside the house shows a staircase through the arched window above the front entrance.

Luke says, "It's one o'clock in the morning. Are you sure you want to knock at their door? They might call the police."

"I have to take the chance. I'm going in with Nat. I think the lady will look at her and know who she is." I heave my backpack over my shoulder.

"Okay, I'll wait here in the dark so no one can see my plates. If it's not the right place, make a quick dash back here so we can jet, okay?" He licks his lips. "Unless . . . do you want me to go with you?"

"No, stay here." I open my door. The cool air slaps my face. I hitch in a breath. The smell of pine trees reminds me of the trees near the orphanage. I shudder.

"What will you do if they're not here?" Luke runs his fingers through his hair.

"Wait, okay?" I lift Nat from the backseat and hold her close. She opens her eyes with the black shadows and looks up at me. It's like Mama is staring into my eyes.

I smile. "I think there's someone here for you to meet." My breath fogs the air.

I climb the stairs to the brick porch and knock. A dog barks but no one comes. *Please, be home*. Nat shivers. I hold her closer and lean on the bell. The dog barks more.

I speak through the door. "Please, Mrs. Murphy, help. Open the door and I'll explain."

No answer.

Tears let loose like hope slipping away.

But then a flash of color moves in front of the side window. A woman's bathrobe.

"Who are you?" she asks through the door.

"Oksana and my sister, Natalia. She's sick. Please, Mrs. Murphy? She needs your help."

"Should I call an ambulance?"

"No, only you can help. Please, open the door."

"How do you know me?" She hushes her dog.

"I met your uncle, Pastor Kostia. A long time ago. Open the door, and I'll explain."

"How do I know this isn't a trick?"

I pause. "Turn on the porch light. Look through window."

The light flashes on. Mrs. Murphy cups her hands on the glass.

I see her eyes. It's her. The one from the photo. I move Nat closer to the window so Mrs. Murphy can see her.

The lady gasps, unbolts the lock, and throws open the door. I know now that things are the way I hoped they'd be. I have the right place. Somewhere in her house there's another girl with the same eyes, the same hair, and the same identical looks.

"How can this be?" she says.

#

A half an hour later, Luke and I are sitting in Mrs. Murphy's living room. Her husband is traveling on business. There are three sofas arranged in a circle. Nat sleeps on one next to me, curled in a ball with a blanket thrown over her. I've explained Nat's disease and how she needs bone marrow, that the best match might be a twin.

Luke sits on the other sofa facing me, and Mrs. Murphy paces in front of the fireplace. She's a little woman with a tiny voice and lots of energy. She flits around the room like a fairy, like she drank a pot of coffee, the bottom of her bathrobe dancing around her ankles when she walks.

There's a large photo of a girl who looks like Nat above the mantel. It's like I'm looking at a healthier, fatter version of Nat. The photo proves the reality that Nat is really sick.

Mrs. Murphy follows my vision as I stare at the photo. "Her name is Olivia. I'm sure you want to see her, but can I ask you something first?"

I nod even though I'm afraid of what she'll ask.

Her brow creases. "How come Uncle Kostia didn't tell me Olivia had a twin or that you were in the US?"

I shake my head. "He didn't know about Nat or me. When I brought Olivia to him, I never told him she had a sister." I bite my lower lip to stop it from quivering, to stop myself from saying too much." I meet her eyes.

"Why?"

I shrug and swallow; my eyes downcast. I don't want to tell her.

She continues. "Pastor said he saw you the next day, but your mom wasn't there. He wanted her to sign Olivia's adoption papers. The next day he returned, but you were gone."

"Ludmila . . . took me to the . . . orphanage." My words come out broken. I stutter because the tears that have been lodged in my throat are trickling down my face. The knot grows the more I hold it inside. Now that I've said this much, I want to keep going. Confessing feels cleansing because I don't know this lady and because I need to help Nat, but I can't tell her that Mama didn't know about Olivia. "I never saw Mama again either."

Luke stares at me, his mouth agape, his eyes wide like he doesn't believe what happened. "Your aunt took you to an orphanage? What happened to your mother?"

I shrug again.

Mrs. Murphy crosses the room and sits beside me. Her hand lies gently on my back, and she nods for me to continue.

"Several days after I was in the orphanage, I ran back to where I lived with Mama, but she and Ludmila had moved. I went to Pastor's church, but he was gone too. I didn't know what to do." I hiccup a sob.

Mrs. Murphy wraps her arms around me and turns me into her. "There, there. Shh." She strokes the back of my head and lets me weep into her chest. "I can't imagine what you've gone through, you poor child." She smells like sweet perfume. "Everything is going to be okay. We're all together now. That's all that matters." She pulls away, reaches for a tissue on the table, and dabs her eyes. "If you hadn't done what you did, we wouldn't have Olivia with us now. We wouldn't have been blessed with the greatest gift God has ever bestowed on us." She reaches for another tissue and wipes my tears.

A thought slams into my mind. If I hadn't separated the girls would Nat be healthy now*? Is God punishing me for what I did? For never telling Mama?*

Mrs. Murphy says, "I'll be right back. There's someone you need to meet." She pats my leg, stands, and moves toward the stairs.

Chapter Thirty-One

Luke shifts to my side on the sofa, hesitantly, like he's not sure if it's okay to sit close to me. "I'm sorry for what you went through. You must have felt so alone." His voice is soft but raspy, probably from lack of sleep. It's after two a.m. and he hasn't slept.

I reach for a tissue and avoid his eyes. His pity makes me feel awkward. I don't know what to say. If I look at him, I'm afraid he'll hug me, and that scares me. I want him to, yet I don't. I don't want him to like me only because he feels sorry for me.

Luckily, Mrs. Murphy descends the stairs, her eyes still full of tears, carrying a bundle of blankets in her arms, a head of curly strawberry hair leaning against her chest. She crosses the room and places my sleeping sister in my arms, her eyes closed.

Emotion floods me, and a sob escapes from the bottom of my heart as I look down at her, holding her close.

Mrs. Murphy says, "This is the baby you saved, your flesh and blood, the child who's changed my life."

Luke slides over so Mrs. Murphy can sit next to me. All of us are on one sofa. Nat still sleeps at the end on the other side of me.

I can't believe how much heavier and sturdier Olivia feels compared to Nat. It's like I'm holding a two-year-old instead of a nine-month-old. Her pale eyelashes curl onto her ivory skin, the color of Nat's and Mama's. She's beautiful like a fresh painting, wearing comfy PJs with soft pastel colors, the kind that make me feel calm. She's warm from sleep and innocence as she curls in toward me, so trusting. Her button nose and high cheekbones are exact replicas of Nat's.

I brush my fingers across her face and feel the smoothness of her cheek, and am overcome with tears of joy. I take her hand, small yet strong, and press it against my face. I kiss her fingers and smell her newness, her clean baby-powder scent. This is my sister, my family, my connection to Mama.

A flash of memory returns . . . the night of the delivery . . . Olivia's frail whimper, her tiny limbs so limp, deathlike. I didn't think she'd live, and that's why I'd chosen her to go to Pastor. I hiccup another sob as I remember how I'd secretly hoped she'd be born dead.

Luke's cell phone rings. "Oh, crap. It's my mother. She's going to kill me."

I turn to him. "Go ahead; answer it. Tell her everything."

Mrs. Murphy reaches for his phone. "Let me talk to her." She wipes the tears off of her cheeks, inhales, and reaches for Luke's phone. "Hello, this is Mrs. Murphy. Your son is at my house." She rises, taking the phone into the other room. Luke follows her. I can hear her, but her voice isn't loud enough to wake the girls.

She says, "No, you don't know me, but Luke is here helping Oksana." She explains my story in brief, that she has Nat's twin. "He'll be home by morning. Here, you can talk to him."

Luke's voice trails in the background, "Hi, Mom. Yes, Yes."

Mrs. Murphy returns to me and sits beside me again.

I turn to her. "Will you come with us to Michigan and let Olivia help Nat?"

Mrs. Murphy's forehead creases. "Of course I want to, but I don't know anything about a bone marrow transplant or what it means for Olivia, or if the procedure is dangerous for her."

"You could ask the doctors, and we could have Olivia tested, but Nat needs her." I'm holding my breath and nod toward Nat's body. "Look at her. She's really sick."

Mrs. Murphy stands and paces, wiping her tears. "I can see that. I have to call my husband first."

"Could you call him now?"

She glances at her watch.

Luke interrupts. "My mom wants to talk to you again." He hands the phone to Mrs. Murphy.

Mrs. Murphy listens, then says, "Certainly. I understand. We'll call her right away." After Mrs. Murphy disconnects the phone. She says, “I need to call your mother.”

I don’t correct her. Katie isn’t my mother, but right now I don’t argue.

Mrs. Murphy opens a drawer and reaches for a pen on a desk. “Luke’s mom said Katie called the police. She didn’t know where you went or why you took Nat. ”

“They didn’t know about Olivia either,” I say in a whisper.

Luke’s eyebrows lift.

Mrs. Murphy crosses the room, sits beside me again, and squeezes my shoulder. “Don’t worry. I’m sure they’ll understand, and everything will be cleared up soon.” She clicks the pen. “Give me their number and I’ll call them.”

Jack must be angrier than when I let the dogs out at the kennel. Maybe he’ll send me away, back to Russia.

After I give Mrs. Murphy the number and she retreats to the kitchen to make the call, Luke glances at me from the other sofa, the one across from me. “You okay?”

I nod.

He slouches down and melts into the billowy pillows on the sofa and shuts his eyes. I can’t believe he’s here and helped us the way he has. Twice now he’s been there for me. I hope he’s my friend for a long time.

My eyes shift to Olivia in my arms. She stretches, revealing her tiny foot. The smallest toe turns in just like mine, like Nat’s and Mama’s. This moment feels sweet like candy—having my sisters so close. If only Mama were here too.

I sigh deeply and close my eyes. I don’t want to sleep, but now that I’ve found Olivia, I’m relieved. Should I pray, say thank you to God, especially now that I have one sister in my arms, and the other within my reach?

#

A while later, someone nudges my shoulder. My eyes flash open. I must have fallen asleep.

Mrs. Murphy stands over me, smiling. “We’re ready to go.” She’s dressed in jeans and a sweater, her robe no longer around her. She’s even tinier, her waist the size of a child’s.

“Huh?” It takes me a second to remember where I am. “You’re coming back with us?”

She nods.

"Yes!"

Olivia sits next to Nat on the sofa. They're both awake, sharing a red plastic toy ring, handing it back and forth. They're giggling at each other. I gasp, my hand covering my mouth. Olivia's smile looks more like Mama's than Nat's. Olivia is beautiful and alert, almost chubby. Tears fall, and I reach out for her. She glances my way, hesitantly, then crawls toward me into my arms. I pull her close and kiss the top of her head. "I never thought I'd see you again."

Mrs. Murphy smiles with tears in her eyes. "I still can't believe this is happening."

"Me neither."

Luke, who just woke, yawns and says, "That makes three of us." He grins and runs his fingers through his messy hair.

I turn to Mrs. Murphy. "You're really going to come to Michigan with us?" Even though she said she is, I want to hear it again to be sure.

She nods. "We'll talk to the doctors, of course. I want to help. I just have a lot of questions."

"Thank you!" I stand and twirl with Olivia in my arms. She giggles. I pause. "Wait, did you talk to your husband and Katie?"

She nods again. "Everything is set. I've been working while you've been sleeping."

"I'm sorry I fell asleep. What did Katie say?"

She lifts Olivia from my arms. "She was ecstatic that you and Nat were okay. She cried. We both did. She wanted to talk to you, but I told her you'd fallen asleep. Maybe you can call her on the way back."

Katie and Jack know about Olivia. I'm grateful that Mrs. Murphy spared me the burden of being the deliverer of that news. At least, for now, I won't have to talk to them about the night the girls were born.

"What time is it?" Luke asks.

"Around five-thirty," Mrs. Murphy says, moving toward the kitchen. "Come and have a quick bite before we leave. I'll follow you two in my van."

Nat reaches up for me to hold her. "You have another sister. Isn't she cute?"

Nat smiles and glances at Olivia like she already knows who

I'm talking about.

I follow Luke and Mrs. Murphy into the kitchen, eager to head back to Michigan.

Chapter Thirty-Two

The sun peeks through the early morning clouds, shining onto the freeway when Luke's phone rings again. I'd drifted off to sleep, lulled by the humming and bouncing of the truck. Drool drips down my chin. Nat sleeps in the backseat, strapped in Olivia's extra car seat. Mrs. Murphy, who follows us in her van, insisted we use the car seat for Nat, and I agreed.

Luke answers his phone. "Oh, hi, Mrs. Engle. Yes, we're meeting you at Mercy Medical, right?" He pauses to listen. "Okay, we'll follow the signs and meet you in the ER. We're about forty-five minutes away." He pauses again. "Sure, hang on." He hands me his phone.

I don't want to talk to her, but I know I have to. "Hello."

"How's Nat?"

I turn in my seat to see her head bobbing. "She's sleeping."

"I wish you would have told us everything and not taken Nat out of the house. Do you know how frightened we were?"

Now she's going to preach to me. I don't answer. I did what I thought I had to do to get Mrs. Murphy to believe me, and I didn't want to leave Nat.

"Are you there?"

"Yes." What does she expect me to say?

She sighs like she's frustrated. "I'm so relieved that you are both safe. My imagination was going wild when we realized you were both gone."

I'm silent.

"I can't believe what you were hiding all this time, never opening up to us."

I'm silent.

"Will you tell us more soon? You know, about what happened in Russia?"

"There is nothing more to say. I don't want to talk about it."

She sighs again. "Okay, we will see you soon."

"Bye." I hand the phone to Luke, who presses a button to disconnect and gives me a sideways glance. "Did she give you crap for leaving?"

I nod.

He says, "Sometimes my parents lecture me about stupid stuff too."

I think he's trying to make me feel better, but he doesn't understand. Katie isn't my parent, and I'm not used to people telling me what I can and can't do.

#

When we arrive at the hospital, Jack and Katie are standing outside the ER door. Katie's bundled in her white coat with the fur hood, and Jack's wearing a long business-looking wool coat. Luke and Mrs. Murphy park beside each other, and we climb out, gather our stuff, unbuckle the girls, and head toward the entrance. When Nat sees Katie her arms flap in excitement. Katie reaches for her and holds her close, planting kisses on her forehead, tears falling down her cheeks.

I introduce Mrs. Murphy to Jack and Katie. They shake hands.

"Thank you for coming," Katie says.

Mrs. Murphy says, "How could I walk away from Oksana and Natalia?"

The twins stare at one another. Katie sets her eyes on Olivia and her mouth gapes open. "I can't believe the resemblance. This is a miracle."

Jack wraps his arms around me. He's never openly hugged me like this. "You are one brave girl, aren't you?"

He's not going to scold me?

Mrs. Murphy says, "She's amazing. A gift from God."

Jack nods like he agrees and shakes Luke's hand. "So you're the infamous Luke and accomplice."

Luke gives him a serious look. "I'm sorry, sir. Er . . . yes, Oksana has a convincing way about her." He shifts his feet and grins at me.

Jack says, "Thanks for your help, for bringing both our girls home safe."

Luke shoves his hands in his front pockets. "You're welcome."

Jack says, "Let's go inside." He leads the way into the building, and we follow. The warm air rushes to meet us as we enter through the electric doors. Jack shows us to a group of seats in the wide waiting room, a cluster of chairs near a large window. "I'll let the receptionist know we're all here now." He turns to Mrs. Murphy. "She'll call the doctor so he can talk to you about the tests."

Mrs. Murphy nods as she sets Olivia in her lap and reaches for a toy in the diaper bag. Katie sits next to her with Nat facing Olivia. The girls' feet touch. Olivia's are in little pink tennis shoes. Nat's are covered with thick purple socks. Olivia's ankles are wider than Nat's, sturdier. She squirms to get down and stands next to Mrs. Murphy, holding on to her leg. Nat doesn't have this skill yet. She can sit, but she doesn't seem to have the strength to stand.

Luke and I sit across from the girls.

Katie says to Mrs. Murphy, "How old was Olivia when you adopted her?"

"She was only a few months old. Our circumstances were different. Like I told you on the phone, my uncle is a pastor in Russia and was able to facilitate the process much quicker than most. He and my aunt actually brought her here. We never had to go over, which was a godsend because I hate to fly." Her eyes get wide. "I have a phobia of heights."

I say, "Where do Pastor and Hannah live?"

"They returned to Russia shortly after he brought Olivia to us."

He must have been in America the day I went to see him—or on his way.

Katie cocks her head like she's going to ask me a question, but stops when I look out the window. I'm not sure how much Mrs. Murphy told her, but this isn't the place to go into any detail. Maybe she realizes it would be better to wait.

Jack takes the seat next to Luke. "The doc is in the hospital, so we shouldn't have to wait long."

A tinkling sound comes from Katie's pink leather purse. "My phone!" She reaches into her bag and snaps it open. "Hi, Laura . . .

yes, they're all here." Katie sighs and glances at me. "What's wrong?" She pauses. "Oh, I see. Sure, I'll tell her. Yes, I'll let you know as soon as we know something."

"What's wrong?" I say. My heartbeat quickens at Katie's frown.

"Boris is sick. Laura thought you should know." Katie nods to Jack like she wants his approval. "Is it okay if we let her go see him? There's nothing more she can do here. We have to wait now."

Jack nods his approval and faces Luke. "I know you've done so much already, but could you drop Oksana off at her aunt's ranch?"

He nods, wiping his hands on his jeans. "No problem. Miss Laura lives up the street from me anyway. Her house is on the way." He touches my arm to go.

"Wait. I want to see Boris, but I don't want to leave Nat." She's asleep in Katie's arms.

Katie says, "Go ahead and go, Oksana. There's nothing you can do here. It'll take several hours before we know anything."

"Will you call me at Laura's?"

She nods.

I stand and kiss Nat on her forehead and turn to go.

Katie reaches for my arm and squeezes it. "We're going to pray, keep our faith. Have Laura fix you something to eat."

Jack says, "Be safe." For once he sounds like he means it. I still can't believe he's not angry with me. He stands and moves toward me, then wraps his arms around me.

It's the closest I've been to him in a long time. He smells like pine soap and men's cologne.

He says, "I'm proud of you."

I choke back the tears that fight to break loose. I'm surprised at Jack's warmth toward me, but I'm more surprised that I'm emotional. He releases me from the embrace, and I avoid his eyes so he can't see my tears.

Mrs. Murphy swings Olivia, who's crawling on the floor, back into her lap. "Bye, I'll see you later. We're family now." She winks.

I smile and turn to go before more tears escape.

Chapter Thirty-Three

Luke drives to Laura's through rush-hour traffic. "I can take you to your aunt's house, but I won't be able to stay. I'm fried, and I'll probably miss school today." He exhales, blowing air up at his tumbled hair, watching the traffic ahead of him. "I have to get some sleep." He turns to look at me and touches my shoulder. "You understand, don't you?"

I nod and look away. His blue eyes look too caring. I don't want to cry anymore, but I'm worried about Nat and now Boris.

"Are you sure?" He touches my shoulder again, and with one hand on the steering wheel he takes the other and reaches for my chin, drawing my eyes to his.

I nod. "Yes, I'll be okay. Thank you for . . . everything. I couldn't have . . . done all this without you."

He laughs. "I have a feeling you would have found a way."

He's right. I smile. "That's true, but I'm not sure how I would have done it. I was determined though, wasn't I?"

He nods. "Understandably."

As he pulls up Laura's long driveway, the mama horse and her colt stand close, grazing. Both look much better than when they first arrived. The colt skips next to his mama, and she raises her head to watch us, more alert now. It's like she's come back to life.

Luke parks his truck next to a white truck that says *Dr. Yates, DVM, Veterinarian* on the side.

My heart thunders in my chest. I reach for my coat on the seat and jump out of the truck.

Luke shouts, “I’ll see you later!”

“Bye!” I slam the door, run into the barn, and stop. Outside Boris’s stall Laura stands close to Mr. Blackwell. Too close. Almost leaning against him. Is she upset and that’s why she’s so close to him, or are they together now? He’s disgusting, but Laura is probably fooled by his good looks.

I run to Boris’s stall. He’s is lying on the ground with his eyes shut, the vet at his side with a needle poised at Boris’s throat. White foam froths out of the corners of his mouth.

“No!”

Laura grabs my shoulders. “Oksy, you’re here. He’s giving him vitamin K. He’s not hurting him. We think Boris might have gotten into something poisonous.”

“Let me see him!” She holds me to her. I wiggle to break free. “Let me go!”

Boris opens his eyes and whinnies.

I say, “See, he wants me.”

Laura squeezes me tighter, shaking me, turning me to face her. “You can’t go in there right now. Talk in a soothing tone. He’s reacting because he senses you’re upset. Once the vet is done, you can go in.”

I relax, and she releases her hold on me. I turn to Boris, peering through the cold bars of his stall. “Whoa, boy.” I keep my voice calm. “You’re going to be okay.”

He lowers his head back to the ground.

“Has this gelding been immunized?” the vet asks.

Laura answers, “Yes, I immunized him when he first came because I doubted the previous owner had.”

“How long ago was that?”

“About seven months ago.”

“Where was this horse before he came here?”

“About ten miles north, living in a mud field full of animal feces and dead horses.”

“Do you know how the other horses died?”

“Nope, there’s no way to know. I assumed they died of neglect. He’s been healthy—up until now.”

Mr. Blackwell turns toward the tack room. I glare at his back. What’s he doing here? Is Laura blind? Why can’t she see that he’s a creep?

The vet says, “Until we get the blood work back, we won’t

know for sure what's causing him to be sick, but we'll treat him for poisoning and hope for the best." He closes his medicine bag and stands. "Is there anything toxic on the ranch?"

Laura shakes her head. "I wouldn't know where. The feed isn't moldy. The other horses are okay."

I say, "Why don't you ask Mr. Blackwell? Maybe he knows what happened."

"Oksana! Why would you say such a thing?"

"Because I don't trust him."

Dr. Yates looks at Laura, his brow wrinkled.

Laura says, "My niece has a vivid imagination. He has no reason to harm this horse."

The vet glances at me and steps out of the stall toward his truck. "I'll stop back later today. Call me if he gets worse, but it looks like he's resting better now. I gave him something for the colic."

My eyes blur from tears. It feels like I have broken glass in them. My gut tells me Blackwell knows more than he's saying. I hate seeing Boris lying in the dirt like he's dying. It reminds me of when I was in the hospital, when Ruzina came to visit me and brought me the apples. She brought me hope.

Right now I must give Boris hope. "I'm here now."

Laura walks the vet to his car.

I whisper to Boris, "I'll be right back." I need to see where Blackwell went. I think he knows why Boris is sick. Where did he go?

I open the back door and see him near the aluminum building where Laura keeps the hay and grain. He's bent over Duke holding a leather lunge line like he's ready to whip the dog. "I told you to stay out of here, to quit your digging. But you didn't listen to me, did you." Anger peppers his words.

The dog's nose and paws are covered in mud like he's been digging in the corner.

Just before Blackwell's arm goes back to strike, I spot an old rust-worn pitchfork and quietly but quickly grab it and charge at the scumbag. "Let him go!"

Mr. Blackwell spins around and sees me with the fork raised above my head. Duke cowers in the corner. "Look what we have here. It's that little spitfire Ruskie who thinks she owns the place. Maybe I need to teach her a thing or two." He shakes his head and laughs, his wiry gray beard bouncing up and down as his shoulders shake.

"You stay away from me or I'll use this. I will." I lunge the pitchfork at him.

"Whoa." He holds his gloved hands in the air. "There won't be any need for that. I never touched the mutt." He turns to Duke. "Go on, get."

Duke runs from between the hay bales with his tail between his legs. He doesn't appear to be injured.

With the pitchfork still raised above my head, I glare at the man.

He turns away, chuckling under his breath, and heads toward his truck. He cranks the engine and drives out the back of the property through the woods. I'm shaking. I move to the back of the hay bale piles where the grain bin is kept and to where Duke was digging. *What was the dog looking for? What is Blackwell hiding?*

There's a pile of freshly moved dirt behind the bin. I poke it with the pitchfork and drag out a large plastic bag. Inside is dark-brown stuff that looks like dried leaves. I open it and sniff. It smells sweet, but I don't know what it is. I don't want to put it back where Blackwell can find it, so I carry the bag to the tack room and put it under an old dusty saddle that looks like it hasn't been used in months.

I want to give it to Laura, but I hesitate. I don't know what it is and can't prove that it's Blackwell's. I return to Boris's stall, open his door, shut it, and lie down beside him. I know I'm not supposed to be in there, but I don't care. He opens his eyes, still panting. I'm not there long when I hear rocks on the driveway kick up from someone's vehicle. It sounds like it's coming from the front of the barn. Shortly after, I hear a voice.

"Pssst, Oksana."

Luke peers down at me from the other side of the stall doors.

"What are you doing here? I thought you had to go home," I say.

"I did. I explained everything to my mom, and she let me come back. How is he?"

I stroke Boris's neck. "He'll be better now that I'm here." I get up and whisper through the bars. "I know why he's sick."

"Why?"

"Mr. Blackwell is poisoning him."

Luke says, "That doesn't make sense. Why would he want to hurt this horse? Are you sure you're not paranoid?"

"Paranoid?" I don't know what this word means.

"Making something out of nothing," he says.

I huff. "Whatever. Figures you'd say that. You're no different than the rest of them." I wave him off.

"What's that supposed to mean?" His tone changes, like I've hurt his feelings.

I shake my head. "You trust everyone because you've never had a reason not to. Well, I have. I've seen the way people really are, and I know how they can trick you into believing they're honest, but they're not. Mr. Blackwell is evil. Whether or not you want to believe me is up to you." I want to storm out, but I don't. I can't leave Boris now. I turn my back on Luke.

"I'm sorry. It's not that I don't believe you. It's just that I don't understand his motive. Maybe if we could figure out why he would do this, then we'd be able to nail him for the deed."

I can't look at him.

"Ah, come on, Oksana. I'm on your side."

I turn around and face him. "Sometimes people are just bad. They don't need a reason."

Luke nods like he agrees. "Where's Blackwell now?"

"He left, but he'll be back because he left something here."

His eyebrows lift. "What?"

I tell him about the bag.

He cocks his head, and his eyes light up like he knows what it is. "Where is it?"

"I hid it in the tack room."

"You have to tell Laura. Maybe it's marijuana."

"What's that?" I ask him.

"It's an illegal drug that a person smokes to make them feel good—to get high. Do you want to show it to me?"

"No, I'm afraid he'll be back."

"Just tell Laura," Luke urges.

"Why? She likes him. She won't believe me, and he'll lie his way out of it."

Luke gets quiet. I think he might agree. Even if he doesn't, he knows I'll hate him if he tells anyone.

"You know what's best, but be careful. This guy might be a psycho drug dealer or something."

I don't know this word *psycho,* and I think I must look puzzled because Luke taps his finger to his temple and makes a circle with it, crossing his eyes. It makes me laugh. He stays a few more minutes, then says he has homework, so he'll talk to me later. But he doesn't leave. He stares at me a little longer. He looks tired, but it's like he wants to say something.

"What?"

"I'm glad you're here and not in Russia." His eyes pierce mine.

I don't know what to say. My face feels hot. He cares about me. No guy has been this nice to me before or has looked at me like he is right now. He doesn't really know me, yet he's kind to me. A funny feeling like a flutter, a good flutter, fills my stomach. I flash him a smile—a real one. He smiles back.

"See you later."

I nod.

He turns to go.

I lie down next to Boris in the quiet of the barn and bury my face in the crook of his neck, the only safe place I know. I hold back the urge to giggle. "What do you think? I think he likes me."

Boris opens his eyes and raises his head.

"Don't be jealous. You're still my favorite." I swing my arm around him and nuzzle his withers. The ground is damp and cold, but I've felt worse. I zip my jacket and pull my hood over my head.

Suddenly, Boris's legs twitch, and he rolls like he wants to get up. I move out of the way and stand. "Come on, boy. Get up. You can do it."

Slowly, he wobbles on his legs and stands.

"You did it! I knew you could." I pat his back.

Laura calls my name from somewhere in the barn. She sounds worried. She must have heard Luke come and go. Shoot, I know I'm not supposed to be in here, but I can't hide now. I holler out to her. "I'm in here."

She runs up to the stall out of breath. "Have you been in there the whole time? Girl, you have to quit scaring me like this! I've been looking all over for you. I thought you went out the back door."

"I'm sorry. I did, but I came right back."

She holds her hand over her heart. "Your mother . . . uh . . . Katie would kill me if you disappeared. And she wouldn't be happy if she knew you're in there with Boris either."

"But look." I point to Boris. "He feels better now."

"You're a genuine horse whisperer, aren't you?"

I'm not sure what that means, but I nod.

"You better come out of there."

"I'm not going to catch what he has. He's been poisoned."

She puts her hand on her hip. "What are you talking about?"

"Mr. Blackwell poisoned him."

Laura laughs. "Why would he do that?"

I shake my head and cross my arms over my chest.

She cocks her head. "You're serious?"

I nod. "He was going to hit Duke with a lead line."

Her eyebrows crease, but before she responds a door closes, and Duke barks like he's trapped a rabbit. A few seconds later, *psycho* man walks up to Laura.

My heartbeat quickens in alarm. Did he hear what I said?

"Hey, Ben." Laura scolds Duke and tells him to hush. "Where'd ya go?"

"I had to get me some chew." He pinches something in a small container and puts it in his mouth. His cheek gets fat again. He winks at Laura. I want to puke. *Is she blind?* He turns to me and smirks.

I show him my back.

Laura says to him, "Oksy said you were going to hit Duke. Is that true?"

He says, "Aw, I wasn't going to hurt him any. He was getting into the feed, that's all. Just wanted to scare him away."

I turn and glare at him.

Laura flashes her eyes from me to him like she wants to say something but isn't sure how to say it. "I don't want any trouble here, Ben. You got that?"

He lifts his hands up in the air. "No trouble from me."

She says, "Why don't you both come in for lunch? I'll fry up some chicken and steam a few veggies."

"I'm not hungry." I lie. I want to tell her about the bag, but I'm not sure if it's Mr. Blackwell's or what it is, and I'm uncomfortable with him standing in front of me.

"Since when are you not hungry? You've had one heck of a night and probably haven't eaten all day. Come on in, and we'll call Katie to see how Nat's doing." She turns to Boris. "It looks like whatever Doc did helped. His stomach relaxed." She turns back to me and tugs my arm. “Come on, you can come back out after you eat.”

“I’m not going anywhere with that man.” I point to Mr. Blackwell.

“Oksana!” Laura says.

The creep says, “She’s just out of sorts because of the sick gelding.”

I ignore them and turn to Boris.

Laura says, “Ben, you go on up to the house. I’ll be there in a minute.”

When he’s out of sight I say, “So now you’re letting him in the house?”

“What’s this really about?” Her voice softens.

How do I tell her I’ve met men like Blackwell and know what they really are, that Mr. Blackwell is no good, that I just know it? How do I explain something that’s invisible to others? I can’t prove anything. It’s just another thing I have, like touch and smell and understanding Boris. I sense when men are lying, and I sense when they don’t really care about people, just like I sense when they do. I cross my arms and look the other way. “You’re just like Ludmila.”

“Who?”

I lick my lips and blaze into her eyes. “My evil aunt who took me to the orphanage!” I shout this at her. My heart pounds loudly in my ears. I can’t believe what I’ve said. I want to take it back, but I don’t. It’s like the door to the barn is open wide. More pent-up words want to thunder out of me.

“You think I’m like her? That I would abandon you?” Her eyes fill with tears. “Oh, Oksy, you don’t know me very well.”

“No, I think I do. You’re stupid.”

“I think what’s really going on is that you’re used to spending time with me, and now you have to share me with someone else.”

I storm past her. “You don’t get it.” My fists clench at my sides. “Why don’t you see what your *boyfriend* has been hiding?” I stomp my feet in the dusty dirt to the tack room down and across the hall.

Boris’s stall door clatters shut, and Laura’s footsteps follow.

“What are you talking about?”

I reach under the saddle where I hid the bag, turn, and shove it in her hands. “This bag.”

She examines it closely, opening the seal, smelling inside.

"Where did you find this?"

"Does it matter?"

"Yes, it does. You don't know who this belongs to."

"You are like all the other women! You will do anything for a man, won't you? Are you sharing your body with this hooligan too?" Spit flies from my mouth.

Her eyes widen and her face blazes red. She raises her hand like she's going to strike me, but stops. "You are out of line. What I do in my personal life is my business." She turns on her heels and storms away.

Tears fill my eyes. I wish I could take back my words, but it's true. I hate her for being such a fool. I thought she was different, but I was wrong. She's like all the other women who will do anything for a man. I am nothing to her. She will choose him over me always.

I run to Boris's stall. Tears trail down my cheeks. He makes a chewing motion, a sign that he's better, comfortable, but if I can't convince Laura about Mr. Blackwell, Boris doesn't stand a chance. Nor do I.

I flee out of the barn, down the driveway, and past the pond and the tunnel of trees. Memories of Ludmila injure my thoughts, fuel my speed. I want to run past the images, but I can't.

Ludmila's grotesque nakedness. The way she hid me in the dark, cramping me in tight corners until the smell of mingled bodies penetrated my nothingness. Darkness's teeth chewed my shelter. Even after I shoved fingers in my ears, I heard their hungry sounds, the pawing, the lies, the pretend love, always wanting, never giving.

Laura will be the same. She wants this pretend love from men.

The wind whips my hood off, so I tug it back on and tuck my hands up inside the sleeves of my coat. I want to run away from the hope. I can't stay here. Laura will abandon me too. I thought she was different, but I was wrong.

I open the gate, let myself out, and shut out Laura's ranch. My racked sobs fill the empty air. The traitorous sun peeks from behind a cloud, pretending to be bright but offering no warmth. A fire smolders nearby, its scent flashing memories of arson in Kapaz.

I want Mama, her shielding arms. *Do you think of me? Do you miss me? Mama, why didn't you keep me?*

I head down the road, consumed with thoughts, not knowing where I'll go. I think about how Laura doesn't believe me and how Jack and Katie never wanted to adopt me. Katie wants me to smile and hug her, but I can't. She wants too much. She doesn't understand. She'll never be Mama. She's nothing like her.

Will my life always be gashed with pain and desertion? If there really is a God, then why can't he help me?

I'm too tired to think about what I will do. For now, I will go to the Engles' house because it's too cold to stay out all night, and I know they're at the hospital, so no one will be home. I don't want to see anyone.

A cool breeze hisses at me, and I stumble in the ditch over discarded cans, cigarette butts, food wrappers, and brittle leaves.

Twenty minutes later, police cars whiz by with their sirens blaring as if they're screaming in agony, feeling my pain.

By the time I reach the house, my feet are numb except for the throbbing blisters on the edge of my little toes. The house is dark. I check for the key in the box off the porch and let myself in. Jasper doesn't greet me. His bowl that typically sits in the corner of the entryway is gone, which means the Engles probably left him with the neighbor.

I kick off my shoes, sighing in relief. My eyes burn from no sleep, and my cheeks feel hot and chapped from the tears freezing on my face. I go to my room and fall facedown on my bed, burying my head in my pillow, not bothering to cry. I fall asleep.

I dream I'm riding Boris in a meadow of tall green grass with pink, orange, and yellow wildflowers. He's prancing like a show horse. His coat shines in the sunlight, and his muscles ripple with each move.

A dark figure appears on a black horse with a red spear in his hand. He's galloping toward us, wearing a mask and laughing. I can't see his face, but I know who it is: Mr. Blackwell. He pitches the spear, piercing Boris's chest. The horse's legs give out. He falls to the ground and rolls over my leg in the dirt. My leg bellows with flaming hot pain. When I open my eyes, Mr. Blackwell is gone, and the sun is shining. Boris is lying dead beside me. I'm alone. I scream for Mama, but I can't move. My leg is pinned and paralyzed. A woman in the distance, her back to me, turns. It's Laura. She runs toward me, her arms outstretched.

I wake to the phone ringing. My leg tingles from its bent position. It's dark outside. My clock says it's eight thirty. I sit up, disoriented, perspiring, and still wearing my coat.

I reach for the phone on the desk and shake my leg that has

fallen asleep. “Hello.”

“Oksy?”

It’s Laura. “Yes.”

“Thank God you’re there!” She exhales loudly. “I didn’t know where you went.”

What could I say?

“Are you okay?” There’s an edge to her voice.

No, I’m not okay. I’ll never be okay as long as she trusts Blackwell.

“I know you’re mad at me. I don’t blame you, but say something.”

“What do you want me to say?”

She sighs into the phone. “I’m coming over. I need to talk to you, to apologize. You were right about Blackwell. I was wrong.”

“How so?” Hope fills me. She believes me now. I want to hear more.

“He’s a criminal, a fraud. I’ll tell you all about it when I see you. You’re going to stay right there, right?”

“Yes.” I smile. Finally she knows Blackwell’s crooked side.

“I’m sorry.”

No one has ever said they were sorry to me before. Is she really? Or will there be a next time with another man?

“Are you mad at me?”

“You should have believed me.”

“You’re right. I was wrong.” She sighs. It sounds like she’s crying. “We can’t prove he tried to kill Boris, but I’m sure he was capable. I’m coming to get you. Jack and Katie are going to stay at the hospital tonight. You’re staying with me. I’ll fill you in when I get there.”

I’m glad they caught him and Laura said she was sorry. I feel better. I’m hungry.

Chapter Thirty-Four

Twenty minutes later, Laura's truck pulls into the driveway, and she barrels through the front door, taking wide steps, her feet clunking on the tile in the entryway. "Oksy?"

"I'm here." I'm in Nat's room rocking in the chair, holding her stuffed duck and thumbing though photo albums of us in Russia and the days that followed. I'm worried about her dying and what my life would be like without her.

Laura crosses the room in three long strides and pulls me straight up out of the chair and into a warm hug. Since she's shorter than me, her face is level with my neck, and her arms are practically around my waist. "I'm so sorry for not believing you."

She's not letting go. She smells like a combo of hay, leather, and manure. I like that smell. She releases me. Her face is red like she's been crying.

I avoid her eyes.

"Can't you look at me? Are you still mad?"

I shrug.

"What does that mean?"

"What happened?" I ask.

"Let's go sit in the kitchen." She takes off her coat and sets it on the chair. "How come you're wearing your coat?"

"I was cold."

Laura places her hand on my head. "You feel warm. I'll make you some tea."

I return the duck to Nat's crib, place the photo album on the dresser, and follow Laura out of the room.

She asks over her shoulder, "Do you know where Katie keeps it?" She heads to the kitchen and opens a few cupboards before I show her where it is.

I sit at the table, groggy, and slip off my coat.

She pours water in a kettle, places it on the stove, and sets two cups on the table. Tea bag strings dangle over the side.

She sits across from me, folding her hands on the tabletop. "I confronted him about the bag you found. He said it was his, and asked if I would like to smoke it with him." She shakes her head, swipes a tear off her face. "'He thought it was funny. 'No,' I said. I thought about everything you'd said and about what he told me when he came looking for a job. He said his wife had died from cancer, and he'd spent all their savings on her medical bills, that he needed a job. I believed him, but then certain parts of the story didn't ring true. He told me his wife's name was Martha, but another time he called her Kathy. When I asked him about it, he said her name was Martha Kathy, but warning bells went off. I told him to leave, but he"—she pauses—"got a little physical. When he realized I was serious about making him go, he got angry and said you were a troublemaker."

She reaches for my hand. "No one is going to call my girl names."

The teakettle whistles so she rises, shuts off the stove, and pours the water into our cups. She crosses to the pantry and pulls out a bag of cookies, then returns to her seat across from me. "I called the police."

"You called the police?" I smile.

She nods and wipes a new tear from her face. "By the time they got to the house, he'd left, but they found him heading out of town. You won't have to see him again. They locked him up. Apparently he has quite a record of swindling people."

"What is swindling?"

"It's lying, cheating, and taking money from innocent people."

"What about Boris?"

"He was eating when I left. Dr. Yates said the worst is over and the poison is out of his system." She motions for me to take a cookie. "I'm not very good at picking men, as you can tell. I think sometimes I'm a sucker for the needy—just look at the horses in my barn. So when Ben told me his sad story . . . well . . . I fell for it."

She stops to take a bite of a cookie. "I like to see the good in people, and maybe that's better than trying to find the bad, except when they take advantage of me. I'm a little too trusting for my own good." She laughs, but I don't think it's funny. Maybe she's embarrassed. "I wish you would forgive me."

A little knot forms in my throat.

She continues. "You aren't like me. You're able to see a person's real character, aren't you? Maybe that's because you've seen too much too soon." She sets her hand gently on my cheek. "You had a rough life in Russia, didn't you?"

I shrug.

She dips and swirls her tea bag, and lifts it out of the cup, "You never talk about your life there. I know it's been tough because you didn't know the language here, but if you want to share anything else, I'm here for you. Sometimes it feels better inside if you talk about things."

That blasted lump in my throat rises again, and I choke back a sob. The one thought that keeps me a prisoner inside myself comes to the surface. "Mama doesn't know about Olivia. I stole her away before she knew she was born." My shoulders shake. I'm sucking air, and tears fall down my face.

Laura leans closer. "I don't understand. How could she not know she delivered twins?"

"She fell asleep." I stare at the floor because I'm ashamed to say *drunk.*

Laura hesitates like she's going to say something, but doesn't. Tears fill her eyes too. "Go on."

"Nobody was there when they were born. Ludmila left me alone with Mama. I didn't know what to do." I stop to catch my breath. "I knew we didn't have the money to take care of one baby, let alone two . . . and Pastor knew someone . . . who wanted a child. I was going to tell Mama, but I . . . never got the chance." I'm rambling now, the words flowing like my tears. "I didn't want my sisters. I wished them dead."

Laura pulls her chair up to mine and wraps her arms around me. "It's good that you're getting this out, talking about it. I'm sorry. Shh, it's going to be okay now. Start over."

"Mama was drunk." There, I said it.

"You must have felt so alone. No young girl should have to go through what you did."

My forehead rests on her shoulder. "But I thought if I gave away my sister Mama would keep me. Why? Why didn't she keep me?" I babble into Laura's shirt.

She holds me tighter and pats my back.

It's easier to tell her everything if I don't have to face her. "There was blood, and Mama kept drinking the vodka. I couldn't make her stop. I thought the second baby was dead, so I took her to Pastor."

"How did you know how to deliver a baby?"

"Sasha showed me. She used to be the midwife, and I would go with her, but I never had to do it by myself." I hiccup a sob. "Ludmila took us away, and I never said good-bye to Mama."

Laura swipes the tears from her face. "I'm so sorry. I didn't know. You poor, poor child."

"I don't understand. Why couldn't I stay? Why didn't Mama come to say good-bye? Why didn't she visit me in the orphanage?"

"I don't know, sweetie, I don't know. I'm sure she misses you and thinks about you. She loves you; I know she does." She rubs my back.

"Then how could she let me go?"

My question hangs in the room like a dissonant chord. Our tea is cold now, and our eyes are puffy from crying.

"I don't understand either." She takes my hands and meets my eyes. "Of course you're hurt. I would be too."

Laura's cell phone rings. She unclips the phone off her belt loop and looks at the screen. "It's Katie." She takes a deep breath before she answers. "Hi, Katie."

Katie screams loud enough for me to hear her voice through the phone. "Olivia's a match. And she's going to donate her bone marrow!"

Laura jumps out of her chair and belts out a "yeeeee-haaaaaa."

At first I startle at the suddenness of her reaction, but then I join her. Together we're bouncing around the kitchen on our tiptoes like crickets in the night.

Inside, bubbles of joy rise to tears. I'm more hopeful now than ever that Nat will live! I laugh and cry at the same time.

Chapter Thirty-Five

I sleep in Laura's guest room that night, and when I wake it's so early the sun is still on the other side of the world, but I feel good. I slept well. No nightmares. Maybe Laura is right. Maybe talking about what bothers me helps. Knowing Nat might get well is a relief too.

Laura's humming and frying bacon in the kitchen. Duke jumps up on the bed, wagging his tail. I pet his ears.

I go to the kitchen and join Laura for breakfast. She tells me Nat will be at the hospital all day today. They're meeting with a team of doctors to discuss her treatment. "Do you want to help me water and feed the horses so we can go to the hospital?"

"Sure." I eat fast, excited to see Boris and help in the barn, but more excited to see Nat. After bundling in a sweater, jacket, and boots, I hurry out, sliding in new fallen snow. Smiling into the cool wind, I welcome the bright sun on my face. Maybe God is answering my prayers for Nat.

I'm watering the bins, when someone pulls into the driveway in front of the barn. I peek out one of the stall windows. It's Luke. My heart flutters as I study him getting out of his truck. I'm excited to see him. He's wearing jeans, his leather boots, and a royal-blue winter jacket. He shakes his head like he's trying to dry his hair. The waves seem curlier than usual, but still as blond.

I set my eyes on the hose, pretending not to see him. The side door creaks open, and a blast of cool air rushes in.

"Hey, Oksana. How's it going?" He shuts the door, closing out the draft.

I look up, pretending to be surprised. “Oh, hi, Luke.”

He gives me a broad grin as he crosses toward me. “I heard they got that Blackwell guy.”

I nod and turn off the hose. “Laura called the police on him.”

He raises his shoulders and shoves the tips of his fingers in his jeans pockets. “I’m glad you’re okay. You didn’t get hurt, did you?”

“No.” My face feels hot, and I hope it’s not turning as red as I think it is. “Laura called him out on it after I showed her the bag.”

“Was it weed?”

I shake my head. “No, it was marijuana.” I stumble over the word, still uncertain how to pronounce it.

He grins. “Marijuana is called weed too.”

“Oh.” I’m embarrassed.

“How’s your sister?”

I give him the broadest smile I own. “Olivia’s a match, and she’s going to donate her bone marrow.”

“Really?” He pauses. “Woo-hoo!” He hollers so loud it makes me laugh. He wraps his arms around me, lifting me off the ground, and twirls me around.

I squeal.

He sets me back on the ground, a little out of breath. “That’s amazing. Does this mean she’ll be cured?”

“Not for sure, but it gives hope.”

His smile fades. “Oh, well, let’s think positive.”

“I’m trying. Laura and I are heading to the hospital soon. Do you want to come?”

He shakes his head. “I wish I could, but I have to go to school. I guess that answers my question. I was going to see if I could give you a lift there today.”

“Oh, thanks, but I really want to see Nat first. Maybe you could take me Monday?” Since it’s Friday, I’m hoping by next week I’ll be ready to go back.

“Sure, I could do that.” He turns and pauses. “Maybe I’ll see you this weekend?”

It’s more like a question than a statement. “Okay. I should be here.”

He flashes me one last smile and turns to go, opening the side door. But this time, when the wind gushes in I’m oblivious to its chill.

#

Although it's only been a day since I've seen Nat, so much has happened it feels like it's been *many moons* ago. I'm still practicing my idioms. When Laura and I get to the hospital, Nat is lying on a bed, and Katie's sitting next to her holding her hand through the side rails. There's a pole on the other side of her with a tube going into her arm. She's watching the cartoon *Dora the Explorer* on the overhead TV and sucking her fingers. She looks weak and frail. My stomach pinches. Jack types on his computer in the corner.

Nat sees me, kicks her feet, and reaches out for the green balloons I'm carrying. I brought two—one for her and one for Olivia. Laura said green is the symbol for life. I take them over to Nat and put them close enough so she can touch them. She giggles and punches them. I'm happy to see her smile, but I don't like the tubes coming from her arm.

The smells in the room remind me of when I was sick in Russia, and I fight nausea. I try not to think about that time and swallow the bile rising in my throat.

Katie reaches for my hand, but I don't take it. She puts it back in her lap, but I see disappointment in her eyes. I know I should let her hold me, but I don't want her to think she's Mama.

"Where's Olivia?" I ask.

Katie says, "She's across the hall in another room, sleeping. Her parents are with her. Maybe when she wakes you can go over and say hello. How's Boris?"

I look over at Laura. She explains the Mr. Blackwell saga and Boris's recovery.

"When will Nat be okay to come home?" I ask.

Jack pulls two chairs in from the hallway and places them in front of Laura and me. We sit at the side of Nat's bed.

Katie says, "It's going to take a while before she's totally well. First, Nat will have chemotherapy, where they'll drip medicine through her veins like this." She points to the pole and the line running into her vein. "The medicine will get rid of the bad cells so eventually the doctors can transfer some of Olivia's good cells. We won't know for a while if Nat's body accepted Olivia's marrow."

"Will she go bald?" I ask.

"Yes, she'll lose her hair."

"Why?"

"Because the medicine kills some of the good cells too," Jack explains. "It's complicated."

We're interrupted by a knock at the door.

It's Mrs. Murphy. "I thought I heard voices." She walks toward me in her short, quick steps and squeezes my shoulder. "It's great to see you again."

Her hands are tiny like a child's—as are her feet. Everything about her is little, even her nose. Everything except her energy.

I say, "How's Olivia?"

"She's a little confused by all this, but she'll be fine. She's much better than Nat here." She nods toward my sister and waves her hands when she talks, except not like Bryce. Her hands aren't forming words. They're choppy and free-flowing, and I'm certain she's going to knock over a vase on the table if she gets any closer.

I hand her a balloon. "I brought one of these for her. Can I see her?"

"Her father is getting her dressed. She'll be over in a minute."

I say, "He came too?"

"Of course. As soon as he could." She smiles.

I'm so thankful Olivia has both a mother and a father. "Thank you for agreeing to help Nat."

She waves her hand like it's no big deal, but worry lines crease her forehead. "We can't imagine turning our backs on Nat. We're family now." She squeezes my hand. "As are you."

Even though she acts like it's no big deal, she wrings her hands nervously.

Katie says, "Olivia went through a series of tests yesterday. It wasn't easy for her, or her parents."

Mrs. Murphy chuckles. "It's definitely harder on us, isn't it? Kids are much more resilient." She turns to me as if trying to change the subject. "I still have so many questions for you. I'd love to know about your life in Russia, what your mother was like, and how you ended up here. Someday Olivia will want to know and will be asking questions." She pauses and looks at Jack and Katie.

She waits for me to say something, but I can't. She's holding her hands again, maybe trying to keep them still. She flashes a look around the room and then to me. "Oh dear."

"I'm Katie's sister, Laura." Laura extends her thick hand to Mrs. Murphy.

"Oh, nice to meet you." Mrs. Murphy seems relieved that Laura broke the silence.

Laura says to Mrs. Murphy, "I'm not sure Oksana is ready to talk about Russia right now. Perhaps we could wait for another time?" Laura winks at me.

"Oh, I'm sorry. Sure, we can certainly . . . talk about it when you're ready. No hurry. Sometimes I don't think before I talk." She tucks a piece of hair behind her ear.

Jack stands and gives Mrs. Murphy his seat. "Here, please sit down. We've all been through a lot in the last twenty-four hours."

"Thank you." She sits on the edge of her seat, looking uncomfortable, like she's going to bolt out the door any minute.

"How often do you write to Pastor?" I ask.

"We correspond around the holidays, birthdays, and special occasions. Sometimes I call . . . you know, when there's been a death in the family, or big news, but not very often. It's expensive. He wrote about you before the adoption. I'm sure he and Hannah would like to hear from you. I doubt they know you're in the states."

"Could I have their address and phone number?"

"I'd be happy to give it to you, but you'll have to wait until I get home later today. I don't have the information with me."

"You're going home already?" Panic fills me. I glance at Katie, who seems to be listening. She nods like it's okay. Nat has fallen asleep.

Mrs. Murphy says, "Yes, just me. Dave will stay with Olivia. I have to wrap some things up before her surgery."

"What surgery?" Why does she need an operation? The room spins.

Jack says, "The doctors have to put Olivia asleep before they can take her bone marrow."

The memory of the hospital in Russia smacks my senses: the burn of the needles, the taste of the thick, bitter medicine rolling on my tongue. I gag.

Laura says, "Oksy, are you okay? You've lost all your color." She rushes to my side. "Put your head between your knees."

Katie reaches for the plastic tray on the table and hovers it near my hand. "Vomit into this."

The room blurs and turns black before my head goes limp. Laura guides its heaviness toward my knees. Why does Olivia have to have surgery? Why can't there be a simpler way?

A cool rag at the back of my neck refreshes me, helps me fight the nausea. “I’m okay.” I inhale deeply. The dizziness passes.

Jack hands me a cup of water.

Katie and Mrs. Murphy lean forward in their chairs, their eyes wide.

“I’m sorry for Olivia. I didn’t know she’d have to do that.”

Mrs. Murphy says, “That’s why you’re sick?” She heaves a sigh. “You poor child. Don’t worry. She won’t be asleep for long. The doctors know what they’re doing. Children are sedated every day. “

She’s kind to say that, but I know she will worry. And so will I.

Laura pats my arm. “You okay now?”

I nod and turn to Mrs. Murphy, looking for a diversion. “What did Pastor say about me?” My voice rasps. I watch Mrs. Murphy’s expression closely, my body tensing into a tight ball.

She smiles. “He said you were a beautiful girl with a deep love for your mother, mature beyond your years, and that you made him promise we would take care of Olivia, love her, and make sure she always had plenty to eat.”

“Do you think he knows where my mama is?” My voice cracks.

“I don’t know.” She puts her hand on my shoulder. “But I’ll get you his information, and maybe you could call him or write to him.” She glances at the door and stands nervously like she’s ready to go.

Mr. Murphy enters the room, carrying Olivia, who’s wearing pastel pink pajamas with purple hearts and a pink bow in her curly hair. Her complexion is almost as rosy as her clothes. She smiles brightly. I’m sad for Nat when I see how much healthier Olivia looks. I hand her the green balloon, and she giggles, reaching for it.

Mr. Murphy is freckle-faced, thin, and short, and wears a mustache. His hair matches Olivia’s color. Mrs. Murphy introduces him to Laura and me. We shake hands, and shortly afterward Mrs. Murphy says she’ll be back late tomorrow. Mr. Murphy and Olivia escort her out.

Chapter Thirty-Six

The hospital room is quiet from the Murphys' absence, but Mrs. Murphy's questions about Mama hang heavy between Laura, Jack, Katie, and me, the answers waiting to be spoken. I can feel the tension and wish Jack or Katie would hurry and ask so I could get everything out in the open.

Katie finally starts. "So Pastor didn't know you were taken to the orphanage?"

I shake my head. "The last time I saw him he came to our apartment looking for Mama, for her to sign the papers, but she wasn't there."

"Where was she?" Katie presses.

I shrug.

Jack says, "I'm curious—why didn't you take both girls to Pastor? How did you choose which one to take and which one to keep?"

Now I must confess. Or lie. I glance at Laura.

She nods for me to continue, reaches over, and holds my hand. It gives me strength. "Olivia was the second baby to be born, and the weakest."

They wait for me to go on.

"Mama didn't know Olivia was born. It was easier to take her and hope that Mama would never find out." There, I said it.

Katie says, "How could she not know she delivered a child?"

Laura presses my hand.

"Because she had fallen asleep from too much vodka." My eyes shift to my lap.

Jack says, "You delivered your sisters alone? Without any help?"

I nod.

"Oh my God," Katie says, and places her hand over her heart.

Jack asks, "Why did you take Olivia and not tell your mother?"

"Because I didn't want her to have to feed two babies *and* me. We didn't have money. She couldn't find work." I pause. "I wanted her to keep me." My voice is barely audible. Nat shifts in her sleep, and Katie reaches out and holds her hand near the side rails.

Katie says, "What made her decide to take you to the orphanage?"

I meet Katie's eyes. "She didn't. My Aunt Ludmila did, Mama's sister. I never got a chance to say good-bye to Mama."

Katie gasps. "What? Did she know your aunt took you?"

I shrug. "I don't know. Ludmila said Mama knew that she signed the papers, but Ludmila is a liar. I went back to our apartment to look for Mama, but she and my aunt were gone."

Laura says, "I'd like to talk to you about something that's been weighing on my mind. This might sound crazy, but I think it'll help everyone."

Katie says, "You knew about all this and didn't tell me?"

Laura shakes her head. "Oksana only told me yesterday. Today was the first opportunity I've had to talk to you about it." She clears her throat. " I'd like to take Oksy back to Russia to search for her mama."

"What?" Katie's mouth drops open. "That's crazy!"

My heart races in excitement. Laura wants to take me home?

Laura raises her hand at Katie. "Hear me out, okay?"

Jack has his hand in his chin, deep in thought. "This is a moral issue, Katie. If her mother really didn't know what happened, then—"

"Maybe we should talk about this later." Katie nods toward Jack like she's looking for support, then nods toward me. "When Oksana isn't here."

"No, this is about me. I want to talk about this now."

Laura says, "I think Oksy needs to have the chance to tell her mama about Olivia and say good-bye to her. I seriously believe that if she can resolve some of these issues, she'll be able to move on."

"How do you feel about this, Oksana?" Jack asks.

"I want to go, to find Mama." My stomach is flying like a bird in the sky, full of hope.

Katie's biting her lower lip and folds her arms across her chest. "I think this is a bad idea. You're our daughter now. Obviously your mama wasn't able to provide for you. Going back is only going to give you false hope. We're your parents now. You have to forget your life there."

Hope dangles in front of me. One minute it's within reach, and the next minute it's snatched away. Tears fill my eyes.

Laura licks her lips and leans forward in her chair, gripping the seat like she's trying to stay calm. "You can't make her forget her life there. We don't know her mother's circumstances. Oksana doesn't know either. It's wrong not to resolve this. Oksana spent thirteen years with her mother. She can't just pretend her mother never existed. It's part of why she can't attach here. Don't you see that? What if her mother has been looking for her? What if she got sick after the delivery and didn't want Oksy to leave?"

Katie's cheeks flash red, and she grits her teeth at Laura. "I don't need you butting in here. Oksana is *my* daughter, not yours. Quit putting ideas into her head."

Laura bites her lower lip. Her eyes fill with tears, and she stares at the ceiling, visibly frustrated and hurt, shaking her head.

Jack, who's sitting next to Katie, reaches over and takes Katie's hand, but she yanks it out of his grasp.

Katie says, "Certainly the orphanage officials would have investigated this." She turns to me. "Your mother signed the papers and gave up her rights by not claiming you, never visiting you."

Anger boils inside me. How would she know? "Maybe Ludmila lied to her."

Jack says, "Katie, I think Laura is right. We have to make sure Oksana's mother actually knew what happened to her."

Jack agrees? Is he saying this because he wants me out of his life or because he knows how much this means to me?

He shifts his eyes toward me. "It's not that I'm eager for you to leave."

It's as if he read my thoughts.

He continues. "I want you to stay here as our daughter, but I also understand why this must be resolved." He turns back to Katie.

Her arms are still across her chest. Tears trail down her cheeks. She turns to me again. "What if—she—wants you to stay there with her? Will you? You're a US citizen now. We are legally responsible for you."

She wants to own me like I'm a prize. Is she trying to trick me into staying? Why can't she understand like Jack does?

Jack says, "You have to be prepared for the worst, Oksana. It's possible you might not find her, or . . ."

His sentence trails, but I know what he was going to say. What if she's dead, or what if she doesn't want me? "I can't think of that right now. I have to hope I'll find her."

Katie wipes her tears. "And you think going back there is going to change everything?"

I don't answer. I'm angry at her for not understanding.

Laura reaches for the tissue box on the table and hands it to Katie.

Katie plucks a few and dabs her face, but doesn't look at Laura. Her shoulders slouch. She heaves a sigh and glimpses at Jack, who sits with a frown, then to Laura, who's stone-faced. Then she throws her arms up in the air. "This is crazy. This feels all wrong." She looks to Jack one last time, like she wants him to agree with her, but he doesn't say anything. "Great, this is just great!" She gets up and stomps out of the hospital room, her heels clacking on the tile.

A part of me feels like I'm going to *jump out of my skin* with excitement, like I'm close to winning the battle by getting my chance to go back home, but why do I feel sad inside? Maybe it's because this is the first time in my life it feels like people really care about me, the first time people are fighting for me. But it's also because I don't like leaving Nat, especially now.

There's something else too. I'm afraid. I don't want to admit it to myself, but it follows me like my shadow. What if Mama doesn't want me? What if she never wanted to keep me?

Chapter Thirty-Seven

For the next few days, I'm consumed with thoughts of going home to find Mama. Ever since Laura made the suggestion and Mrs. Murphy called with Pastor's phone number and address, I can't think about anything else. When it's daytime, I think about it being nighttime there. When it's nighttime here, I think about it being daytime there. I wonder where Mama is and what she's doing. I study the globe and the weather in Russia. All I have to do is type in Kazak, Russia, and a website appears with photos from the city. I recognize the architecture, but the buildings in the photos are ones I don't remember. Maybe they were there, but I never noticed.

One afternoon, when Nat is allowed to come home for the night, Katie doesn't say much. She's tired from spending most of her time at the hospital. She naps and doesn't fix her hair like she usually does. Laura brings homemade lasagna over for dinner.

Jack seems relieved. Maybe he called Laura and asked her to come.

I change Nat's diaper and set her in her high chair. She's weak, but she whimpers like she wants to eat, and I hand her a piece of buttered bread.

Katie sits at the table but acts like she's still sleeping. She won't look at Laura or me. It's like she's angry with us, keeping inside herself.

Before we eat dinner, Jack reaches for Katie's hand and says a prayer. "Heavenly Father, thank you for giving Oksana the courage to bring the Murphys into our lives to help Nat, and thank you for this food. Please help both our girls to heal quickly."

I look at him, puzzled. Why do I need to heal? I'm not sick.

His head is still bent, and his eyes are closed. "We hope Olivia's bone marrow will heal Nat, but Oksana needs to know that her family is here in America, right here in this kitchen, ready and willing to heal her broken heart. Amen."

If I make these people my family, I'll feel like I'm stabbing Mama in the back.

Laura says, "Amen." She's sitting next to me, and reaches over and squeezes my hand.

Katie stares at her plate.

What does Jack mean about having a broken heart? If my heart was broken, how would it pump blood to my organs? I'd be dead. I'm sure the phrase is another idiom, so I don't ask. I don't say anything. I pick up my fork and eat.

After we clear the table, Laura says, "Let's play Catch Phrase."

"What's that?" I ask.

"It's a guessing game of word phrases," Laura says.

I'll probably lose since my English isn't as good.

Katie pushes her chair away from the table. The legs scrape against the tile, and her slippered footsteps dragged across the room toward her bedroom. A door shuts with more force than usual. The sound bounces off the walls, reminding me she's still upset.

Jack says, "I better go talk to her."

Laura says, "No, it's probably better if I talk to her since I'm the one who brought up the subject of Russia." She and Jack look at me but neither move.

I get the hint. "You want me to go, don't you?" They don't disagree even though I want them to. I don't know what I'm going to say, but obviously Jack and Laura think I need to try. "Maybe she's worried about Nat."

Jack says, "It's more than that."

I bite my lip, push back my chair—the legs scraping the floor—and mince my steps toward Katie's bedroom. I knock, but she doesn't reply. Laura stands in the hallway watching. She waves for me to go ahead, so I open the door a crack and see Katie lying across her bed with her face buried in the blue-flowered blanket.

I go in, shut the door, and stand next to her bed. I smell the sweet perfume she leaves in a decorative bottle on a mirrored tray on her dresser. *What should I say?* I sit on the edge of her bed and wait for her to notice I'm there, but she only cries into her pillow.

"Katie?"

She stops and sits. Her eyes are puffy, and her hair is flat on one side. "I don't know what to think anymore." She wipes the tears with a balled-up tissue. "I want to be a mother to you, but you won't let me. I live in her shadow—this woman who you love and who has this hold on you. She's intangible. Is she real or made up? What will happen if you don't find her? How will you feel if you do find her and she says she can't take you back? What then? Or what if she wants you to stay with her? How will you live? What about your schooling, your future?" She hiccups a sob. "What kind of mother am I if I let you go?"

She wraps her arms around me, smashing my face against her shoulder.

I pat her back, this gesture foreign to me, but I think it's what she wants me to do. I don't say anything. I don't have answers.

She breaks free from her embrace and wipes her tears, black mascara streaking down her cheek. "I'd like to go with you, but I need to be here with Nat. You understand, right?"

I nod. "Yes, Nat needs you here. I don't want to leave her, but I know she will be okay if you're here." I'd rather go to Russia with Laura anyway, but I don't say that. Somehow I think Katie knows. Does this mean she's going to let me go? My heart explodes with excitement, but it feels wrong. If only Katie wasn't angry anymore.

She squeezes my arms. "I want you to come back—especially now that you found Olivia, and Nat will miss you." She touches my cheek and pushes the hair out of my eyes.

I shiver at her tender fingers and know what she wants me to say, but I can't lie. I don't know if I'll come back. I don't know what's going to happen, but I need to find Mama. "I'm sorry."

That's the best I can do.

Finally, she wipes her eyes and says, "You need to go back to search for her. I know that's the right thing to do. It's just hard." She swallows like she's holding back more tears. "We'll take up a collection at church so you'll have something to take to help your mother or to give to Pastor's church."

"Thank you." I'm excited for me but sad for her too. A part of me wants to tell her she's been kinder to me than anyone ever has—besides Laura—but I can't bring myself to say the words, not without feeling like a traitor to Mama.

Chapter Thirty-Eight

An hour later, I call Pastor Kostia. I think it'll be morning there, but maybe it's too early. The phone rings several times, and just when I'm going to hang up I hear Hannah say a groggy hello.

"Hannah, this is Oksana," I say in Russian.

"Who?"

"Did I wake you?"

"Oksana? Who?"

"It's me . . . the sister of the baby you gave to Mrs. Murphy."

There's a long silence, and then she squeals like she finally understands, and she tells Pastor that it's me. "Where are you? Where are you calling from?"

"I'm in America. I met Pastor's niece and my sister."

"How can you be in America? I don't understand."

"An American family adopted Natalia and me, but I want to come back. I need to find Mama. Have you seen her?"

"Praise the Lord, child. I worried about you. I prayed for you. Wait, wait. I must get up and put my robe on. Just a minute."

I hear rustling and then she returns. "What did you ask me? Have I seen your mama?"

"Yes. Have you?" I speak my native language, and it feels good and strange at the same time.

"There were a few times I thought I saw her with your aunt, but I can't be sure. They were together at the soup kitchen, but there are so many people that come I can't be sure. Why?"

"I need to find her. I don't know if she knows where I am."

"What?" She gasps. "How can that be?"

"My aunt took me to the orphanage. I never got to say good-bye to Mama. Can I come and stay with you for a while to look for her? I won't get in the way, I promise. Aunt Laura wants to come with me, help me find her. Would you have room for both of us?"

She laughs, and I can picture the dark spot in her smile. "You won't get in the way. You're welcome at our church anytime. We will make room for you and your aunt. Pastor and I will ask around about your mama."

"Really?" I bounce on my toes, even more hopeful.

We talk about when I think we'll arrive, and I promise to call her once we have our arrangements made.

#

A week later, Laura says our *ducks are in a row,* and we'll leave in a few weeks. Bryce and his mom, Beth, will take care of the ranch. The school knows I'll be gone indefinitely, and I know I'm at risk of failing a grade, but that doesn't matter to me as much as seeing Mama.

But before I go, Olivia has the bone marrow surgery. Jack says it is better if I go to school. It will give me something to focus on. I don't object because I don't want to be at the hospital if something goes wrong, but I can't focus.

During English class I get a pass to go to the bathroom. The door closes with a whoosh, and I stand in the stall, caged in with the shadows of my worries, my forehead smack against the cold door. Closing my eyes tight, I pray. *Dear God, please help my sisters live.* A vision of Olivia on a hospital bed appears. She smiles and asks me if I brought her a balloon. For the rest of the day, I'm calm.

After school, Luke takes me to the hospital. Several girls wearing jealous expressions watch as I get in the truck with him. Oblivious to their stares, he talks about his horses, their names, and who's the dominant one, who's the follower. He's trying to keep my mind off of my sisters, but it doesn't work. Twisting the bottom of my shirt, I stare outside at winter's cold temper. Gray skies and snow squalls chase us and dampen my hope. Does the ugliness of the day mean something is going to go wrong?

Luke's father is a doctor, and he says Nat has a good chance of getting better, especially now that we found Olivia. His dad said thousands of these procedures are done every year.

Really?

Luke reaches across the seat and takes my hand as if trying to press confidence into me. He parks the car and holds my hand on the way into the hospital. I let him. It keeps me warm outside and inside.

Katie meets us in the lobby. Despite her lopsided hairstyle, she's smiling. "Olivia is out of surgery. Everything went well." She hugs me, and it's like a surge of energy fills my insides with rich, warm chocolate milk. Maybe I'm getting used to her embraces.

I sigh in relief. Did God answer my prayer? Will he answer my other ones too?

In Olivia's room, multicolored balloons hover near the ceiling, floating like crayon-colored clouds. She smiles when she sees me. She looks the same and rubs her eyes like she's waking from sleep. Now that I see she's okay, I want to see Nat.

Across the hall, Nat rests in an isolation room. Since she's getting lots of medicine, she has to be protected from outside germs. Luke and I dress in masks, cloth shoe covers, and gowns.

Katie gives me a serious look. "Nat's hair is falling out in clumps. Try not to react when you see her."

I want to cry but plaster on my best fake smile and enter. A radio plays soft Disney music. Books are splayed across her bed. She's sitting up, with the tube pole to her right, dripping fluid into her arm, poison that's making her hair fall out. I know she needs the medicine, but a part of me wants to rip it out. I wish prayers worked faster than they do.

Katie says, "Look who came to see you, Nat!"

There are only a few stray strands of hair left on the right side of her head near her ear. I inhale sharply and swallow. "Hi there, baby sister."

She reaches up for me.

I lift her into my arms, and her bony knees hug me around my waist. "Pretty soon you're going to be all better, and you'll get to ride Boris with me." I make a pretend horse sound and gallop in my place. "Neigh!"

She giggles.

I read her a few books and notice the last glob of hair falling out. Plucking it off her shoulder, I stuff it in my pocket, wanting to keep it with me always. Luke watches in silence. Nat gets sleepy, and Katie says we have to go. Visits have to be short. Luke drives me to Laura's, where I'm staying while Nat's in the hospital.

Questions ping-pong in my mind. How will I leave Nat? What if I never see her again? What if she dies?

No! I can't let myself think that will happen. I will pray more. Jack and Katie love her and will take care of her. Someday I will return here.

But how? I'm torn in half like the divided highway we're traveling. Each road leads in a different direction.

Chapter Thirty-Nine

Beth arranges a farewell lunch party at the ranch with Laura, Bryce, Luke, and Megan. Jack and Katie agree to come and bring Nat for a short time. She's still getting medicine through the tube, but not all day. She wears a cute monkey hat and a mask around her nose and mouth. We gather in Laura's kitchen since it's too cold to picnic outside.

Everyone brings something to eat and little wrapped gifts. Pink, purple, yellow, and green balloons hover over the food table. There's a square cake with blue icing and "Good Luck, Oksana" written on it.

"No one has ever thrown me a party."

Megan says, "Not even for your birthday?"

"No."

Katie says, "Well, we'll have to make up for lost time when you get back."

It turns awkwardly quiet, like there's something on the table no one wants to talk about, and everyone pretends they can't see it.

Bryce hands me his gift. I'm shy about tearing off the wrapping paper. Inside is a small journal book with a picture of a white horse on the front. The horse looks like Boris.

Bryce says, "Write every day so you can tell us about it when you return."

Megan gives me a pen set.

Luke says he brought me something, but he doesn't want to give it to me in front of everyone.

Megan says, “Woo-woo,” in a teasing tone.

Luke’s face turns red.

Katie gives me an envelope. “This is from the church. They raised over five hundred dollars for you to take to help your mama or give to Pastor’s church.” She nods to Laura.

Laura’s mouth drops open. “How generous of them! We’ll make sure it gets put to good use.”

I nod. “That was very kind.”

Katie says, “I’ll hold on to the money until you leave.”

“Give it to Laura before we leave. She can keep it safe.” I don’t want the responsibility of holding the money. Someone in Russia could steal it from me.

Katie reaches on the table for a blue and pink polka-dotted wrapped gift. “Here’s something else.”

I peel off the paper to find a book full of photos of Olivia and Nat with hair, and me with Boris, and a few of Jack and Katie. There are old pictures of Laura’s barn and Jack and Katie’s house too.

Katie says, “You can show your mama your new family, where you live and, of course, Boris.”

I can’t picture me showing Mama these people—total strangers from two different worlds, but I thank Katie.

Luke is the last one to leave the party. “Your gift is in the truck. Come out with me.”

We bundle in our coats, and I follow him out. The wind whips off my hood, and strands of hair fall into my face. He’s says, “Get in. It’ll be warmer.”

He switches on the heat blower, drives away from the house down near the pond , and parks. The setting sun glows orange, reflecting off the ice on the pond, spotlighting Luke’s face.

I turn toward him. “So what did you bring me?”

His eyes twinkled with mischief. He reaches around to the back seat and grabs an envelope and a little box wrapped in tissue paper with gobs of tape.

“Open the box first.” He brushes a strand of hair out of my eyes.

“Did you wrap it?”

He grins. “How can you tell?”

I chuckle as I unwrap the paper layered in tape. No boy has ever bought me a gift. I’m not sure how to act. Inside the box is a necklace with a tiny charm of the United States flag. I pull it out. “Thank you. It’s very pretty.”

Luke reaches for the necklace. “Let me put it on you.

He unclasps the end, and when I turn, he swings it around to the front and fastens it at the back. His fingers send shivers down my arms, a tickle that usually makes me feel cold, but I’m warmer than I’ve been in a long time.

He lifts my hair over the chain and spins me around to face him, then holds my hands, pulling me closer. Our faces are inches apart. He stares at my lips. “I’ll miss you. I want you to come back. I want America to be your home.”

My face feels hot all the way down my neck, and I don’t want to move. I’m sure he can hear my heart hammering in my chest.

He tilts his head and presses his lips against mine, tenderly, affectionately. My body leans into his. I smell a musky, clean scent like deodorant. I taste the flavor of hope and love, and for one instant I have the desire to stay here and never leave. But I know it won’t last. Men never stay. I pull away before he lets me go first. It’s better this way.

He doesn’t look disappointed, only patient, like he can wait. There’s passion in his eyes. I stare at them longer than I should. “Thank you for your kind gift.”

He brushes the back of his hand across my cheek.

I shudder.

“Don’t open the card until you’re in Russia. Come back to me, okay?”

I nod ever so slightly.

Chapter Forty

My filled suitcase lies open on the bed in my room. I stuff one last pair of socks into a corner space. Jasper nudges the door open with his nose and jumps up next to me, resting his head on my packed clothes. He lets out a heavy sigh.

Jack taps on the open door. "Can I come in?"

I nod.

He takes a few more steps inside, and the room suddenly feels small. "You have everything you need?"

"I think so. I came here with so much less."

He chuckles. "It didn't take us long to Americanize you."

Me, an American? It sounds strange but it's true. I've gotten used to luxuries.

Jack plucks a nesting doll off my dresser and twists the bottom from the top repeatedly. "I know it's important that you go back, but school is important no matter where you are—here or there. Education is the key to your future, and without it you won't be able to use the gifts God gave you." He pauses and meets my eyes. "We want what's best for you, and that might not be what you think it'll be. You're a smart girl, and once you put your mind to something, you'll achieve it because you're stubborn for the right reasons." He smiles.

I nod.

"But no matter what happens, remember that you have a family here, a future, and parents who love you."

Are his eyes red around the rim? Certainly he's not going to cry. I've never seen a man cry before. Nor do I want to. And no man has ever told me he loved me before either, not even Sergey. I'm uncomfortable, but in a good way. I think. Ever since Jack found out about Mama, he's been softer to me, more patient. Maybe he understands now.

He returns the doll to the dresser and places his large hand on the top of my head. He messes up my hair, then walks out the room. I smile at his weirdness, and I'm glad he didn't try to hug me or kiss me, or anything gross like that.

#

Jack will take Laura and me to the airport. Even though Nat is home, she can't be around people and germs. There's a light frosting of snow on the lake out my window. The world looks white. The sun bounces off the snow, and I squint. Will I ever stand in this room again and admire the clean, open view?

Katie stands in the doorway, holding Nat. "Do you have the photo album packed?"

"It's in my backpack."

She sucks in her lower lip like she's trying not to cry.

Nat reaches for me to hold her. Running my hand across her bald head, I say, "You be a good girl and get well."

"Bye-bye," she says in baby talk.

We've never heard her say good-bye before. Katie and I laugh.

"Good job, Natalie!" Katie says. "Will you give Oksana a kiss too?"

Nat puckers her thin lips and smacks them against my cheek, giving me the wettest kiss I've ever received.

Tears flood my eyes.

Katie throws her arms around both of us. "My two favorite girls. God has blessed me."

How can she say that when I'm leaving and may not return and Nat is sick? How can she continue to love God?

I wrap my arms around Katie because she wants me to, but I want to remember what this feels like, this moment—her safe arms, her sweet perfume, Nat's tiny hands in mine, standing in my room that I may never see again. The mirror over my dresser reflects the moment, presses the image of the three of us embracing, creasing the seam of Katie's love for me in my mind.

She scoops Nat into her arms, turns, and dashes out of the room like she can't bear to watch me leave.

I will not cry. If I do I might not stop. I don't want to leave Nat, but I promise, no matter what, I'll see her again.

Jack loads my suitcase in the car and drives in cold silence to Laura's. He left early enough for me to say good-bye to Boris. As Jack loads Laura's travel gear, I run to the barn, my breath fogging the air on the way. Boris is wearing a green blanket and munching hay.

"Hey, buddy."

His eyes shift to mine, and he saunters to the door, chewing.

I unbolt the lock and go to him, tears brimming my eyes. I throw my arm over his back, hug him tight, and bury my face in his neck. "I won't see you for a while," I blubber, "but don't forget me. Laura will take care of you until I return." I drink in the smell of his hide, the hay, and manure, memorizing the feel of his smooth warm body beneath my fingertips. "Be a good boy." I pinch the dirt out of the corner of his eyes and kiss his nose.

I don't tell him I may never return, because even if Mama wants me to stay I will come back here someday.

On the way back to the car, I brush the tears off my face with the sleeve of my jacket. Jack and Laura chat in the front seat. I climb back into the warm car, and it's like the weather has changed, as if there's a storm—Laura's tornado. She rambles like she's nervous, talking about the horses; did she remember to tell Beth about Firefly's medicine? Did she remember to ask her to bring the mail in? Did she leave the vet's number in a place Beth could find it? She twirls her hair—something I've never seen her do. Maybe her worries will help keep my mind off of leaving Nat.

At the airport, Jack insists on carrying my bag to the check-in counter, but before Laura and I part for the terminal, he pulls me into the largest hug I've ever had. It feels like I'm in the arms of a bear, a cocoon, a hiding spot.

He says, "Take care, kid, and don't cut your hair. Be proud of it."

Maybe he says this because he has no hair. Could be, but it *dawns on me* that he and Katie have never shunned my hair, asked me to hide it, or begged me to cut it. Just for fun, I reach up and swirl-rub the top of his shiny bald head, giggling.

He smiles, his eyes wide, seemingly surprised. With red eyes, he stands on the other side of the gate until he can no longer see us.

#

Exhaustion slurps my energy as we board the plane. I haven't slept well for nights. Thoughts of what I'll say to Mama fill my mind. How will I tell her? Will I find her? Will Nat be okay?

The nightmares returned.

In one dream several nights ago, I searched the old buildings where Mama and I used to live. I climbed stair after stair, looked in every run-down corner, and couldn't find her. Other times, I couldn't remember what she looked like. I dreamt she was holding me, the smell of vodka on her breath, dirt on her shirt. Her bony ribs pressed against me as she stroked the back of my hair. Then Ludmila's deep, husky laugh filled the room. Startled, I let go of Mama and fell into a deep hole, screaming.

I woke and my heart raced, my clothes damp from perspiration. After several nights of the same dream, I feared sleep.

Maybe I'll be able to sleep on the plane. It's an eleven-hour trip. Laura brought three equestrian magazines full of photos of healthy quarter horses. There are articles on riding, showing, and caring for them, but I can't concentrate. So instead, I pretend to read them. After we're in the air for an hour, Laura hands me a little wrapped gift. It's an electronic held-hand game called a Game Boy.

She says, "You're a real American teenager now." She shows me its features, how to play a game about Mario and Yoshi, and how to win. The tinkling music coming from the device makes the man across from me crease his brow and glare. Laura shows me how to turn the sound off. By the time we land in Moscow, I'm really good at winning points.

The gray world returns before we touch ground. We're surrounded by ominous clouds. It's *raining cats and dogs*. It's like we're in a black-and-white television set and all the color has drained. The airport walls and floor are old and worn, and the people look solemn. Few people laugh or take the time to talk to strangers. Was it like this before and I didn't notice? Maybe it's because I've been living in a colored TV that I notice the difference. Even the color of my clothing is more vibrant than the people around me.

I'm home! But instead of feeling excited, a burn festers in my stomach, a gnawing fear. One that I'd forgotten.

We see a woman holding a sign with our name on it. She must be the guide Pastor Kostia arranged to take us to the train station.

Laura says, "Thank God I don't have to find my way around here. I'm way out of my comfort zone."

People rush around speaking Russian. It sounds strange, and I realize how much I've adapted to English. I haven't spoken my language in a long time. I say hello to Vera, our guide, and tell her who we are. My voice sounds peculiar. Laura stands to the side while Vera and I talk. I introduce them to each other. Vera smiles at Laura and points ahead. We follow.

Laura says, "Now I know what you felt like when you first came to America. Oh, my! Let's hope I don't faint."

Does she notice that none of the women at the airport except us wear leather boots, jeans, and plaid shirts?

Vera loads our suitcases in the trunk of her car and drives us to the Kazaksky train station. The rain turns into big flakes of white snow and causes a traffic jam around the city. Cars bounce and weave in and out of lanes, trying to get ahead of everyone else. Horns blare. Laura holds her backpack in her lap and squeezes her eyes tight every time a car gets too close. She licks her lips over and over, and I fear they'll be swollen by the time we get to Kazak. We pass an accident scene and see a man with a bandaged head standing on the side of the road next to his crashed car. The ambulance pulls away.

Laura says, "Are they just going to leave him there?"

I say, "He must be okay. Maybe he's waiting for a ride."

"I can't believe they're not taking him to the hospital. I hope we don't end up like him."

I recognize the small turret and the clock above the entrance to the railway station. The building has fancy architecture and is lit up well as dusk settles in. Vera will travel to Kazak with us. We wait in the station for a few hours before we board. The coal from the engine gases the air. Everyone is quiet, and after we settle into our little bunks in our rail cars we sleep, or try to sleep.

Even though I'm close to home, I feel like a stranger.

Chapter Forty-One

Early morning sunlight streaks through the clouds and bounces off the snow resting on the ground, highlighting Hannah as she waves at us from the train platform. She wears a large furry hat and a big black coat. She looks like a bear, and I almost don't recognize her until she smiles. Pastor Kostia stands beside her. He's thin and worn. Have I been gone that long for him to have changed so drastically? Or is it because I'm used to seeing Jack's big body that Pastor looks small in comparison?

We embrace, and I introduce them to Laura. We pay Vera and tell her we'll let her know when we're returning so she can accompany us back. I tell her I might not be going. No one disputes this, but Laura doesn't understand what we've said, and I don't translate. I try not to think about returning to America.

Pastor drives his little black car toward the city to the church on Bauman Street. We're snared in traffic, exhaust fumes wafting from passing vehicles. Soon, I recognize the buildings—the tall arched cathedrals etched in painted detail, bell towers in onion domes, the river that divides the wealthy from the poor, the city hall on Liberty Square, and the entertainment center near the Kremlin. The buildings look older, foreign, so different from the bland ones in America.

Laura says, "The buildings are amazing, so much detail in their designs. They make our churches in the US look like cardboard."

Then we cross the bridge that leads to the poor section, where the buildings look more sinister, dirtier, and abandoned. Bubbles float in my stomach as I study the people on the streets who wait for buses and walk to work. I'm already searching for Mama's familiar face.

"Have you seen Mama?"

Hannah shakes her head. "I'm sorry. We've inquired, but nothing." She reaches behind in her seat to where I'm sitting and pats my hand.

I'm disappointed but not surprised.

Pastor says, "I came back the next day. I didn't know where you went or what happened to you."

Laura's forehead wrinkles like she's puzzled, but I know what he means.

"I was already at the orphanage, and Mama was already gone."

"I'm sorry," he says.

"I returned to the church too, but you were gone. I thought you'd left forever."

Hannah pats my hand again. "Poor child. We are together now."

#

Laura and I stay together in a tiny room at the church. There are two small cots, and across the hall is a bathroom. We eat our meals with Hannah and Pastor. Laura insists that Pastor accept money for our food, so before we search for Mama we exchange American dollars for rubles.

When it's finally time to search the streets of Kazak, Laura and I bundle up in hats, gloves, and our winter coats. We've switched to boots so we can trudge better in the snow. My hands shake but my heart sings.

We see many faces along the way. Laura's mouth gapes at the drunks lying in the gutter, the cheap painted women loitering in doorways. The city seems larger and more frightening now. Panic fills me. How will we find her? No one looks familiar.

I take the path to the old building, our apartment, where we used to live. The way there doesn't seem as long as I remembered. This time I notice how dark, dirty, and cracked the streets and paths are—drastically different from my home in America. The buildings are run-down Some are condemned. There are no wide spaces with green grass or pastures with grazing animals. The air is thick, and a foul taste lines my mouth like grime.

We approach the tall building, our apartment, and I stop. My stomach fills with fluttering bird wings. There's no longer a condemned sign barricading the door, but it doesn't look like the building is in better condition than before.

"This is where my sisters were born."

Laura takes my hand and squeezes it. "This is where you lived?"

I nod. "For only a short while."

Pity lines her brow. "Do you think your mama will be here?"

"No, but someone may know where she is."

I take Laura up the stairs. Babies cry, doors slam, men shout, and women shout back. Rotten garbage litters the stairwell. The familiar smell of wet socks reminds me of Ludmila. We hold up our sleeves to our noses. When we get to the door where Mama and I lived, I knock. An old woman answers. She says she doesn't know Mama. She's lived there for six months. I ask her if she knows Ludmila, but she doesn't know her either. I ask other men and women standing and sitting in the hallways, but no one knows her.

I can't wait to leave the building and the memories. We go to the market in the center of town, and I show Laura the vendors and the orphans. Her eyes fill with tears. I don't look at the children. I want to forget. I think I see Ludmila's back and run to her, but when the woman turns, I see she's a stranger.

Laura stops at fruit stands and art stands, where artists have painted black-and-white landscapes of buildings in Kazak. She asks which one I like, and she buys it to frame and hang at the ranch. She buys hand-painted matryoshka dolls for Megan, Natalia, and Olivia. I help her choose my favorites.

We're ready to go back to the church, when I turn and see a man who looks like Ludmila's friend. He's the one who knows rich men. He's leaning against a building, smoking a cigarette, his hair longer and greasier than before. I don't want to talk to him, but he could be the connection I need.

"Excuse me. Have you seen Ludmila?"

He stares at me as if he's trying to remember who I am. Then he smiles and shows me his yellow teeth. He inspects me like I'm a piece of food he's going to eat, then glances at Laura, then at me again. "How much you pay for this information?"

"Nyet," I say. I don't want to give him a dime.

He throws up his arms and walks away.

I follow. “Da, okay, I will pay you, but you must tell me what you know.” I don’t trust him, but I have no other leads.

He says to pay him first. I dig in my pocket and hand him a hundred and fifty rubles. He asks for more. I glance at Laura, who nods. I give him two hundred rubles, and he tells me where she lived the last time he saw her. It’s a long walk from here and a darker side of the city.

“How long ago was that?”

“Maybe two months.” He stuffs the money in his pocket and turns to go.

A strong wind kicks an icy chill down my neck. Snow bursts from a cloud, pelting my face with icy slaps. It’s getting dark. Laura slips on the pavement, so we hold on to each other as we trudge back to the church.

I’m quiet at dinner, but Laura tells me not to despair because we have a lead. We’ll go there tomorrow. She holds my hand and prays, “Dear God, please give us the endurance to find Mama. Show us the way, and give us all the strength to cope with your will.”

I ask her what “will” is. “Why do you pray for what he wants?”

She says, “Sometimes what we want isn’t what’s right for us. Only he knows our true path.”

I don’t like this. Why must he be the one to decide?

Chapter Forty-Two

The next morning the sun kisses my pillow as it sparkles through our window. The snow stopped sometime in the night. I slept like a stone on the edge of a cliff. I didn't move, but I felt like I could fall out of bed. I didn't dream. Maybe it was from the cold air and the exercise yesterday. I'm eager to leave and search again.

After breakfast we bundle up and head out. The cold air stings my cheeks, and I bury my chin in my collar, wishing it was summer. We search the block that Ludmila's friend mentioned, but there's road construction, and parts of the street have been blocked off. We go into buildings and ask, but no one knows Mama or my aunt.

Laura has an idea to leave small photos of me with the people we meet and ask them to pass on the information. We take a photo of me from Katie's album and make copies at a local store, cutting my photo into small pictures and writing a note on the back. I sign my name and ask Mama to go to the Orthodox Church on Bauman Street. The photos are black and white and not the best quality, but they might help. We leave them, telling people if they see Mama to give her the photo.

Laura leans against buildings, taking breaks, sighing often. "The poverty here makes me sad. I had no idea."

She doesn't finish her thoughts, but her silence tells me she's uncomfortable. Our roles have reversed. Now I'm in charge, leading her. She has to trust me. The wrinkled lines of worry arch on her brow.

A hooker applies red lipstick and blows Laura a kiss.

Under my breath, I say, "Don't look people in the eye. Avoid their stares." I teach her. "They can see your fear. They can hear it throbbing."

"I'm not afraid." Laura doesn't say this with much confidence and gives me a sideways look. "Okay, I admit it. I'm a horse in a sea of whales."

I grin as we slog through the slush of snow, but each time we ask about Mama and are met with blank stares, my shoulders sag and my hope dwindles.

We stop and eat *obed*, lunch at a local café, and sit near the window drinking hot tea. I order for Laura since she can't read the menu. Our waitress brings us *pelmeni*, minced meat in a dumpling, and borsch, which is a vegetable soup. Laura doesn't complain about the taste. She'll eat anything, which is what I do in America, but she makes a funny face when she swallows.

A small woman walks past the window with her head bent. She's bundled well and turns her head to block out the cold. Her profile looks familiar. Could it be Mama? I jump out of my chair and run out the door, calling "Mama," but when the lady turns, she's a stranger. I return to Laura, who holds my hand and prays.

We trek the potholed streets for hours longer as clouds seed the sky. We pass the blind, the old, and the weak. Sirens wheeze in the distance. When the sun dips and stars attempt to prick the sky, we head back to the church for supper. There's a soup kitchen line like the one I stood in long ago.

So much inside me has changed since then, yet the people are the same—poor and hungry. I'm a different person, seeing this with fresh eyes. I forgot the desperate feeling of hunger, but standing here now with these broken people reminds me of when I lived here. How could I have forgotten so quickly? My stomach aches and I shudder. Laura and I wait in line with the others.

Tears teeter down my cheeks, and Laura wipes them off, burying my face into her shoulder. When we get to the front of the line and Hannah sees us, she says, "Your mama was here! She was holding your photo."

"What?" My stomach tumbles down to my toes. "Where is she?" I search the crowd.

"She came to the line and asked if it was true that you were here. I told her yes, and she asked where you were. I told her you were looking for her. She said she couldn't stay, but she'd be back tomorrow."

"Did you ask her where she was staying?"

"By the time I had a break in the line, she was gone."

Tears of joy stream down my face. I will find her. I know I will! She came to see me! "How did she look?"

Hannah frowns. "Tired."

Laura reaches for my hand and squeezes it. She wears her wide smile. "You will see her soon. I can't wait to meet her."

I think Laura will be surprised by Mama's looks.

After dinner, Laura and I return to our room. It's dark, and I have to wait until the morning, but I can't sleep knowing Mama's close. I go to bed hoping the night will pass quickly.

The next morning, I'm awake before the sun. Laura still sleeps. I dress and go outside and pace in front of the church, waiting. It's silly because Mama never gets up early, but maybe she'll be so excited to see me she'll wake earlier today. An hour later, I sit on the front porch steps, rubbing the tips of my ears and my toes that have gone numb.

Laura rushes from the church, out of breath. "I didn't know where you'd gone. You scared me. You have a habit of doing that!" She wears her flannel pajamas under her coat, and her hair lies in all different directions. She pulls up her hood and sits on the porch next to me. "Any sign of her yet?"

I shake my head.

"Why don't you come in for breakfast? I'm sure she'll be here soon."

She takes my hand and leads me into the church and through Hannah's kitchen door.

Hannah is baking pies, and the sweet doughy smell makes me hungry. She insists on making us *zavtrak*—breakfast. She makes buckwheat pancakes, omelets, and hot tea.

All I can think about is that Mama will come to the church and not know how to find me through the door behind the altar, so I hurry, eat, and take my electronic game out to the church and wait. It's warmer there. Laura dresses and joins me, and we wait for so long that our stomachs growl for lunch.

We're about to go into the kitchen again, when the church's wooden doors open and a small, thin woman enters.

I strain to see, but the light coming in from the outside blocks my view. I hold my breath. The door closes, and the church is dark again except for the candles at the ends of the pews. The lady walks slowly toward us.

"Mama?"

She stops. "Oksana?"

Laura turns and watches the woman, seemingly puzzled, exhaling a slight gasp.

I run to Mama and into her open arms, but they're sticks, like she's become a living skeleton. She reeks of dirt, cigarettes, vodka, and the scent of poverty that I'd forgotten. She's much tinier than I remembered, her hair lifeless, her beautiful skin replaced with a pinch of dull gray. Her beauty hides behind the strands of thin, greasy hair falling over her face. I doubt she's had a bath in weeks.

"I can't believe I finally found you. I've missed you so much," I say.

She cries and holds me to her bosom and speaks to me in our native language. "I didn't know what happened to you. Tell me, where have you been?"

I was right. Ludmila hadn't told her. "Ludmila took me to the orphanage."

"Here," she says, "let's sit down over there." She slurs her words. We walk to a pew at the back of the church, away from the praying people. My arms are locked around hers, and tears are falling like rain.

"I hate Ludmila. She should have told you what she did. Where did you think I went?"

"Don't say hate. Ludmila does what she thinks is best."

Why does she defend her? "Did she tell you she took Natalia to the orphanage? What did she tell you happened to us?" My fists are clenched at my side.

She studies my hair, my face, and my clothes, like she's seeing me for the first time. "You look good."

"You aren't answering me. Did you know?" The pitch of my voice raises a notch. I'm holding my breath.

She exhales. "Yes, I knew. I let her take you."

The air is suddenly thick, and it's difficult to breath. It's like someone kicked me in the stomach. The room spins. No! "Why? Why didn't you say good-bye? Why didn't you come to see us?"

She looks away. Her hands tremble in her lap. "I couldn't. It would make me too sad. I couldn't come to see you because then I wouldn't be able to leave. How could I see you, then walk away?"

Tears fall down her cheeks. She wipes them with her quivering fingers, revealing her broken, dirty nails. "It was easier for me to pretend you were better off there. I am not a good mama."

Laura appears out of the corner of my eye. She stands at the end of the pew where we're sitting, her brow furrowed, her steps tentative. I'd forgotten she was in the church.

"Oksana, is everything okay? Will you introduce me?"

Mama says, "Who is this?"

"Aunt Laura from America. Laura, this is Mama, Elaina."

Laura extends her thick hand, and Mama touches it briefly.

"You have been in America?" Mama asks.

I nod. "I live with Natalia in America, with Laura's sister."

She glances at Laura again. "Oh, I didn't know." She places her hand on her heart. "I'm happy for you. You are such a good girl, pretty too." She holds her hand against my cheek, and I cover hers with mine, remembering how strong hers used to feel.

She says, "Why did you come back here if you have a new family there?"

"I don't want to be in America. I want to be with you."

She shakes her head. "*Nyet*, *nyet*, you think you do, but what kind of life would you have here?" She looks away and draws her coat closer. "I can't take care of you."

"I'm older now. I could get a job."

Her eyes show me a dreamy look. "Tell me about Natalia. How is your sister? Who does she look like?"

"She looks like you." I reach deep into my pants pocket and pull out the baggie I brought for her. "Here," I place the bag in her hand. "This is a lock of her hair. It's beautiful, isn't it? Like the color of a peach."

Mama gasps and takes the bag, opens it, and caresses the strands. Her eyes glaze in a dreamy way. "Like Sergey's."

"Her hair is falling out."

"Why?"

"She has a disease, but she's getting better." I look down in my lap. Laura, who's standing beside me, squeezes my shoulder. I have to tell Mama what I did. I swallow. "Nat has a twin, Mama, a sister who looks like her. This is why I had to come back to Russia—to tell you this."

Mama's eyes grow wide. "I don't understand."

"She was born after Natalia. You didn't know because you fell asleep from the vodka." I heave in a deep breath, wishing I could cleanse the memory from my mind. "I couldn't wake you, Mama. I tried. I shook you because I didn't know what to do. Nobody was there to help me. I took the baby and gave her to Pastor for his niece in America."

"What?"

"I wanted you to keep *me*." My voice raises a notch.

"Nat has a twin?" Mama's eyes are open wide.

Laura hands me the photo album.

I open the album and show Mama the girls.

She laughs and cries. "Two beautiful girls? I had no idea."

"Are you angry at me for taking her and not telling you?"

"Nyet, you are a good girl." She puts her hand on my cheek again and smiles like she's proud of me.

I hiccup a sob. "I thought you'd . . . be able to keep *me* . . . if I gave her away, but you . . . didn't."

Mama looks down at the floor. "I have nothing to give you. I'm poor." She glances up at Laura. "This is good now." She points to the photos. "You have a new family." She sighs and points to the house. "You are rich." She chuckles. "I could never give you this."

"I don't want that."

She waves her hand. "Tell me about this disease Natalia has."

I explain leukemia and what Olivia had to do to help. I don't know how to say *cells* or *bone marrow* in Russian so I tell her Olivia's blood is healthy. Mama doesn't understand, but I say, "Nat will be well soon."

Mama's eyes shift to Laura again, then back to the photos in the book. "Do they take good care of you?"

I nod.

Laura scoots beside me in the pew and stretches her arm across my back.

Mama says, "Are you happy?"

She doesn't want me. I know this now. She's slipping away. "They are good to me, yes, but they are not my family. You are." I clutch her arm. "Don't leave me again."

She casts her eyes downward.

"Are you still living with Ludmila?" I ask.

She nods, but still won't meet my eyes.

"Does she know you're here?"

"Da, she heard you were looking for me. She saw your

photograph."

"What did she say?"

Mama pats my arm and finally meets my eyes.

"She doesn't want to see me, does she?"

"She wanted me to ask you for . . . money."

"Mama, I'm older now. I can take care of you."

"Nyet, Oksana, I'm weak with the drink. Ludmila is strong, and she takes care of me. I can't ask her to take care of you too. She won't."

"You won't have to. I can take care of myself." It sounds like I'm begging, but I don't care.

She shakes her head.

Tears stream down my face. I don't want them to, but they have a mind of their own. I want to show her I'm strong, but I can't. I breathe deep. "Where are you living? I want to see Ludmila. Tell me."

"It is a hellhole. I don't want you there."

Mama looks at Laura again and says to her in Russian, "Will you take care of my Oksana for me?"

"Nyet, Mama!" I clutch her arm tighter.

She pulls away from my hold.

Laura says, "What is she saying?"

Mama takes my hands and slowly moves them into Laura's. I yank them away and grab Mama's coat sleeve. Finger by finger, she removes my hold and places them in Laura's again.

Mama stutters. "You tell your . . . sisters . . . when they grow up that . . . their mama . . . loved them. Promise me you'll never drink like me."

"You're going to leave me again, just like that?" I bolt out of my seat and catch my breath between my hiccupped sobs. "What kind of mama are you?" I shout this at her now, and the praying people in the church turn to watch. I ask this question even though I know the answer. She's the kind of mother who abandons her children, who's too weak to turn against the bottle.

Laura holds her arm around my waist.

"I hate you!" Spit flies from my mouth.

Mama flinches like I've struck her and squeezes her eyes shut, lines creasing her brow. She stands to go, and Nat's lock of hair flutters to the floor, forgotten, abandoned. Mama walks out of the church, her head hanging low, her steps unsure—like they've always been.

As the door opens and she exits, I collapse in the pew in Laura's embrace, my face buried in her chest. I weep and taste a tad of iron in my throat, like I bit my tongue and it's bleeding. Maybe it's my heart shedding the blood of hope, purging the dreams of being together with Mama.

How will I ever forgive Mama? How will I go on?

As if reading my mind, Laura whispers, "Your world seems like nothing now. Let yourself grieve, then let God sweep you up. Let him hold you high. You're stumbling, but you will climb again. It's the steps in your journey that will bring you to him."

I don't know if I will ever believe in Laura's God, but I know I've fallen, and she's here to pick me up, to love me even though my own mother doesn't know how. It occurs to me that I have survived without Mama because of Laura, Jack, and Katie, even though I've been cold to them.

When no more tears will fall, I look up and see the empty church, my throat raw, the taste of blood gone. The last ray of sunlight spills through the stained-glass window, casting a light on the altar, showing me the truth that I've been too blind to see.

How could I have been so stupid? Mama could never stand up to Ludmila. She's always let others control her life—her sister, the bottle, poverty. She's never been able to stand up for herself or fight the curse or fight for me. Why did I think this time would be different?

She doesn't know what love is. To her it's only an empty promise, a spoken word like *the* or *was*, a verb or noun with no action.

I am nothing like Mama, nor do I want to be. Even without Ludmila, Mama and I wouldn't have succeeded to rise above the poverty. She's too weak. She relies on others to do for her. I want to rely on others to show me the way, strong people who know how it's done, who can teach me how to love.

Laura pats my back. I look at her with new eyes. She's the strong one, the one who takes in the needy, stands up for those who can't, believes in a God she's never seen, and believes in me. She's loved me even though I've never loved her back. Maybe if I trust her, I will gain strength to be someone Mama will never be. I will make money someday to help Pastor feed the poor and Mama.

Laura says, "Your mama loves you and wants what's best for

you. I know you can't see that right now, but someday you will." She closes here eyes. "Dear God, thank you for answering our pray to reunite Oksana and her mama. Help Oksy to see that her mama cares, and give Oksy the strength to have confidence in you, believe in you, and know that you love her unconditionally. Help her to find happiness in America with me and her new family who desperately want to be a part of her life and who love her and accept her."

I think, for the first time, I'm willing to try to take a chance at being a part of this new family.

Chapter Forty-Three

The following afternoon, Laura and I pass food to the poor at the soup kitchen outside the church. It's like I'm in a dream, floating. I'm here, but only in spirit. I barely feel alive, moving like a robot.

Sadness surrounds the poor people who come, but when Laura smiles at them, they smile back. They thank Pastor for blessing them. I'm ladling soup, when I recognize Mama's hand. I gasp and look up. Has she changed her mind?

She's wearing a desperate look—the one I've seen before but had forgotten. It's the one that reminds me of a dog begging for a bone. I hold my breath, and for one fleeting second I think it's me she wants, but then I know. It's not me. She smacks her lips, and her eyes dart right and left. She needs a drink. She stutters and shakes, seemingly nervous, but it's because she's sick. Yes, that's why.

"Ludmila made me come and ask you for money."

She's lying. I know that now. She wants to go to the kiosk to buy vodka. Slowly, I reach into my jeans pocket and pull out all the coins I have and shove them into her hand. I meet her eyes and see her for the first time. I see her filthy hands, her sickness, and her weakness. I pity her. I never want to be like her. She will never change. She will never be strong enough to be anyone's mama.

"Don't buy more vodka," I tell her. "Buy food and find help, Mama. You need help."

She shakes her head. "I can't. I just can't." She panics and claws at the money like she'll die without it. Maybe she will.

I open my palm and she scoops it in to her hand. “Thank you. I love you, Oksana.”

But love is just a word to her. She’ll never understand its meaning. Love is unselfish, something she knows nothing about.

She hurries down the food line and out of sight. I’m glad I came here, happy I saw her because now I can move on. It still hurts. It will always hurt, but I thank Laura’s God that I have another home.

Laura wraps her arm around me, studying me to see what I will do next. “Are you okay?”

I nod and smile. My tears have all dried up. Last night when Laura held me, I vowed I wouldn’t cry any more. Now, I embrace Laura. “Yes, I am okay. I am lucky because I have you.”

Tears fill her eyes. “Thank you.” She squeezes me close. “Yes, you have me, but you have Katie, Jack, Natalia, Boris, and Olivia too.”

“You forgot Luke.” I grin.

She winks. “How could I forget Luke?”

#

Before we leave Russia there is one more person I need to see. I hate to ask Laura to go because she’s done so much already, but I ask anyway. I don’t want to go there alone. I need to see Ruzina, which means I need to go back to the orphanage—the place I dread the most. And it’s a long walk. I hope she’ll still be there, but she should be. She doesn’t turn sixteen for a couple more years.

Laura wants to go, especially when I tell her about Ruzina, but she wants to take a cab. I don’t know the address of the orphanage. I only know how to get there on foot, so Laura agrees to walk there, but only after we bundle ourselves in layers.

On our way, we stop at the market along the poorer section of the city. There’s something I want to buy for Ruzina. We pass the orphanage children selling cards at the curb. Laura smiles at them and gives them each two American quarters.

“Spacibo,” one girl says.

This time I smile at them. One day, I will return here to help the children who have no home, no one to love them. But like Jack said, I will have to study hard first.

As soon as I buy what I want from the market, Laura and I head to the orphanage. I lead the way. It's the afternoon, and light snow falls delicately, dusting our path. The sidewalks are deserted. It's cold, but we walk fast, and sometimes we skip with our arms locked together. I remember walking this way with Ludmila, and I shiver. Laura wraps her arm around me and huddles so close, we clumsily bump hips and giggle.

A half hour later, when we pass through the trees, I nod to my left. "That's where Nat used to live."

Laura pauses as she gazes at the building and puts her gloved hand over her heart. "Oh my."

"Do you want to see inside?"

She hesitates. "We're allowed to go in?"

"No." I motion for her to follow me and turn toward the black gate. "But we can peek in the window. I used to do it all the time."

"I don't want to get in trouble."

I push in the gate that leads to the orphanage, and the rusted hinges creak and rattle. "This way."

Laura must be curious, because she follows me on the sidewalk and to the window.

Cupping my hands over the glass, I peer inside hoping Dominka will be there, but she's not. Only the old battle-ax Veronika is there, bent over an infant, her back to us. Rows of cribs line the wall, each with at least one child, some with two.

Laura stands beside me gawking too. A soft gasp escapes her lips. "So many babies and only one worker? They just lie there. Are they alive?"

"Yes."

"But none of them are crying. It's so sad." Her voice softens. "Thank God Nat isn't here anymore."

Veronika turns toward us, so we duck.

Laura hurries to the sidewalk, toward the gate. "Come, let's keep going. How much longer before we're where Ruzina lives?"

"Just through the trees ahead and down the path. We're close."

Laura is silent as we push past the gate and travel down the sidewalk. It's like her mood has changed, but I understand, especially after seeing America and all the care Nat gets now. That's the way it's supposed to be.

When I see the red-bricked building in the distance, I stop. A dark-gray cloud hovers over the orphanage like the shadow of evil. The building seems darker and more solemn than before. Perhaps it's because I've seen America and the green pastures in Michigan. I stare and tremble.

Laura follows my eyes. She doesn't say anything, but she doesn't have to. There's sadness in her expression. She knows this is the place where I used to live because I've described the building, the food, Mrs. Myasha, Nicholas, and Ruzina.

"I don't know if Mrs. Myasha will let us in. We might have to sneak. Is that okay with you?" The air is so cold I can see my breath.

Laura hesitates. "I don't know. We don't want to end up in jail. Is there another way?"

"Maybe we can wait outside and ask someone to bring her to us." I motion for her to follow me. My heart pounds in my ears. I try not to think about when I lived here, but the air smells like old garbage, reminding me how I used to feel.

Laura walks beside me as I climb the cracked steps to the front door. A girl with dark eyes and hair opens the door as she was about to leave the building.

"Excuse me," I say in Russian. "Does Ruzina still live here?"

The dark-haired girl pauses as if considering whether to tell us the truth, seemingly suspicious of us. "Da, she is here. Why?"

I reach into the pocket of my coat and hand her five hundred rubles, which should be enough for her to buy lunch at McDonalds. "Will you get her and bring her to us here?" I point to where Laura and I are standing.

The girl's eyes light up when she sees the rubles. She takes the money, nods, and returns inside the building.

Laura and I stand in the sunlight against the brick wall, a little hidden and shielded from the wind's cruel breath. What will I say to Ruzina? What will she say to me? Will she be happy to see me?

The door opens and Ruzina appears, looking hesitant, like she's not sure what she'll find. She's wearing my old coat, the one Mama gave me years ago. Her red hair hangs to her chin, a little shorter than it used to be, but she's as tiny as before. I doubt she's grown an inch. She's probably less than five feet tall. There are dark circles under her eyes, like she hasn't slept. When she sees me, her mouth drops open.

"What are you doing here?" Her voice is soft and as light as a musical note. She continues out the door toward me, smiling, her gray eyes wide.

"I came to see you." I wrap my arms around her—something

I've never done. She smells of the stale air of the orphanage. I don't let go. Slowly, she hugs me back, relaxing in my arms.

She breaks apart and says, "I've been wearing your coat to remember you."

"It looks good on you." I lie. The sleeves hang over her arms, and the shoulders are too wide. I turn to Laura. "This is Laura, my aunt from America."

Ruzina lifts her hand, waves, and smiles at Laura. "*Kak vy pozhivayetye*."

Laura says, "I've heard so much about you." She pulls Ruzina in a tight embrace, but Ruzina's arms fall to her side, like she's not sure what she's supposed to do. Of course, she doesn't understand Laura's English, so I translate.

When Laura finally lets go, Ruzina turns to me. "Why are you here?"

I reach inside my coat for the gifts I bought her from the market. "To bring you these."

"Apples?" She takes them from me, turning them over in her hands. "They're so shiny. Thank you."

"I didn't forget what you did for me when I was in the hospital in Kazak." I reach in my pocket and hand her a piece of paper. "Here's my address so you can write to me. I'll write to you too."

She nods. "Thank you." She takes the paper, juggles the apples, and puts the paper in her coat pocket.

"How are things here?"

"The same." She glances at Laura, then at me again. "How is America?"

"It's different, but good. I wish you could come with us. Laura has a ranch with horses.

She nods. "I'm happy for you. I wish I could come too."

It's unfair that she can't come, that no one is coming to get her. I don't want to leave her here, but I don't have a choice. I hope now that Laura has met her, she will help her get to America too. She has to. I reach into my pocket again and pull out half of the money from the church in America. "Here, this is to buy stamps and other stuff."

Ruzina's eyes get large as she scans the money and looks over her shoulder, like she's checking to see if anyone noticed the exchange. "Thank you." She puts the money in her pocket and pats it. "I still have the money you left me too. I'm saving it for when I leave here."

"We can't stay. I don't want Mrs. Myasha to see me. Write to me. I will look for a way to bring you to America too." I know this must happen soon or she'll be left on the streets to fend for herself.

She nods and smiles, tucking the apples inside her coat.

"I'm glad I got to see you," I say.

"Me too." She smiles at Laura, turns to me, and actually hugs me first.

When Ruzina steps away toward the door and out of my life, Laura's eyes fill with tears. This is a good thing. Maybe Laura's compassion will help bring Ruzina to America sooner.

On our way back to Pastor Kostia's, Laura cries. "It breaks my heart to see all the orphans without family. Ruzina seems like such a sweet child. It's not fair."

I explain the laws in Russia and how orphans must leave the orphanages when they are sixteen. Ruzina was thirteen when I left, but is probably fourteen now. She'll have to leave the orphanage soon and will have to fight for everything she needs.

Laura says, "Let's hope that doesn't happen. We need a plan to bring her home."

"Really? You'll do that?" I smile that Laura thought of this herself.

She nods.

I reach for her hand and squeeze it, happy and skipping along the sidewalk, already thinking about how we could make this happen. "Thank you."

#

On the plane ride back to America, when Laura sleeps beside me, I take Luke's card out of my backpack, the one I didn't trust myself to read until now.

The card is written on blank notepad stationary. Inside, in sloppy handwriting, is his note.

> *There are evil people in the world. I think you've seen more than your share, because I can see the hurt in your eyes, and it makes me want to throw my fist into the wall, hurt those people who hurt you. Worse than the evil are those people who don't do anything about the evil. My*

dream is for you to find your place in the world where you can bring hope to those who need it, to those who have felt your pain. For selfish reasons, I hope that place is in America. I know, I probably sound too mature to write this, but since I might not see you again, I needed to say something profound, so you will remember me. Be safe and come back.

Luke

I chuckle at him trying to sound wise. I like him. Inside, I'm bubbling. I can't wait to see him again. Pressing my fingertips to my lips, I remember how his felt when they were on mine.

#

When Laura and I exit the plane in Detroit, my stomach flutters. We descend the plane like before, but this time my feet hit the pavement and grip the earth with more purpose, more confidence. I know now this is where I need to be. This is the place Laura says God wants me to be.

I can't wait to see Nat, but I'm nervous about seeing Jack and Katie. Will they pity me? Will they be happy to see me?

As we turn the corner out of the gated, secured area at the airport, Jack, Katie, and Nat are the first people in line. It's like I'm seeing Jack and Katie for the first time. They look the same but different, maybe because I've changed.

Katie's smile spreads across her face—her clean, calm, and in-control persona so different from Mama's. She wears jeans and a pink ruffled blouse under her hooded jacket. A cross necklace dangles from her neck. She has a new hairstyle, with one side longer than the other. I like it.

Nat, wearing a white fluffy bunny hat with ears, waves from Jack's arms. She looks thin but happy.

A knot forms in my throat, and I know I'm going to cry, especially when I see Jack's eyes turn red and fill with tears. "Welcome home," he says, and places Nat in my arms.

I hug her close and cover her face with kisses. She giggles.

Katie wraps her arms around me, her tears gushing. "I'm so

glad you're home safe."

For once, I freely return the embrace, breathing in the smell of her sweet perfume, welcoming the scent, the fragrance that reminds me of her love, of her desire for me to return her love.

I smile. "I'm happy to be here too."

She sobs openly now, like I've said the words she's waited her whole life to hear.

Jack says, "I want to join in this group hug too." He circles his arms around Katie and me holding Nat. "We missed you."

I reach up and pat his bald head. "I missed doing this."

Everyone laughs.

Epilogue

Laura invited us, the Murphys, and Luke to her ranch for a picnic, an announcement, and to celebrate our "Gotcha Day." It's been two years since Natalia and I were adopted. The summer sun glows orange in the bright-blue sky, casting a light as bright as my mood.

Jack pulls the car into Laura's driveway, and I get out to open the gate. The familiar smells of horses, hay, and the pine trees along the driveway welcome me. Katie's in the backseat with Nat reading *The Very Hungry Caterpillar* as the car tires crunch on the gravel driveway.

The Murphys, who are visiting from Indiana, are waiting for us under the oak tree, where Laura has set up our party table.

Luke's throwing a ball for Duke. He waves and smiles at me, and my heartbeat quickens.

Nat squeals when she sees Olivia. After Jack lifts her out of her car seat and sets her down, she runs toward her sister. She never walks anymore. Her peach fuzz hair has grown into short curls. Finally. She's healthy now—no more chemo treatments. She's in remission, and the doctors don't expect her to have any more problems. She giggles and runs into Olivia's arms, and for a second I think they'll topple over, but Olivia keeps them balanced.

After we climb out of the car and say hello, we gather around, and everyone sings "Happy Gotcha Day" to the tune of "Happy Birthday."

Jack says a prayer. "Dear Heavenly Father, we thank you for

this day and for giving us the blessings of two daughters. Thank you for showing Oksana the way back to our home, our hearts, and our family. We thank you for our friends here today and for the opportunity to eat this food, especially the cake. Amen." He smiles and winks at me.

Laura claps and sings, "Aaaa-mennn, A-men, A-men." Her notes are flat, and Duke cocks his head. For a minute I think he might howl. Luke and I laugh. Then Laura reaches her hand out to me to *high-five*. I slap her hand and grin because in Russia high five is when someone elbows you in the mouth and knocks out your teeth. The American gesture is much more pleasant.

Laura stands up on the picnic table's seat rest. "I have an announcement to make."

We listen.

"Lottie foaled last night. Do you want to see her colt?"

We all shout in unison. "Yes!"

I say, "I can't believe you waited this long to tell us!"

She says, "I wanted to celebrate you first. Now we can celebrate the colt."

We run to Lottie's , which is next to Boris's. Lottie is the most recent rescue horse. She stands in the corner, and her foal suckles her teat while standing on wobbly legs. Lottie's eyes are closed.

"He's so cute and little," I say. "What will you name him?"

"Phoenix," Laura says.

"That's a weird name. Why Phoenix?" I ask.

"It comes from the Greeks a long time ago when there was a mythical bird named Phoenix—the symbol for immortality. The story goes that this bird died and rose again from his ashes. Since we're celebrating the girls' 'gotcha day' today, I thought the name would be appropriate. After all, it's like we're celebrating the girls' rebirth here in the United States. What do you think?"

I don't know what to say. I shrug and Laura hugs me. Ever since we returned from Russia, Katie seems okay with sharing me with Laura and lets me spend most weekends with her.

Laura says to me, "I'd like you to have him."

"Really?" He's perfect. I'm excited, but when Boris neighs from his stall, I pause. "I have to ask Boris first. I don't want him to think he's being replaced." I mosey over to him, and everyone waits while I whisper in his ear.

"You'll always be my number one. There's no need to worry."

He nuzzles my neck with his nose.

Several minutes later, I return. "He said it's okay as long as I make time for him too."

There's a round of applause.

Luke says, "Doesn't sound like you'll have time for me though."

I can't believe he said that in front of everyone. My heart does clumsy cartwheels. His blue eyes are holding mine like he's waiting for me to say something. "Yes, I promise to have time for you too."

He grins and reaches for my hand.

Nat and Olivia giggle and shuffle in the dirt, creating dust, oblivious to our discussions.

Laura says, "I have more news."

The Murphys, who were chatting with Jack and Katie, stop to listen.

"I've decided to make the arrangements to adopt Ruzina. I should be able to bring her *home* to us in three months!"

I'm stunned. I knew Laura had been asking Pastor questions about a possible adoption, but I thought it was going to take her longer to make the decision. For once I'm the one saying "woo-hoot!"

The colt startles at our noise, so we move outside, back to our party table.

I can't believe Ruzina will actually be here on this ranch with me. We've written back and forth a few times, but not until Pastor Kostia went to see her. I had sent her several letters and hadn't heard from her, so Pastor made a trip to the orphanage. Ruzina told him she mailed me two letters, but I never received them. In Russia, the government sometimes intercepts mail. So instead of mailing the next ones, Pastor Kostia collected them from her and faxed copies of them to me.

Ruzina's letters were funny, despite her situation. She talked about the other kids and what she was learning. She was far chattier in her letters than in person.

Jack snaps our photos as we stand around the table, and Mrs. Murphy cuts the cake. While she passes out pieces, Katie hands me a little wrapped box.

"What's this for?" I ask.

Katie shrugs. "I wanted to give you something special."

I unwrap the paper and open the box. Inside is a silver-linked bracelet with a heart charm dangling from the end. The links are thick and feel unbreakable, different than the cheap one Sergey gave me so long ago.

"Do you like it?" Katie asks.

I nod, not trusting myself to speak. Tears lodge in my throat.

Katie unclasps the hook and places the bracelet on my wrist. "The heart is a symbol of our love for you. The links are strong like our bond. You'll be our daughter forever."

"Thank you." I throw my arms around her, this time not holding back. Tears fall down my cheeks and onto her shoulder. The pain that used to be in my heart—the empty one of missing Mama, the one that used to make me turn inside myself—has almost disappeared. Now there's a warm glow that makes me feel safe, like the arms of someone who cares, like Katie's arms.

Jack, Katie, and the Murphys, Luke and Laura, and my sisters—my family—are here now celebrating me. No longer are the links of my family scattered in the dirt. They're a part of me, like this gift. I touch the bracelet and feel its strength, assume its power, and know that this family gives me the love I've always wanted, the love I never had.

I look to the sky, its open expanse reminding me that somewhere in the world Mama struggles. I pray for her because I don't know what else to do for her. I don't know if prayers work, but I'm starting to believe that they can't hurt. It's a choice—to believe. And I'm trying to make better choices than Mama did. Someday I will return to Russia and help orphans. Maybe Ruzina will go with me.

Ruzina and I promised to gaze at the sky every day at eight o'clock p.m. my time, which is seven a.m. her time, so she won't feel alone, so we know we're thinking of each other. I look up now as two birds fly side by side, joining other pairs and forming a *V* in the sky. Ruzina is probably sleeping now, but I hope that soon she will have a new life here, one she never had the opportunity to taste or feel, the one she'll have with us. Will she learn how to love? Will it be too late?

At one time, we had a lot in common—loneliness and parents who forgot us. Will being together in America help us forget? Or will the memories open our wounds, spilling the blood onto those around us?

I don't have the answers, but I hope for the best. I can't wait to show her this world.

After we eat cake and ice cream, Luke and I saddle Boris and Firefly and head out for the trails, eager for a few moments alone, my heart thumping at the possibility of Luke stealing another kiss.

THE END

Acknowledgements

Scattered Links was inspired by our Russian adoption journey in 1997. However, none of the events in this book took place, and all the characters are a product of my imagination.

When we traveled to Russia, adopting an unplanned additional child would have taken much longer and perhaps multiple trips. There were occasions where families went to Russia to adopt one child and returned to the states with more than one, and many times the children were siblings.

Before we traveled on our adoption journey we faced many obstacles, but we continued to believe that God would bring us the child we were meant to raise, the child He had planned to be a part of our forever family.

Looking back at the days and months before the adoption, we were naïve as to what it would take to raise a post-institutionalized child, a child who might not have received the early nurturing that's so important in their development. We believed that love would be enough to conquer any attachment issues.

That's not always true.

Fortunately, for us, we have been blessed with a child who's well-adjusted and doesn't struggle with RAD, reactive attachment disorder. However, many parents of adopted children and foster children haven't been as blessed. The parents and children suffer from the problems and consequences of this disorder. Parents don't understand their children and some "re-home" them like pets.

It's important for adoptive families to realize that children who've been bounced from home to home or in and out of orphanages are special-needs children. It takes more than love to nurture them back to health. It's often a life-long commitment to show them and guide them on how to trust enough to bond appropriately.

Special thanks to Megan Spinks LCSW, ACSW, an attachment therapist, who was able to give me insight into parenting a child with an attachment disorder; to Terry and Alisa Leek who let me hang out with their amazing Arabian horses where I asked never-ending questions about horses; to Magical Meadows in Warsaw, Indiana for inviting me to watch therapeutic riding lessons for special-needs kids; to Debbie at Rymar Ranch, Lecanto, Florida for teaching me proper riding techniques and horse gear lingo.

Also, a special thank you to the Dare to Dream Youth Ranch, Ft. Wayne, Indiana, whose purpose is to rescue abused, neglected and dying horses. Laura's farm was modeled after yours. I love what you do for horses and children!

Thank you to Olivia, my favorite Ruskie, horse-whisperer and animal lover, for listening to my endless chatter about this novel. You are a gift from God and an inspiration to those around you. Of all the children in the world, God chose you to be a part of our family, and we have been blessed.

To my editor, Susanne Lakin, who encouraged me to confidently publish this novel, thank you. To my beta-readers and favorite plot *bouncer*s Robin McClure, Janelle Leonard, Angelika Weidenbenner, Christie Fitzpatrick, Cindy Leininger, Alexa BeMent, and Alyshia Marie Hull.

Thank you also to my number one and number two fans, Dad and Mom, Maurice and Marie St.Germain, who gleefully read my work. Thank you for teaching me how to dream, reminding me that anything is possible, and that there are always two sides to every story. You two are a huge part of who I am. Thank you for your amazing love!

People I interviewed: Rick Barry, my go-to American/Russian guy, and Konstantin Rysyanin, our Russian friend and translator during our adoption.

Thank you to the other adoptive parents who spent time answering my nosey questions: Mary Wooten, Stacy Dumbacher, and Susan Leo.

Michelle Maly, your endless love and commitment to minister the orphans in Odessa, Ukraine is beyond belief. Thank you for helping the world to see and care for all orphans.

A Bag of Rocks

By an anonymous writer with RAD, Reactive Attachment Disorder. Shared from the blog, Forever Parents. (http://www.foreverparents.com/2008/03/a-bag-of-rocks.html)

When you carry a bag of rocks around, day in and day out, you will inevitably become tired. No matter how far you walk, how hard you work, how much you try, you are still tired. Even sleep is ineffective, because you are sleeping with your bag of rocks, and when you wake in the morning you continue throughout the day carrying the bag of rocks.

Some people would ask, "Why not just let go of the bag of rocks? Stop carrying it around with you, just put them down. Can't you see that would make it easier?" But, you see, I am afraid that if I let go of the rocks there will be nothing left. The rocks are all that I have, all that I have carried with me throughout my life, all that I trust. Certainly, carrying these rocks around makes me tired. But being tired is familiar, and safe. Would you let go of all that you have in the world, if you were not certain that by doing so you would gain more?

And yet (the irony is) we cannot have the certainty of more, until we let go of what we have. As long as I am carrying this bag of rocks, my arms are much too full for me to accept anything else. Even when you offer me a bag of feathers I don't dare to take it, for how can I trust that the load you are offering me is truly a load of feathers without opening the bag? Others have offered feathers, but given lead. How can I know that the bag you offer is not heavier than my current burden unless I let go of my bag of rocks, freeing my hands to open your bag? And I cannot let go of my bag, for if I put it down it might be taken from me. Or, even worse, I may find that my arms ache far too much for me to pick up the bag again, and then I would have nothing.

Can you understand why I would despair? You ask me to give up all that I believe that I have, all that I believe that I am, and yet I cannot. The fear of having nothing–of being nothing–is far too great. You want me to give up my hatred, my anger, and my pain (but most of all my pain, for the hatred and anger are mere masks for the grief and fear I hold inside). It will make me better, you say. And yet, how can I trust you, without first giving up all that I am holding on to? And how can I give up all that I am holding, if I do not trust you? Can you not see the confusion I am living with, the overwhelming fear that controls my actions? Can you not see why I push you away? Why I cause harm to myself, and to you? Can you not see why I am afraid?

Please understand, I don't want it to be this way. I do want more, I really do. Perhaps you may have noticed how hard I try, before the despair seems too much to bear, before I give in. If only I could give up these rocks, I would have peace. I would be happy. I want to believe it, but I can't. So I continue walking, dragging my bag of rocks, and wishing for something I can never have.

I wrote this just over a year ago, as an attempt to explain to my therapist why I was holding on to so many of my destructive behaviors so stubbornly. I finally found the courage to let go of the bag and try something new–and yet at times I still go back to that bag of rocks, because it is so familiar and safe, and the new ways are still uncomfortable and scary. I am considering adding more to this piece–as I no longer feel the hopelessness I ended on a year ago.

In the meantime, I hope this piece can help parents of RADs (reactive attachment disorder) understand why it is so difficult for their children to trust, and why they may fight so hard against what you can clearly see is best for them.

Study Guide Questions

1. Describe how Oksana's life was different in Russia than in the US.
2. Therapeutic horses have been proven to help special-needs children. What do you think contributes to the success of this theory?
3. Do you think RAD, reactive attachment disorder, is more prevalent in post-institutionalized children or foster children?
4. What did Oksana leave Ruzina in the orphanage?
5. How many children are being re-homed as a result of RAD? (Re-homed is when parents place their RAD children in other homes because they can't cope with this disorder.)
6. What does our country do with unwanted children versus other countries? Is there a better way?
7. What were the emotional scenes? Did you cry? Why/why not?
8. If Oksana were a real character alive today how would her past affect who she is as a mother, employee, or wife?
9. What did you learn from reading this novel?
10. What genre would you say this book fits? Is it for young adults or women?
11. What tense was the book written in?
12. Would you have preferred to read it from Katie's point-of-view too?
13. Do you think children with RAD can become well-functioning adults? Why/why not?
14. Why do you think Oksana was closer to Laura than Katie?
15. Were the characters believable? Why/why not?
16. Abandonment and trust are two themes in this novel. Can you think of a time when you felt abandoned and how that affected your trust?
17. Was the ending believable? Why/why not?
18. Why do you think children fantasize about an absent or neglectful parent?

Michelle's Other Work

CACHE a PREDATOR, a geocaching mystery
Amazon Bestseller
Available at Amazon

ÉCLAIR, a children's chapter book series for first – third graders.
(To be released in 2014)

SPARK, The Willow Series, a young adult supernatural suspense novel
(To be released in 2014)

About the Author

Michelle Weidenbenner is a full time writer and blogger at Random Writing Rants where she teaches teens and adults how to get published. When she's not writing she's winning ugly on the tennis court. No joke. It's ugly.

Message from Michelle

Thanks for investing your time in reading my book. I'd love to hear from you. Follow me on Twitter @MWeidenbenner or on FB at:
http://www.facebook.com/randomwritingrants
My email address is: mweidenbennerauthor@gmail.com

If you enjoyed reading *SCATTERED LINKS* would you take a few minutes to write a review?

"I can't write without a reader. It's precisely like a kiss—you can't do it alone."
— John Cheever

I appreciate all my readers. Thank you.

26691828R00155

Made in the USA
Charleston, SC
16 February 2014